I0788721

RUTHLESS KING

MICE AND MEN BOOK 1 (THE WAR OF ROSES UNIVERSE)

LANA SKY

Ruthless King

Ruthless King By Lana Sky

Copyright © 2020 by Lana Sky
All rights reserved.

This is a work of fiction. Names, characters, businesses, places, events and incidents are either the products of the author's imagination or used in a fictitious manner. Any resemblance to actual persons, living or dead, or actual events is purely coincidental.

ACKNOWLEDGMENTS

Thanks so much to everyone who supported this draft along the way, including the many beta readers who provided encouragement! Please keep in mind that this story includes dark, graphic, and explicit content matter that is not suitable for readers under the age of 18—or for readers who are uncomfortable with the following subject matter: age gap relationships, explicit sex, mentions of sexual abuse, and graphic depictions of violence.

1

—

DON

"Though this be madness, yet there is method in't." ~ Hamlet.

While I wasn't the smartest kid in the world, I had one trait most don't—ambition. Ambitions so grand I envisioned myself one day ruling the world—and I wasn't satisfied with just imagining it. Sure, the dumb fantasies were no different than what most punks aspire to at that age, but I'd wanted more. More than a kid raised in the streets was entitled to.

More than I deserved.

Mama called it "dreaming," thinking too big for my britches but, bless her soul, she was naïve when it came to the way of the world. She never taught me that dreams don't mean shit in the long run, or that success has a price—desperation. You have to take it. With pain, with blood, by any means necessary, you take what you want.

And the easiest way to do that? Through force. Young Donatello learned that violence could garner him whatever he craved. Cars. Booze. Women.

But I also learned that there isn't one damn thing that can't be ripped away afterward. Despite the odds, I'd gotten my wish once, gaining everything I'd dreamed of and more. The funny thing is, I was so fixated on what I lacked, I didn't even know it. Greed was the one constant I knew, and I only ever had one goal. Money. To have more of it than God himself, enough to have this entire city in the palm of my hand. I got that wish too—my name was feared, be it Donatello or the various monikers assigned to me by rivals. *Il Mostro. The Butcher. That Violent Cunt.*

Back then, I'd been stupid enough to assume that fear meant something. That fear equaled power. In his own esteem, the old Donatello was a force to be reckoned with—and if that smug little punk could see the man I am now, he'd scoff, unable to recognize himself.

A man who scrapes for what he has and appreciates every damn cent. Who knows what it means to be humble. To suffer. To bide his time and keep his fucking mouth shut.

This new man ain't no *Butcher*, for damn sure. From crook to legitimate businessman. Hell, it sounds like some shitty fairy tale, but reformed or not, a man never forgets his past. If he's smart, he'll even learn from it.

Now, of all times, I remember a particular piece of advice—coincidentally given to me by the last bastard I ever killed myself. His name didn't matter; he was some balding, pudgy little asshole who read Hamlet once, and thought that made him a fucking intellectual. Funny, because that "intelligence" didn't pan out so well for him in the end. I will give him this much, though—he made an impression on me in a way few have.

"Though this be madness, there's a method to it, see. Like Shakespeare?" he'd ranted, right before I'd put a bullet in his skull.

The madness was selling me out. The method? Using back-channel deals to frame me for extortion. In his mind, it all made sense. He wasn't trying to set me up to save his own skin, see? By slithering his way into my inner circle like the lying cunt he was, he was merely doing me a favor by revealing how easy it could be to fuck me over. His betrayal was all for the greater good.

Unimpressed by that genius rationale, I'd reacted the only way I knew how back then.

Fast-forward almost a decade later, and karma gives me a cruel, new perspective. Finally, I understand just what the dumb son of a bitch was getting at. He wasn't smart; hell, he wasn't even trying to be. Logic doesn't mean shit when you're *desperate*; when you have nothing else to fall back on but insanity.

In such a mental state, everything starts looking like a good idea —like what I'm doing right now.

It's insane to stand here before two armed guards, holding a gift wrapped by some lady in a store who assured me a woman would "enjoy such a thoughtful present." She even tied it with a goddamn bow.

It's insane to wear this pathetic smile and pray to God my act holds up.

It's methodical insanity.

"We're Fabio Botelli's guests," I say, gesturing to the slender man beside me. Just like I'd told him, he keeps his mouth shut, his smile as dumb as mine.

One look at these guards, and I know they're no bumbling rent-a-cops. *Ex-soldier* is written all over their stiff posture and the cautious way they glance me over. Considering the reputation of the man who owns this property, I'm not surprised.

Nerves ripple through my belly, catching me off guard. I feel like a punk again, stepping up to the head of the *famiglia* for the first time, wearing my Sunday's best. Little did I know, the dress shirt sported a fucking pizza stain on the collar. Old Giovanni had taken one look at me and scoffed, seeing through my act. He'd turned me away that time, warning that he didn't work with "boys." He only hired men.

This inspection feels no different, though one would hope a couple decades of experience would improve my chances. A week after that initial meeting, I'd returned to Giovanni, but with the added prestige of having shot one of his rivals at point-blank range. Bloodstains carry a bit more weight to them than pizza sauce. The old man had taken me on then and taught me the importance of casting an image. Of sowing a reputation based on fear. He bought me a brand-new shirt, and I made sure never to stain it. Hell, I still have it, a reminder of that valuable lesson.

If he could see me now, Giovanni would shake his head in disbelief. "You look plain, Donny," he'd scold. "You are a lion among men dressed like a fucking sheep."

In this city, aptly named Hell's Gambit, *sheep* wear Italian designer suits and grease their hair to shine. They smile awkwardly before those in authority and simper just long enough to go undetected. Those sheep? They dine with the wolves, a position preferable to figuratively starving. Hell, I'd bleat if I thought it would help.

Luckily that aspect of this ruse doesn't seem necessary. The guards share searching glances, and then one inclines his head. "This way, Sir."

He gestures to the massive oak doors propped open to allow guests inside. With a few tense steps, we're in, joining an advancing line of other guests.

Relief surges through my blood, mingling with the shot of whiskey I'd taken for good luck. I fall into step behind a woman dressed in a black gown and catch sight of myself in a mirror hanging on the wall. A crazy son of a bitch stares back, his eyes only slightly bloodshot, his hair the neatest I've seen it in days. His smile is charming, but the strain in his expression gives it all away—he's desperate. In a sense, he looks like Mr. Hamlet did when he pled for his life before me.

What supposed method might explain this man's madness?

That's easy. Survival.

I'm here because the only other option is to lie down quietly and let the brutality of this city swallow me whole. I can't, not even newly reformed as I am. Luckily, Mischa Stepanov, owner of this massive residence, has done the one thing worth prostrating myself at his mercy. An act powerful enough to change the entire Vanici legacy for the better.

He's decided to present his daughter to the world on a silver platter.

So, call me insane. I'm here, ready to grovel.

And apparently, I'm not the only one. A queue of well-dressed guests extends both ahead of me and behind. On polished shoes and pointy heels, we tread over a floor burnished to shine, and into a home displaying breathtaking gothic architecture. A large central staircase dominates the entryway, and past that is a winding set of corridors capped by vaulted ceilings and grand arches. Eventually, we're herded into a massive grand hall, every bit as impressive as the name would imply. Instantly, I find the rumors were true after all, and this isn't some elaborate trap. The fearsome leader of the Russian mob has decided to throw a birthday party of all things, in honor of his eldest daughter. Fresh roses litter nearly every available inch of space. Soft white accents lessen the intimidating atmosphere cast by the house itself and the security presence out front. As the swell of elegant music reaches my ears, and I spot dedicated servers mingling with trays of food, some of my unease lessens.

"You see, Vincenzo? There's a method to my madness," I tell the boy beside me. He doesn't look convinced, an eyebrow cocked, his mouth flat in a hard line. Balancing the gift on one hand, I flick his nose the way I used to when he was a kid, always giving lip. "Stop your pouting and smile, damn it. You have a *principessa* to charm."

"A princess, huh? You've lost your mind," Vin grumbles while tugging at the collar of his tux. Hell, it might be the first time in years that he's worn one—I know for a fact that he spends more time hiding in the library of his fancy school these days, than dressing to impress. If he didn't share my eyes, and the signature Vanici grin, I'd doubt we were related. My heir, the genius, who'd have thought?

What he makes up for in ambition—to become a doctor, of all things—he lacks in political savvy. Sadly, even a doctor must

and the quality of her male counterpart's suit, they could purchase the entire Sigerelli stock for fun.

"Hooked nose, a scar on his chin… He's Giovanni Rossi. Runs a casino, but that's just his day job," Vin murmurs around his own fake grin. "Pompous. A dick. We don't like him."

"That's my boy," I mutter back. Unlike his namesake, this Giovanni is a pathetic whelp, unworthy of the Rossi name. His own father didn't allow him into the fold, but he still has his uses. "Now, tell me *why* we don't like him."

"Because he's not only a dirty crook, but a backstabber," Vin replies under his breath. Spotting us, Giovanni inclines his head in greeting, and Vin's the first one to return it with so much enthusiasm I'd think it genuine if I didn't know any better. "We still show him respect, though," he adds as we approach an unoccupied corner. "Even if he no longer runs the *famiglia*."

"And why is that?" I ask, my head cocked, tone critical.

The answer is so obvious, he shoots me a sideways glance. "Because you keep your enemies closer than your friends."

"Damn right. Speaking of enemies…" My eyes narrow as I spot a figure holding court across the room, and a worrying ripping sound comes from the gift tucked beneath my arm. I grasp it with both hands, fighting to keep my expression neutral. "Who is that?"

I nod in his general direction, though Vin has no trouble seeking him out. A white suit sets this man apart from the rest of the crowd—but not in the way he probably expects.

"Antonio Salvatore," Vin hisses. His handsome façade cracks as his lips twist into a snarl. "He runs the *famiglia* now, but we definitely don't like him because he's a—"

This description, I voice for him. "A sick son of a bitch. Dickhead. And a murderer." Even if I could never prove it. His hallmark is a signature of all the crimes he has a hand in— cruelty, brutality, and callous rage. Turning his head, the bastard catches me staring and winks, puffing up his chest like he's some big man.

A different me would have slit his throat here and now. I just smile. "You stay away from him," I hiss to Vin.

He nods in agreement, only to raise an eyebrow at a sudden thought. "But you haven't spoken about this guy much. Mischa."

He's scanning the massive grand hall of the Stepanov manor— and I don't miss the appreciative gleam in his eye. Despite his studious tendencies, he has enough sense to know power when he sees it on stark display. He's impressed.

And I'm unnerved.

"Why come here if we weren't invited?" he questions, cutting his eyes up to mine, as perceptive as ever. "What makes this Mischa so important you'd drag us here on Uncle Fabio's coattails?"

I turn away, avoiding those searching looks he excels at. The bastard will make a damn good surgeon one day. Or a cop in another universe.

"You don't party, Don," he points out, refusing to let the subject drop. "Ever. Hell, any other day, you'd be sloshed by this time of the night—"

"You want to know why we're here?" I slip my arm around his shoulders and jerk my chin to indicate our surroundings. "Take a look. View more than the surface beauty. Tell me what you see."

I see deceptive white accents and enough fucking roses to choke someone to death on the stench. But beneath that? I see power. The massive hall alone is large enough to fit the entire floor of the hotel Vin and I booked, with room to spare—and it's just a fraction of the manor itself. Well known for his swagger, Mischa spared no expense to celebrate his daughter's exploits. Decadence oozes from every corner of the space, from the ivory tablecloths to even more sprawling floral centerpieces.

I figure it'll take months of showers before I stop smelling like fucking flowers.

But roses aren't enough to sway the men gathered here. No, this gesture of fatherly love serves another purpose entirely. Even someone as disconnected from our world as Vincenzo can instantly pick up on it.

"He must have more money than God," he mutters in awe, and I'm reminded of the boy I used to be who'd craved to own just that. "And a lot of sway to get you to even enter the same mile radius as Antonio Salvatore."

"And then some," I grudgingly admit. "He's only been active in this territory for about six years, but he now controls the entire *mafiya,* which—their exploits combined—gives him a hefty sum of dark money to draw on. Not to mention that his allies outnumber everyone else two to one. Only a fool would dare to challenge him."

And under his control, this city has transformed, forgetting all about the legacy of the *famiglia* and its once feared ex-leader. Or so I'd hoped.

Maybe I'd been the naïve one, thinking that I could quietly return and just meld into the business sector, newly focused on legitimate enterprise. I'd tried that—only to be thwarted at nearly every fucking turn. Someone doesn't want me back, and if I were a betting man, I'd place my money on Antonio Salvatore.

The funny part is that we came up together, both pupils under Giovanni's tutelage. There were three of us once—Antonio, myself, and another man I considered to be my brother, Gino Mangenello. While I went on to lead in the old man's place, Antonio was too busy lusting after everything I had to achieve anything on his own. Some might say he still won in the end. Now he rules over the fragments of the *famiglia*, but it's a shadow of its former glory. Case and point—he's here sniffing after Mischa just like I am.

I'm sure he's done everything he could to scuttle my latest deal, but I managed it regardless, and now I own legitimate shares in the city's port. It isn't much, but it's something, more than enough revenue to fund Vin's education. With a new advertisement campaign, I hope to extend that holding.

And with Mischa Stepanov on my side? No one could stand in my way, and I technically wouldn't be breaking any of the vows I swore to myself all those years ago. Perhaps, just bending them a little.

"A fool would challenge someone like that," Vin agrees, a note of seriousness in his voice. "Which is why we just snuck into his party even though Fabio told you we couldn't come?"

"We didn't sneak in," I counter gruffly. Spying a man dressed in black lurking on the outskirts of the room, I point him out with a grim warning, "Do you really think we'd make it past the front door if we had? Besides, Fabio always says no to everything. He worries worse than you do."

"Fine, we didn't sneak in," he admits. "We just kindly hijacked Uncle Fabio's invitation and spent five grand on a silver mirror to impress some crime lord's daughter."

"It's a nice gift," I say grudgingly, eyeing the pale blue wrapping paper and its nice white bow. The saleslady was right—it looks fitting for any princess, be her legitimate royalty or not. Meeting Vin's disapproving stare, I shrug. "Here is another lesson for you —in this world, my boy? You've got to pay to play."

"What would you call it? A down payment on my future?" His sneer reveals his true thoughts on that statement, but I smirk, satisfied. At least he's thinking like me for once.

"Exactly. And you might like this girl. I hear she studies in Vienna, at a school just as fucking pretentious as yours." He purses his lips at that, but I know him well enough to sense he's intrigued. Vinny admires smarts the way most men do tits. "She's a musician too. Blond. Beautiful, and—"

"And she's the kind of girl who has her father throw her some stuffy ass party for clout."

I bark out a laugh. Every now and again, he reminds me that beneath the book smarts, he's one hundred percent Vanici. "Like that makes a difference? Now, look sharp!" Ruffling his hair again, I shove him forward.

Speaking of his future, the time for jokes is over. Switching to a sterner tone, I tell him, "No heiress will pick you out of the crowd if you stick to me like a baby up his mother's skirt. Take this gift and go mingle—" I hand him the box. "And stop slouching. Remember who you are. Vanicis cower before no one."

"Except Mischa Stepanov."

"Hey!" I smack him on the back so hard he coughs. "No one. You got that?"

"Whatever you say, Don," he mutters under his breath. Nonetheless, he strolls off with his head held high, the way I taught him.

The same way my father taught me—Vanicis always keep our fucking chins up. You make eye contact with only those who matter. Shove your way past anyone bold enough or dumb enough to stand in your way.

Bow to no one.

We may not have much, but we are Vanici.

Daughter of a Stepanov or not, this *mafiya* princess will be lucky to have him. Willow is her name, and the things I told Vin weren't all bullshit. They say she's blond like her father. Thin. A swan, apart from the family of raptors she sprung from. For what it's worth, they've kept her out of the public eye, limiting the information known about her. I hear she's beautiful, at least. Like Vin, she runs in better social circles than the criminals her family controls, attending the best schools in the world.

Even if he won't admit it, Vincenzo deserves a woman like that. With his pretty pianist wife, he can play doctor all he wants, and an alliance with the Stepanovs will give him a hand up in the world I would have killed to possess at his age. Nestled in their powerful orbit, he'll be untouchable.

More importantly, he won't have to scrape like me.

He won't be like me.

The only problem?

As Vincenzo stated, we weren't exactly invited.

Why? I'd be a fool not to consider the most obvious of reasons—my reputation has preceded me, even after all these years. It would certainly explain why the man has rebuffed all my attempts to meet and why Fabio balked when I even suggested attending this little party.

Perhaps Mischa doesn't want to associate with such a monster, though from the rumors, he's no saint either. The same man who singlehandedly fought a bloody war for over a decade doesn't seem like the type to shy away from an old phantom from the past. Besides, if the man saw me as a real threat, I doubt we would have made it past security at all.

They're professional, the kind of men it costs good money to keep. Loyal. Subtle. Intimidating. A least twenty men cover this room alone. Dressed in black, they stand guard at strategic positions throughout as a constant reminder of the vigilance a man like Mischa lives under—and for a good reason. In our world, even a girl's debutante party could invite danger.

Danger I know well. Unease prickles my skin as I watch Vin meld into the assembled crowd of criminals and socialites. It's comical in a sense—politicians and crime lords alike, all gathered to kiss the ring of one man.

And, as if on cue, he appears beneath an archway at the back of the hall, drawing everyone's notice.

I stiffen at the sight of him, but not out of fear. Hell, maybe it's jealousy? Some men need whiskey to make it through the night while others…

They bask in the bosom of family like something out of a fucking sitcom. Despite his reputation, I've only seen him in person a handful of times. Tall, built like a bear with the cruelty and wit to match, he requires no introduction, nonetheless.

Basking in the attention, he starts forward, a beautiful brunette on his arm. A mature grace gives her a poise I doubt a nineteen-year-old girl would possess. His wife, I presume.

They say she too comes from a powerful web of families—the proud, ruthless Vasilevs and the callous Winthorps. Standing beside a man nearly twice her size, she looks every bit the welcoming hostess I'm sure she is.

But no sane woman could live with a man like him without possessing some ruthlessness of her own. Even my Olivia, with her soft, gentle ways, had a temper. Mischa's wife, I'm sure, is no different—and the elegance of this soiree is no doubt in part to her efforts. Though, judging from the size of her belly, Mischa looks well on his way to expanding his brood of daughters to display.

My jaw clenches as I take a step forward and consider approaching him now. Would he really refuse a direct meeting here?

In theory, he shouldn't. Donatello the Butcher is dead. Brick by brick, he rebuilt his life in the sun—and I don't intend to look back. Though while my days in the *famiglia* are over, I still have something to offer Mischa and his *mafiya*—an alliance. For peace. For stability.

For outright greed.

With Mischa's resources and my assets, we could secure this city for years to come with plenty of spoils for us both.

Emboldened by that thought, I take another step, tracking the couple across the room to a raised dais festooned with white roses. Clearing my throat, I adjust my collar and try to compile a fitting greeting.

"Hello, Mischa. Thank you for presenting your daughter on a silver platter? Have you met my nephew?"

Not exactly tactful, but it might do. So intent on my quarry am I, I don't realize someone's beside me until they grab my forearm, triggering years of instinct. My hand slaps against my pocket before I even remember that I'm unarmed. Those empty fingers curl into a fist regardless, poised to attack in any way possible. Tense, I jerk my head around and sigh.

"I thought I told you that you were not welcome," a man scolds. One look at him, and some of the tension drains from my muscles. Some. Rather than prepare to fight, I brace for a scolding like a boy caught by his mama with his hand in the cookie jar.

"Don't look so grumpy, Fabio," I gruffly reply, shrugging him off. "It's a party. Don't tell me you're tired already, old man?"

Though he's my age, thirty-five, he looks older. Gray has already started to color his auburn hair, a testament to his gift for worrying, though the trait is a double-edged sword. His obsession over detail makes him a sought-after accountant employed by everyone from the governor, to Mischa Stepanov himself.

"If it makes you feel better, I promise to be on my best behavior, scout's honor." I slap a hand over my chest for emphasis. "Trust me, Mama. You don't have to be up my ass tonight. Relax, I'm here for business."

"I wouldn't have to be 'up your ass'—" He grimaces with distaste at the wording. "If you weren't swaggering about the place, drawing notice. I saw how you looked at Antonio Salvatore. The least you could do is be subtle."

"This is me subtle, Fabio," I say, though I submit to letting him herd me toward the back of the room where we're more hidden among the crowd. Eyeing him, I'm forced to admit, "You look good tonight. Aiming to snag this Stepanova for yourself?"

He cuts a confident image in a tailored black tux, his hair perfectly coifed. It's easy to overlook the fact that he barely comes to the middle of my chest. For what he lacks in stature, the man more than makes up for in reputation.

No one in this room is more respected.

"At least you remembered her name," he grouses while snatching a glass of champagne from the tray of a passing server.

"The adding an 'a' at the end for a woman?" I gloat, pleased with myself. "This old dog can learn some new tricks."

"That's the simple way of putting it. These Russians are sticklers for respect. Though like that matters any to you." He takes a hearty sip from his glass as his cheeks flush pink. In a hoarse whisper, he confesses what has him so frazzled, "Even after all the years I've known you, you always manage to surprise me. Really, Don? Sneaking into the home of the head of the *mafiya* on my invitation. I'll be lucky if I don't wake up to a horse head in my bed tomorrow."

"He's the *mafiya*, not *famiglia*," I correct. "It's my kind that butcher horses—though Giovanni was partial to severing a finger or two instead. He was an animal lover, you see. I'm sure Mischa would just kill you. Or castrate you outright as a friendly warning."

Wincing, Fabio downs nearly half of his glass in one go. "Thanks for the reassurance, Don. *Cavolo!* Why am I even letting you talk me into this?"

"Because I'm invoking Olivia's name," I say softly. It's a low blow, but desperate times call for desperate measures. Sure enough, Fab's strained frown reveals the appeal hit its mark. "You're too good of a man to resist that," I point out, but in no way am I pleased with myself.

Olivia. I can clearly remember the last fucker I killed... One would think I'd never forget her face. Never.

But as my last dose of whiskey wears off, the painful truth seeps in—I can't even recall what she sounded like.

"She was twice the social charmer you are," Fabio says. Some of the worry lines around his mouth soften. "If only she could see you now. She'd probably piss herself from laughing at the sight of you stuffed into a suit. Could you find no tailor to fit you properly? Though I suppose it's too much to ask for a miracle—"

"Hey! I can't help it that I spent more of my life fighting in the streets than mingling with the upper class," I grumble, tugging at a sleeve of my jacket. Contrary to Fabio's snide remarks, it was expertly tailored by a man I trust, not to mention damn expensive. Alas, fine material and expert craftsmanship can only go so far.

My life didn't offer me the same pampered safety as a Willow Stepanova, or a Giovanni Rossi, who never wielded a weapon in his life.

Wars may begin and end, but battle scars will always remain.

"I should have known you wouldn't be able to resist drawing attention to yourself, even unintentionally," Fabio grouses. "It's in your nature, you damn, prideful Vanicis."

I feel my upper lip quirk into a grin. "Yes, us damned, incredible Vanicis. For all of your worrying, look at Vin." I nod to where he stands. Head held high, he's taken my encouragement to heart, radiating that trademark charm. Joy swells in my chest, overpowering even my own doubts.

My smart boy may have some inclination toward politics yet.

"My God, Donatello," Fabio exclaims, slapping a hand over his chest. "It's been years since I've seen you smile. And the last time you had just killed a man. The blood on your chin negated the effect a little."

"I think every father cracks a grin when he sees his baby boy out in the world." The seriousness of the moment flattens my mouth again. "Forget me. You ask why I came here? For him. I can't protect him forever."

Fabio sighs, inspecting his now empty glass. "There are real fathers out there who don't treat their own sons the way you treat Vin—let alone their nephews. Donella would be proud of you for how you've looked after him. I know she's looking down on us both right now, cursing us to hell and back for letting Vincenzo wear a tie that clashes so harshly with his skin tone. Really, Don? Navy?"

I shrug, gritting my teeth—but he's right. I can hear my little sister nagging from here. Even back when we had pennies to our name, she was so fixated on keeping up appearances. It was that pining for more that cost her her life in the end. When she didn't achieve the fairy tale ending she envisioned for herself, not even her son could keep her from a bottle of pills. One day, she took too damn many.

"A tie is a tie," I snap, shaking my head to banish the memory. "No matter the color, let's just hope it catches the younger Stepanova's eye, huh?"

The girl hasn't made her entrance yet, though I sense her arrival is imminent. Her parents are positioned expectantly by the dais, and an air of impatience buzzes through the shifting crowd. Already, anyone with something to prove has jockeyed for a prime spot near either of the two entrances she's bound to come in through.

"I feel like we're watching one of those animal documentaries about the breeding season," Fab remarks, ever the intellectual.

I'm not so tactful. "Welcome to the world that awaits those of us without wives," I tell him. "It's all one big pissing contest."

Some have gone through greater lengths, it seems. I catch a flicker of movement from above and spy a shadowed hall overlooking this space. An amusing thought makes me chuckle. Could the little *principessa* be lurking up there, gloating over her crowd from above?

From her vantage point, she'll have a good view of the contenders, including a familiar figure who managed to score one of the best spots available.

"Smart lad, Vin," I mutter with pride. "Smart lad."

Finally, a commotion near the back entrance draws my attention, along with everyone else in the room. Visible from beyond the archways, a retinue of people approach, Willow presumably among them. I surprise myself, eagerly craning my neck for a glimpse of this elusive *mafiya* princess along with everyone else.

"Don." I barely register Fabio snatching at my forearm until he digs his nails in. "Don!"

I swivel my head toward him in alarm. That wasn't his usual worrying tone. Constricted, his gaze is focused straight ahead and whatever he sees makes him clench his jaw. "It seems you weren't subtle enough."

Confused, I turn to look in the same direction and instantly find the source of his concern. Mischa Stepanov. Apparently, my party crashing has not gone unnoticed—and judging from his frown, the man has no intention of rethinking his slight.

I'm no pussy. I've stared down grown men armed with way more than a corsage of roses more than once in my life.

And I can safely say that none of those foes ever looked at me the way he does. With raw, searing anger that transforms his expression into a snarl. Funnily enough, I know that look well, seeing it every time I look in the fucking mirror these days.

There's no other word for it—hate.

"Wait here," Fabio mutters before slipping through the crowd. He reaches Mischa within seconds, presumably speaking in that smooth, confident way he excels at.

But even his skills can only go so far.

I know hostility when I see it. Alarm for Vincenzo mingles with anger, festering, building… I have to dig my nails into my palms just to wrestle it under control. I've come too far to fuck up now. Too far…

But only respect for Fabio keeps me from crossing the room and confronting the man directly.

All this time, I've written off his shunning of me as arrogance. To him, I could be just another greedy son of a bitch desperate to lick up his scraps. God knows I ignored more than my fair share of ass kissers when I was the *famiglia's* head.

But now? There is no mistake—he knows damn well who I am. Which rumor or horror story sparked his ire, I wonder? My past? The men I've killed? The crimes I've committed unchecked? Or maybe the man—with his many children—heard about what I did to the one I'd sworn to protect.

Her. Even while I look for Olivia at the bottom of every bottle of liquor, another face haunts me at night. Torments me, her dark eyes searching, her lips hollowed around a silent scream. Nothing keeps her away for long. Not booze. Not time. Not prayer.

My little Safiya…

No! I fight back her memory as my breathing quickens. Teeth gritted, I refocus every brain cell I have on Mischa. No matter the reason, he's gone out of his way to prove his point. I'm not welcome in his orbit.

"Don?" Vin's already by my side, scanning my face. "What's wrong?"

"Nothing." I snatch the present from him, but even as I force a smile, I know he suspects the truth. "But we need to leave," I murmur as Fabio glances at me with an unmistakable warning. From the corner of my eye, I see that retinue of security start to peel away from the perimeter one by one, converging in our direction. Grabbing Vin's arm, I practically drag him after me. "Now."

"Why? What's wrong?" he asks, but he doesn't resist as I hook my arm around his shoulders and head for the entrance of the ballroom.

"Just a minor hiccup," I say, glancing back to find Fabio following us. "I'll explain later. But who needs a fancy shindig anyway? I'll buy you whatever drinks you want back at the hotel. We should celebrate before you return to London."

He's still frowning, but he's too smart to argue now. Guilt taunts me for bringing him here in the first place. Together, we exit the manor the way we came, skirting the scrutiny of Stepanov agents with every step.

A guard we pass on our way into the foyer touches a headset affixed to his ear, frowning, his gaze on me. Never before have I so bitterly regretted playing by the rules and coming here unarmed. Would Mischa be above mounting an attack right at this moment?

I can't tell. Someone knew to expect our hasty exit, at least. We've barely made it down the front walkway when my driver pulls up. Not of my own employ, he's a hire from the hotel, but judging from his blank expression, I doubt rushing his clients from fancy venues is an unusual occurrence.

"I'll take that, sir," he says, stepping out to retrieve the gift from me and set it in the trunk.

As I climb into the back seat, I make a mental note to tip him extra. Fuck, if he can get us off this property within the next few minutes, I'll employ him my damn self. Fear of Mischa isn't what sparks my impatience. Adrenaline rushes through my veins, making me think more clearly than I have in months. Calculating. The icy way I cringe from these days. Like the world is against me and fighting tooth and nail is the only way out.

It was the dark impulse I'd relied on back in the day. The cruelty that led me to do more than just kill a man. No, I had to make him suffer. Make him bleed.

Ensure that anyone watching would swear then and there to never cross me.

If I were still that man, Mischa's silence would not be tolerated so kindly. I'd march up to the bastard, put a knife to his throat, and demand he faces me like a man and states his issue outright. It's the way things should be fucking done…

"Don?" I don't even realize I've been holding my breath until Vin sprawls out on the seat across from me.

"Some party," he gripes, oblivious to the danger. Or so one might assume by looking at him—but his brown eyes are alert, darting toward the windows at the imposing manor looming above.

Tension stiffens my muscles, and the twisted thoughts come faster. *I've raised Vin too soft. Too weak. He has to learn for himself that nothing in this world comes for free. You've got to fight for it. Rip from the bastard who has it. You win.*

Sweat dribbles down my neck. I'm clutching the end of the seat just to keep myself in this car. I feel like I'm damn near close to exploding from this goddamn suit entirely by the time Fabio wrenches open the door and sticks his head inside.

"Sorry to cut your fun short," he says to Vin. "But I need your uncle to handle some very important business for me. I'll make it up to you, though." He tosses something to him that I can't make out in the dark. "Take my card for the week. Have some fun on me. The kind of fun stuffy Donatello might disapprove of."

"Thank you, Uncle Fabio." Vin grins though I suspect the boy's idea of a good time is far from what Fabio may have in mind.

"I bet you'll find a series of charges from a bookstore," I taunt.

But as Fabio meets my gaze, I realize the true depth of the situation he has the sense to hide from Vincenzo. He's worried. Judging from the prominence of the wrinkles around his mouth, I suspect this little incident will take all of his cunning to smooth over.

I don't even have the chance to ask him why before he leaves, closing the door behind him. Just as quickly, the driver takes off, whisking us away from Stepanov manor with a briskness that significantly improves my chances of offering him a job.

"I would have liked to see what she looked like," Vin says wistfully. "Given all the pomp and circumstance, I bet I dodged a bullet. Rich men tend to overcompensate, and going off the expense of that party, that guy must have a lot to make up for."

He sounds so damn confident that I snort, shocking myself. Gradually, that icy, unfeeling thinking process gives way to the warmth I've clung to all these years. It's like I can breathe again, and I eye the boy, feeling an ache in my chest. If my love for him could grow any more, I'd explode from the force of it by now. God bless him; he's kept me sane.

"You're quiet because you know I'm right," he teases.

"I hear she's beautiful," I counter. Beautiful, rich, and off-limits to him.

Fuck. If anything, tonight proved that securing his future won't be as easy as catching the eye of some spoiled debutante.

But I'll find another way.

Any way.

"You have that look again," Vin scolds, crossing his arms, already over the fancy event. His posture slouches as he adjusts his glasses on the bridge of his nose. I recognize that studious expression—the second we return to the hotel, he'll probably sequester himself in his room, eager to pore over whatever medical texts he lugged on the plane ride here.

Just like that, I have to question if he truly is my nephew.

"What look?" I demand.

"The 'woe is me. I'm Donatello, the toughest, saddest son of a bitch in the world. I do things like dragging my Vincenzo to extravagant birthday parties even though I can count the number of times I've worn a suit on one hand.'" He hams up his performance, mocking my voice, and puffing up his chest. "'I beat myself up for every little thing because I don't know how to operate outside of perfection.' You can relax, Don. I'm not mad."

His smile wrings a similar one out of me, and I choke out a noise that could be a chuckle. The little bastard. Ever since he was a boy, he's had a knack for cutting to the heart of a situation and turning it on its head in one go. He certainly turned my world on its head—for the better.

He deserves so much more than I can give him.

More than some spoiled *mafiya* girl.

"You can be sappy when you want to, you know that?" I toss back.

"Yeah. And I'm fairly sure that your matchmaker story was bullshit. Just admit it. I think you wanted her for yourself." He wags a finger disapprovingly at me. "You're old enough to be her father. That's gross, Don."

"Sure, Vin. I wanted a spoiled little socialite nearly half my age. The girl wouldn't know what to do with me."

"Maybe she could get you a better suit for one?"

"Oh? Is this your way of coming out to me, Vin? Turning down a beautiful, rich brat in the name of fashion? I'd love you all the same if you were gay, you know."

He laughs harder. "No. This is my way of saying you need a woman in your life. At least then I won't have nightmares while I'm at university of you waking up in a pool of booze mixed with your own vomit. It's time to settle down, old man."

"Why settle?" I raise my hands and lean against the leather seat. "I already have an heir to carry on my legacy. Besides, I was married once. What use is another woman? You're all I need, Vincenzo." I'm not laughing anymore. I don't think I've ever been so serious. So earnest. Vin squirms in discomfort, but I don't shy away from adding, "You are my heir. My legacy. The future of the Vanici line rests with you. You will carry it all, and look damn good doing so. I don't need anyone else."

"You do," he says softly. His eyes take on a distant gleam that triggers an ominous dread. I'm tensing before he even whispers her name, "What about Safy?"

Every time, it hits with brutal force, this pain—affecting me more than the remnants of my old icy mindset. I crumple beneath the guilt. Like a wave, it crashes down, drowning out everything else. The need to breathe. Think. I can't even see as the world goes black.

In the midst of that darkness, her face appears in my mind. So innocent. So trusting. My little Safiya.

Only Vincenzo can ever bear to say her name. Why? He doesn't know the truth, believing she died in a horrible accident all those years ago. I fed him that lie myself.

"Don?" I blink to find Vin nearly leaning out of his seat, his eyes on my face. "I'm sorry," he says. "I know you don't like to talk about her."

I look away, fighting the emotions down to the depths of my soul where they belong. The guilt, and the pain, and the regret. Gradually, I forget her—that face, those eyes. I banish her memory—for now. She always comes back.

Every night. Every nightmare. She always returns.

"You're here now," I rasp, turning my attention back to Vin. "You."

He nods solemnly. "You're lucky to have me," he says. "I, at least, know how to wear a suit."

2

DON

I barely get one glass of whiskey into Vin before he's already heading up to bed.

"That fancy university has made you soft, whelp," I scold him, horrified by his nearly full drink. "Be thankful that as a doctor, you won't be expected to out drink a Russian informant while trying to secure a deal for a shipment."

He raises an eyebrow. "I thought you were doing everything on the up and up these days?"

I scoff, but he's right. While he's been slaving away to earn those good grades, I've been on my own journey toward self-improvement. The new Donatello Vanici makes his wealth through legal means only. My first step in that direction was securing partial ownership of Hell's Gambit's sole port. The next goal in mind? Plaster the city with enough advertisements to overcome any hostile parties who might be trying to undermine me, be them Antonio Salvatore or Mischa Stepanov himself.

I've already covered the airport to capture any incoming businessmen looking to make connections here. I'd say that in a year, I'll have my own shipping empire. Hell, even without the *mafiya* or the *famiglia* on my side, I'm nearly there anyway. Most of the legitimate commerce flowing into this godforsaken place comes through me.

And I'm proud to say that I haven't stolen or extorted a single dime.

But going on the straight and narrow overnight can't help a man's reputation. There are still plenty of my enemies waiting to strike a blow—from law enforcement to jaded old families. The Salvatores being one of them.

And, as it seems, the Stepanov clan.

"Take Javier when you go up," I command, swiping my hand through Vin's hair. Like a good boy, I'd left the old bodyguard here while at the manor, but I know better than to let Vin wander around alone.

"I don't think I need a nanny, Don," Vin says, but the argument is half-hearted.

"A nanny wouldn't look half as badass holding a gun as Javier," I counter. One of the first professionals I hired after leaving the *famiglia*, I trust the man with my life—more importantly, I trust him with Vin's. "Humor me. If you won't carry a gun on you, at least stick close to someone who will."

He eyes me sideways with far more maturity than a kid twenty-one should possess. "You're drunk, Don." His tone is resigned, belaying a truth that causes me to snatch up my glass rather than face.

He relays it regardless, "Though, to be fair, you're always drunk."

"I prefer the term 'inebriated,'" I counter, saluting him with my drink. At least I'm not falling down pissing myself like my father. A few shots of whiskey on the regular keep me dulled enough to think with some ounce of sanity, let alone sleep until morning. Considering my track record when I was sober, I think it is a fair trade-off. Some nights it actually helps.

Vin disapproves of the habit. "Night, Don," he says in that soft, sad way that makes me flinch with guilt.

"Night, Vinny!" I choke down my drink entirely and call to his retreating back, "As soon as you're married and practicing as some renowned doctor, I won't have to hide behind a bottle ever again."

The sad part? I'm not joking. Maybe then, I'll finally know peace. If my liver holds up, that is. I'm on my third glass when the seat beside me is taken by a figure who wrinkles his nose in disgust.

"How did I know I'd find you here?" Fabio grumbles while waving down the bartender. Rather than hard liquor, he orders a glass of water with a lemon wedge. Typical Fab.

"Shouldn't you be dancing with the younger Stepanova by now?" I ask, raising an eyebrow.

"Stop sulking," Fab scolds. "And for your information, no one got to dance with her. She never showed. At least not before I left."

Frowning, I eye the gilded clock mounted over a fireplace at the other end of the bar. "We left what? Four hours ago?"

He nods, grabbing for the water glass the bartender sets down before him. "Four hours. You should have seen it. We were all milling about like scurrying cockroaches as the *hors d'oeuvres* dwindled. Soon it became a bloodbath for the last glass of champagne. It seems our little Stepanova found other entertainment tonight. A shame." He shakes his head with a wistful sigh. "She was spared a hall of lecherous old men hoping to charm her in pursuit of her father's favor. I'll have you know that poor Antonio Salvatore looked like he might piss himself in disappointment."

I chuckle at the mental image before another takes its place— Salvatore skulking around, hoping to claim the girl for himself. I wouldn't put it past the sick bastard to want someone so young. He can't keep a real woman long enough to tell the difference.

Eyeing Fabio, I ask, "Mischa ever say why I wasn't welcome at his little party?"

I'm more curious than I let on. Anxious too. My foot bounces against the rung of my stool, and those dark thoughts start to gnaw through my alcoholic daze. Virgin mother Mary above, the man is lucky I'm reformed.

"No," Fabio admits, but his grim expression confuses me even more. "I know a death glare when I see it, however. I explained you were my guest, but it did no good. I'd go as far as to say I may have just lost the Stepanov accounts from my clientele because of my association with you."

"Bullshit," I declare, lifting my glass and slamming it against his. "You're the best damn accountant in the game. He'd be a fool to dump you, regardless of your ties to me."

"I'm still convinced you haven't told me everything about what's going on between you two," Fabio suspects, eyeing his lemon wedge. "That look... You don't build up that kind of animosity for nothing. Come clean now, Donatello. You fucked his wife, is that it? She's pretty enough for your tastes with that sweet, wholesome thing and all. If one of Mischa's little whelps is yours, that would explain his feelings a bit."

I scoff at the prospect. "No. Though, if I had, considering how fertile she is, I'd probably have an army of children by now. Then I wouldn't be pining for Mischa's approval, pissing myself with worry every time Vin leaves the country, and I certainly wouldn't be spending my nights at the bar like some pathetic *stronzo*. Bartender!" I flag the man down and shove my empty glass toward him. "Another."

"I'll try to find out," Fabio says softly. "If only to satisfy my own curiosity. The man deals with Salvatore, so it can't be a moral standing. You may be no saint, but I'd bet my soul on you getting into heaven over him."

Even I have to chuckle at that assessment. "Antonio Salvatore may be a cunt, but he's never killed half as many men as I have," I point out. At least not with his bare hands. The pussy prefers to hide behind mercenaries, covering his tracks. Or, as in the case of Gino Mangenello, manipulating others into doing his dirty work. Still, sin is sin, and I've spent my fair share of time in the confessional to be unable to judge anyone.

"It's not a contest, Don," Fab says.

"No. Though if it were, let me add up the score, then. Antonio Salvatore may have gone through four wives in his lifetime, but he lost them all to divorce—"

"His latest one died in a car crash, remember?" Fabio interjects. "The Salieri heiress."

"Yes, but he didn't *fail* them." My voice breaks, but the arrival of a fresh shot of whiskey provides the perfect distraction. I down it and mutter, "He never had to scrape pieces of their brains from his living room floor with his bare hands—"

"God damn it, Don," Fabio exclaims, clearing his throat. He looks visibly pale, though he should. His sister was the woman in question.

My Olivia…

Could I prove that Salvatore was behind the attack that killed her? No. But I more than got my revenge on the sick sons of bitches who carried out the plan. Gino Mangenello suffered the most of them all.

"Another," I demand, striking the counter. But the promise of another drink isn't enough to shut me up. "As vile a cunt as he is, Antonio Salvatore never failed to protect that horrid fucking family of his—"

"Protect?" Fabio sniffs. "The bastard is no father of the year. I've heard more than one rumor about his little girl sporting bruises —the one who lives with him."

"While he may beat his children senseless," I say over him, "he hasn't sold one of them—"

"Enough! Don't even compare yourself to him," Fabio snarls. He levels me with a hallmark stare that serves as one of the many reasons why his reputation is so respected in our circles. Despite all his pomp, Fabio always tells the truth, no matter how cruel it may be. A skill both valued in an accountant as well as a friend.

"What happened wasn't your fault, and you've made the best of it," he insists. "And as for that last thing you mentioned…"

"Selling a child, you mean?" I choke down the rest of my drink and gesture for more. "Vincenzo mentioned her tonight. He whispered her name, and I don't even have the heart to tell him that I'm the reason she's gone."

"You were mad with grief," he says. "That doesn't make it right, but there is no telling what a man would do in that state. I remember how you were back then. God knows, you could have done so much worse…" He shivers, and the horror unfurling across his face is a testament to how hard I've worked to change. Never again will I be that man.

I've gotten clean.

Gotten a soul.

But even so, most days, it feels like God is merely mocking me, testing my patience by the day. What might he throw my way that could finally put me over the edge?

"We all have our lot to live with, Don," Fab says. "Stop punishing yourself. You want to know why? Because even after what you've done, you live with it. You've done your best to repent, and I think you have."

Repent. He makes it sound so damn righteous to forsake the criminal underworld I was raised in. Try to forge a path on the right side of the law. Raise Vincenzo with the skills that will never force him to make the mistakes I did.

"Look at our precious boy," Fabio points out as if reading my mind. "He's studying to be a doctor. *Madonna!* Donella is dancing in her grave."

A tired smile tugs on the corner of my mouth. "She should have married you, you know. Rather than run off with some punk half the man you are. It's the Vanici in us, always leading us to stubborn defiance of our hearts. The only downside is that Vin would have turned out about a foot shorter and two feet wider."

He rolls his eyes and stands, fishing a gold money clip from his suit pocket. "Bah! Vin is fine just the way he is. I wouldn't be half as fanatic a guardian as you are. But as much as you love him, you need to try showing some of that to the man in the mirror."

I scowl at my reflection, barely visible on the polished surface of the bar counter. In that man's dark gaze, I see only evil restrained by sheer willpower. I see violence. A lost soul destined to burn in the fires of hell where it belongs.

Then I blink, and I see a smaller face. Rounder, with wide, searching eyes and a hopeful smile. I don't banish her this time. Reaching out, I stroke the edge of a tiny cheek, feeling only cold, hard wood in response.

"She would be nineteen by now," I say, though I barely hear myself above the surging thump of my own heartbeat. The sound chugs away, mocking me with every steady beat. She's dead, but I still live on. Stubbornly, this body lives, enduring the abuse I've put it through.

"Her birthday was in the spring. Little Safy. Nineteen." I chuckle at the thought of it, picturing her dancing at her own debutante ball. The pain returns like a lance, ripping me apart—but still… My heart keeps beating on. "I promised her once I'd throw her a grand party, can you believe that? She was so excited. God forgive me, I promised her—"

"You've spent too damn long punishing yourself," Fab snarls in disgust. "Enough. I think it's time you strive for a little happiness, huh?"

He sets down a crisp stack of bills. It's more than enough to cover the tab with a hefty tip to spare.

As he turns on his heel, he adds over his shoulder. "Oh, and Vin made me promise not to tell you, but he's already used my card to charge a special gift to help cheer you up. It's in your room."

He winks, and I'm genuinely unnerved. Vin and Fabio's "gifts" are rarely of the desirable variety. But hell, at least I'm distracted by the prospect enough to take another drink and clear my head.

"It better not be another glitter bomb or whatever the fuck those things are called," I grumble, cringing at the memory of the pink sparkles I'd spent weeks trying to wash from my hair the last time the pair felt benevolent enough to give me a present.

Fabio just laughs. "Goodnight."

When I finally tear myself away from the bar, I approach the group of rooms we rented on the hotel's top floor. It was an expense well worth Vin's supposed introduction to high society. I even gave him the pick of the lot with encouragement to enjoy himself with whoever he chose.

Deep down, I know the boy is too much of a goody-goody to take me up on the offer. In contrast to his, my room is a simple suite. I enter it, scanning the narrow space for any hint of Vin's "present."

I don't have to look too hard. On the bed is a silver tray sporting a small white cake, upon which someone wrote in blood-red icing the phrase, "Best Papa." Surrounding it is a crudely formed smiley face crafted out of what appears to be silver condom wrappers and a handful of the best damn cigars money can buy.

"Little bastard," I scoff, swiping my finger through a dollop of icing. I'm smiling as I sample the taste. It isn't bad, though it could be made of shit, and I'd appreciate it no less.

My boy. God bless his devious little soul.

Though maybe more devious than I thought…

A flicker of movement makes me pivot, instinctively reaching for my—still empty—pocket. The lack of a weapon I can easily rectify the second I can get to the safe in the closet. Though, as my eyes narrow over the intruder standing in the corner of the room, I let my hands fall, all thoughts of fighting forgotten.

Damn. An appreciative whistle escapes me as I stand straighter and inspect my visitor fully. For the first night in a while, I wholeheartedly regret dulling my senses with so much alcohol.

That's the only explanation for why I might have overlooked the woman watching me from beside the bed. Slender and blond with dark eyes that swallow most of her delicate face, she brings a new meaning to the term present.

"Vinny, Vinny, Vinny," I murmur on a long exhale as my gaze drinks her in. While a bit on the thin side, a tight black dress clings to her like a second skin, revealing more than enough curves to work with. Perky little breasts and a nice round ass to start.

My cock stirs for the first time in weeks, and the sensation triggers a legitimate concern. How long has it been since my last lay?

Too damn long.

"What a damn fine son you are, my boy!" Appreciation thickens my tone, but the blond doesn't simper in gratitude for the compliment.

Instead, she raises her hand, and I stiffen as the light glints off the object she holds. I recognize the shape instantly, and—if anything—my pulse surges faster, excitement heightening my senses to a manic state of amusement.

The little minx has a knife.

3

WILLOW

TWENTY-FOUR HOURS EARLIER...

One of my composition professors is an accomplished pianist who has performed with various orchestras worldwide. Undeniably talented, he also happens to be a virulent misogynist. Working with him was a trying nine-week-long test of my patience.

I did learn something from him, though—a valuable lesson when it comes to dealing with men outside of my family—most are vain, selfish creatures unable to think beyond a pretty face. It's an aggravating realization to come to, but there's also power in that knowledge.

There is power in destroying some pompous lecher's perceptions of success.

"A young girl shouldn't be studying music, wasting her beauty away," he'd scolded me during our first lesson. *"You should be living your life, thinking pretty thoughts, and finding a husband to whisk you away."*

He'd shouted, of course, presuming that I was deaf instead of mute. With an eyebrow raised in feigned pity, he then suggested I, *"Take a less intense course this semester. I'm disinclined to make any adjustments to compensate for a disability as I don't think it would be fair to the other students. I'm sure you understand, dear."*

I did understand. After all, he had a point. "Compensating" his notoriously ruthless schedule for one lone woman would have been a crime against humanity. So, to ease his concerns, I'd proceeded to play a concerto so complicated he promptly kept his mouth shut for the rest of the class.

"Disabled" or not, I went on to pass that semester with top marks.

Still, I could kick myself for channeling his banal thinking now. Maybe, in some warped, twisted sense of logic, the bastard had a point? On the eve of her nineteenth birthday, a girl should think nothing but pretty, happy thoughts. Fantasies starring men her own age, or silly daydreams, perhaps?

Especially if said girl is rich, well-protected, and healthy. Her life is perfect, and she should be grateful, not fearful. I know firsthand—it could be worse.

Therefore, fully content, someone in my position should be looking toward the future—not at a billboard innocently placed in her path as though fate itself intended it to be there.

Stopping short, I blink several times. Shake my head. I even pinch myself on the wrist so hard the pain lances up my arm.

Nothing makes the sight disappear.

Ironically, I should have been too distracted to even notice such an obscure advert but, for whatever reason, I couldn't miss it.

And it can't be real.

His face, staring at me from beneath a glossy veneer, must be the result of some horrific waking nightmare—and it could be… If it weren't for the faint wrinkles around his eyes. I never picture him like this. Aged. Weary, and yet in so many ways, exactly the same. Dark, brooding eyes glowering at the world before him, his mouth curled in a beguiling half-smile.

There's no mistaking him for anyone else—this is Donatello.

Pain rips through my stomach as though I've been punched, building with every new detail I notice. Even in a photograph, vigor screams from his coifed, dark hair and bronzed skin. Both could be the work of Photoshop, yes.

But the man I knew would be too proud to craft such a façade.

It's him. In the background stretches an expanse of water and a succinct title reading: *V Development Group: We build the future you desire.*

A future…

I blink again and rub at my eyes for good measure. This can't be real. Only in my imagination could such a cruel parallel be cast by that one word.

Because by just looking at him, one would never know of the so-called "future," he ripped from me. The life he brutally stole. The beloved friend who put a little girl through unimaginable horror.

Closing my eyes can't erase it. They burn beneath the assault of memories, and it takes everything I have in me to choke them back. Squash the emotions the way my father taught me to.

"Focus, Mouse," Mischa would scold while training me with simple defensive moves in the courtyard of our home. *"You always let your anger get in the way. Move past it! Focus!"*

It was that mindset that drew me to studying music. Sheets of notes required more than just emotion to play effectively. They had to be analyzed rationally, every note carefully planned.

I try to do that now, pushing past the jumbled emotions clawing through my heart.

At the end of it all, one reality remains—I am not that girl anymore. He should mean nothing to the person I am in this moment. This rich, sheltered woman. This accomplished, scholarly musician. Nothing…

But like some lingering infection, he's already inside me anyway, seeping into my veins with every frantic surge of my pulse. The memories descend one after the other, until I'm drowning in them. All I can think about is *him*. Donatello, the man who left me for dead. So sweet, his laugh could infect an entire room of people with joy. One smile from him could charm the sun from the sky.

His love was poison, but as a child, I gladly took every ounce he had to give.

And after seven long years, I've healed from him. Through grit, and luck, and pain, I salvaged the life he tried to destroy. I've found a new family with which to enjoy it. A new protector. A father.

A new life.

Nineteen is a significant birthday in the world I belong to now, denoting so many things—freedom first among them, womanhood overall. The day a girl shakes the bonds of childhood forever and takes her rightful place in society. It may be more symbolic in this case, given my real birthday was months ago—but I am no longer Safiya Mangenello, and Willow Stepanova will achieve this milestone with fanfare.

On this one day, I should be the happiest…

"Miss?" a voice beckons from the exit of this private terminal. I look over to find a man with black hair shorn close to his head, standing at the door. His dark suit and watchful gray eyes set him apart from any other airport customer—even before someone would happen to notice the gun professionally tucked beneath his jacket. He's tall enough that I have to crane my head back to meet his gaze.

For his benefit, I force a smile, but I can't seem to make myself move. Not yet. Slowly, I return my attention to the billboard, praying that it's vanished, only a delusion after all.

Dark, glittering eyes meet mine mockingly, crushing that hope. He's still here—in more ways than one. An address in the corner of the advert refers to a location in Hell's Gambit—a port city so close it's laughable. I scan it over and over, burning every last letter into my memory. Only then do I turn away and continue forward.

With every step, trivial observations creep into my brain, and I gladly let them, trading the past for stupid, nineteen-year-old thoughts. I'm overdressed. It's still stifling hot this early in summer. Sweat slips beneath the collar of my blouse as I exit the airport for the sweltering fresh air. I'd give anything to trade this beige wool skirt and sweater for the light linen shifts I used to wear as a child.

Holding the door for me, my father's trusted bodyguard, Evgeni, stands beside a cart containing many of my suitcases. He smiles the moment I'm in view, but I know him too well. His eyes scan my face with undisguised concern.

"It seems your mood has changed between you stepping off the plane and now," he teases. "I'm sure you heard the news? About your not-so-secret birthday party, that is." He makes a show of cupping his hand around his mouth, his voice a mock whisper. "I think your papa's invited half the world by now."

I blink to show I'm unsurprised, and he chuckles. As suspected, I know. Mischa couldn't keep a secret, even with me out of the country. He's too proud, not to mention unsubtle, in posing many "hypothetical" questions regarding which kind of party ornaments I might enjoy during our video calls.

"You're too smart for your own good," Evgeni remarks as we approach the black car waiting nearby. "If I didn't know better, I'd think you made your flight come in two hours early on purpose. Your papa had a whole grand welcome planned, but you've managed to skirt it. So far, at least." He winks, alluding to the event I've both dreaded and anticipated for weeks.

"Don't be too mad," he says as we approach the sleek sedan my father sent to collect me. He loads my suitcases into the trunk and faces me, rubbing his hands together. "If my daughter got into that fancy school of yours, I think I'd at least throw her a party, even if she hated them."

I smile warily at that, but I can't shake a niggling sense of dread that has loomed over this date for weeks. Mischa means well, I know he does—but he has no idea what the symbolism of this birthday means, not even after seven years since he adopted me.

Nineteen. It's a chilling reminder of everything I've lost. It's a sickening anniversary of the day I became someone else apart from who I was born as. A shadow. A mouse. Someone trapped in limbo between two worlds. Two families.

I can't forget his voice…

"I will throw you a grand debutante celebration when you come of age, little cucciola. No other shall compare…"

"I'm not supposed to tell you," Evgeni warns, his voice cutting through the memory. Blinking, I turn to find him watching me in a way that warns distracting me was his goal. "So if you snitch, I'll deny it, but I hear he's gone all out for you, your papa. He even bought a suit. Give it a chance; you may find that you enjoy having a little fun."

He crinkles his mouth, seeming so much younger than a man in his early thirties.

"Come on, let's get going." Clapping his hands, he ushers me into the back of the vehicle and then claims the driver's seat. "And, only for you, I'll let you decide if I let your papa know in advance that you got in early. If you want, you can mount a surprise all your own. Turn the tables, so to speak. Should I call?"

Even the thought of arriving to fanfare and drama makes me cringe.

"Thought so," Evgeni says with a nod.

He takes off toward the countryside, and the sprawling fields and swaths of green forests usher in a nostalgia potent enough to distract from everything else. I've been so desperate for the change in scenery, and a sigh escapes me, soft and wistful. I've missed this place. While away in Vienna, longing for my old home plagued me constantly. The stone manor, with its familiar walls, draped in ivy and the abundant rose gardens dotting the property. I've missed Mischa and his booming laugh, and my mother's soft grace. I've missed the many children who fill the manor with more noise and clamor than the busiest orchestra.

But beneath those charming memories, my past festers. Ripped open by one chance sighting, not even the delightful views from my window can soothe the wound. He corrupts me, creeping into my skull. Donatello, dwelling in a nearby city. It almost seems too cruel to be reality. I've pined for home, but now I wish for nothing more than to be back on the plane.

It's strange. Time used to seem endless when I was a child. Despite how overwhelming a stretch it feels like now, in reality, I'll only have a few short months before I'll be back in Vienna—an education made possible only by the man who took me in when everyone else in my life turned their back.

Mischa deserves my focus, no one else.

"Don't stress about the party," Evgeni calls from the front seat, still troubled by my expression. Apparently, he thinks the party is the cause of my unease, but I don't have the courage to correct him. "It isn't until tomorrow night, after all. If you really don't want it, I'm sure your father would cancel it if you asked him."

He's right, and I purse my lips at the prospect. Mischa would do anything I asked him to—but a man like him isn't the type to plan parties without a reason well beyond some trivial age milestone. Years ago, another man spoke of my far-off debutante debut in more stark terms. *Your ball will be the best in the world,* he'd boasted. *No one will doubt which family you come from.*

Mischa's pride is entwined with this celebration as much as his love is.

As I settle into the back seat, I try to imagine what such a party might look like. Something grand, but presumably no different than any gala or performance I've suffered through this past year. And yet, it promises to be worlds apart from the modest events that peppered my childhood. Before…

My life was even more sheltered than it is now. Most girls would be embarrassed by the lack of traditional milestones, I think. I had no real mother to guide me then—mine was too busy partying. No, my modest presents were always clumsily wrapped by a man who could master a weapon but never understood the concept of a ribbon. Still, he tried if only to make me happy. Even my cakes, he would bake himself, coloring the icing whatever happened to be my favorite hue that year. Without fail, he'd attempt to write my name across the top and always run out of room, forcing him to condense it into his affectionate moniker—Safy. Afterward, he would sing to me in Italian despite his preference that we practice English at home. To make me laugh, he'd sing in as high a pitch as he could, straining his deep baritone so that it comically broke as the song went on. *Happy birthday to you, my Safiya…*

His voice has never left me. Long after he turned his back on me and walked away, I can still hear him, echoing inside my skull. *"Do with her what you will,"* he'd said to the stranger keeping me restrained. *"I don't care."*

My throat thickens as my eyes blur, obscuring my view from the windows. Desperately, I blink back any threat of tears, choking them down. The past is the past—and I made peace with mine a long time ago.

Or maybe I haven't…

The billboard just gives me an excuse to confess the obvious—he will always live in my head, smiling that goofy, deceitful grin while balancing my lopsided cake on one hand and a present on the other.

"Miss Willow?"

I look over to find the back seat door open and Evgeni standing on the other end. The car has stopped, I realize. Before me looms a stoic structure formed of gray stone and creeping ivy.

"We're home," Evgeni says, extending his hand for me. "True to my word, I haven't called to inform anyone. That's bought you a few minutes of peace, but the sooner you face your parents, the sooner everyone else can pretend you won't notice the parade of caterers streaming in through the back."

Eager for a new distraction, I scramble out and crane my neck to take in the house fully. As my gaze drifts over the familiar architecture, my lips quirk, and my heart swells with pride.

"It might not be some fancy university," Evgeni remarks, "but I guess it does hold some charm, doesn't it?"

I nod. Stepanov Manor is relatively old by most standards, lacking the modern embellishments that adorn the fancy mansions of the wealthier students at the conservatory. Even so, its worn stone walls convey a familial softness no other dwelling could come close to. Expansive emerald lawns lush with rose gardens create a world apart from the harsh reality waiting beyond these walls.

It's paradise. Always, when I'm here, it's like being transported to another realm, one where the harsher realities of the world could never encroach. A place where someone like Donatello Vanici doesn't exist, and where my only identity is that of a beloved daughter.

But, as I approach the servant's entrance, I have no delusions about the cost of such peace. Much like my idyllic childhood, all of this security and luxury is made possible by the sheer efforts of one man who rules it all.

And no matter how beautiful it seems…

This paradise is paid for with blood.

4

WILLOW

"Pretend to be surprised," Evgeni warns as he hauls my bags through the servant's entrance. We're alone in this spacious back hallway, but already telltale signs of the impending party are obvious. Stacks of boxes clutter the space, leaving barely enough room to reach the nearby breakroom beside the stairs. An audible commotion warns of a flurry of chaos taking place throughout the house. Paramount among the noises? Child-like shouting.

"Hurry." Evgeni nods to the stairs and winks. "I'll have these brought up and unpacked later. You have maybe five minutes before the others sniff you out, so enjoy it."

I start up the back stairwell feeling my throat tighten. The wooden floors creak beneath my steps as if welcoming me back, and I can't resist trailing my fingers along the worn beige walls. Excitement tinges the air, giving the old structure a renewed sense of wonder. Six months away might as well have been six years. Before I even reach my bedroom on the second floor, I have a grim suspicion as to what might await me. As expected,

55

I've barely pushed my door open when I see it, draped over my bed with loving care.

My hand falls to my side as the door sways, obscuring the sight from view for a split-second before revealing it again in breathtaking glory—a gown fit for any debutante.

I'm immediately flashed back to over seven years ago, the first time someone presented me with a similar dress. That garment had been part of a ruse in which I was meant to smuggle drugs for a criminal. It might as well have been a funeral dress.

The presentation this time is admittedly far different. I creep toward it, tallying up the differences as I go. A soft, creamy off-white, this gown spans the length of my childhood bed. Tentatively, I run my fingers over a bodice formed of delicate interlocking lace and marvel at the feel. Silk, I suspect, buttery soft to the touch.

It's beautiful—but much like my first white dress, the purpose of this newer one is more figurative than anything else. Wearing it, I'll be a dove, finally let loose from her protective cage.

I'll be presented to the world as a Stepanova.

"Do you like it?" a voice calls tentatively from the doorway. I turn to find Ellen, my adoptive mother, standing there, her blue eyes as perceptive as always. "I thought I'd heard someone moving around this wing two hours too early. Welcome home!"

She approaches me, cradling her swollen belly with one hand and her neatly coiled brunette hair with the other. As she eyes the dress, a hesitant smile flits across her lips, making her seem even younger than she already does. If she claimed to be my age, I doubt anyone would be able to tell the difference from a glance. The only flaw in her delicate beauty is a series of faint, silver scars on the left side of her face, strategically obscured by a few loose brown curls.

"I know it's a bit much," she admits, referring to the dress. "I wasn't sure of the style, but Mischa insisted. What do you think?"

Whatever she sees in my expression emboldens her to approach the bed.

Gingerly, she drapes the fabric over her arm before turning to me. "May I?" she asks.

I nod, and she positions the garment against my body, circling to stand behind me. I catch sight of myself in a floor-length mirror in the far corner. The girl I find staring back could be a stranger, but I can't tell if it's because her dress is so beyond my usual fashion scope.

Or because her face is so unnaturally blank.

"It's going to look stunning on you," Ellen murmurs while smoothing a stray bit of hair behind my ear. "You are stunning. I know I've blathered on about it so many times, but…" Her lips strain to conceal another smile. "We are so very proud of you. Mischa can't stop talking about your accomplishments, and the girls were pestering me all week about your arrival. I'm surprised you even made it inside the house without getting ambushed—"

"You're back." As if on cue, a slender boy slips across the doorway, proving her point moot. Whip-thin, with wild blond curls, he's like a miniature version of Ellen. Her smile widens as he draws up to her side.

"Why didn't you tell me she was home already, Aunt Ellen?" he demands, his tone as inquisitive as always.

"Eli, darling, I've only just found out, like you." She pinches his cheek playfully, laughing as he swats her off. Turning to me, she cocks an eyebrow, her gaze skeptical. "It seems Miss Willow thought she could sneak in and circumvent the surprise your papa has planned for her."

"I told him she wouldn't like it," Eli smugly declares, crossing his arms. The motion makes him look older than eleven. He's grown so much since I've been gone. Some of the baby fat has left his cheeks, revealing a bone structure enhancing his resemblance to the woman standing beside him. Wearing a plain white shirt and jeans, he could be a carbon copy of Mischa as well.

More nostalgia constricts my chest. I remember the days we used to play together in these very halls. At night, we'd sneak out to the gardens and race beneath the moon. I couldn't love any brother more, be them related to me by blood or not.

But he's not the first, a cruel voice in my mind whispers. I try to ignore the memories, but they unfurl anyway. Those of another boy, older, but no less tolerant of me. Always patient, he used to braid my hair to keep it clean before we played hide and seek. Wide from behind his glasses, his brown eyes only ever radiated kindness and joy. Vincenzo...

"Will?" Eli's voice draws me back, and I find him watching me with that mature curiosity again. Before he can say anything else, I step forward, my arms outstretched. He blinks, but within seconds he's throwing his arms around me as Ellen gently moves the gown out of reach.

"The twins, reunited at last," she says with a wistful sigh.

I smile at the moniker—our combined nickname, despite our difference in ages, setting us apart from the other faction of this growing family. *The little ones.*

And as if conjured by the thought alone, the oldest of said faction comes storming into my room, several inches taller than when I saw him last.

"Get ready, Mama," he declares, placing his hands on his hips. Dark brown curls fall haphazardly into his eyes, the same piercing blue as his mother's. His stern, serious expression is all Mischa, however. "The girls are fussing again, and—Willow!" Argument forgotten, he throws himself toward me, muscling in beside Eli. I extend my arm around him, marveling even more at his height. Not so little anymore, he comes up to Eli's chest, who is already an inch over my modest stature.

"Careful, Ivan," his mother warns. "You'll knock her over. She's only just got home… Oh, not again!"

Cocking my head, I can easily pick up on the sound that triggered her alarm—high-pitched shrieking growing louder by the second. The next figure to teeter through my doorway just so happens to be the source of the noise—a toddler with blond curls and amber eyes wearing a tiny pink dress.

Spotting her mother, she bursts into tears. "Jona kicked me!" she declares, scampering forward to bury her face in Ellen's skirt. "She kicked me and took my doll!"

"It was Aljona's doll," Ivan corrects, pointing a finger at her disapprovingly. "You took it from her first. Then you broke it and gave her the pieces."

"Marnie!" Ellen inclines her head sharply, suddenly stern. "Is that true?"

The little girl stiffens, her cheeks flushing pink with guilt. "She started it."

"Oh, is that so? Where is Jona now?" Ellen asks, smoothing her fingers over her daughter's curls.

Ivan rolls his eyes with an exasperation well beyond his six and a half years. "Where else?"

From behind him, Eli flashes a crooked grin, and I can sense what's on his mind—*nothing's changed.*

"Let's find her and sort this out," Ellen says tiredly. Looking at me, she shrugs. "Would you mind juggling one, while I juggle the other?" She coaxes Marnie toward me.

Sniffling, the girl tugs on my hand until I scoop her into my arms and then proceeds to hide her face in the crook of my shoulder. As I start after Ellen, Marnie lifts her head long enough to murmur, "I missed you, Willa."

I tighten my arms around her, surprised by just how much I missed her too. How I missed them all. My first year away should have been a godsend. For once, I was no longer a burden, free to earn back every bit of kindness Mischa and his wife—my adopted parents—have bestowed upon me.

Now that I'm back, I can't ignore the feeling that's been itching at my psyche long before the resurgence of Donatello.

Doubt.

Guilt.

That unsettling, lingering pain I've tried to suppress for seven years. It's foolish to dwell on anything other than gratitude—I know that. Mischa and Ellen took me in and loved me as their own, but there is no denying the truth lurking underneath. That despite their affection and generosity, I've never really belonged here. It's obvious to anyone looking from the outside in. After all, my age and features set me apart from the Stepanovs in ways that nothing else could. Eli and I were "the twins" for more than just our closeness. We were both misfits in this world.

Cherished, wanted misfits, but still misfits all the same.

"Is your papa in his study, Marnie?" Ellen calls from the base of the grand staircase that serves as the heart of the manor. Lost in thought, I barely manage to catch my footing on the next step.

"I think so," Ivan says, answering for his sister. "And Jona will be hiding behind him, of course."

I chuckle internally, forgetting my dilemma for now. Mischa Stepanov strikes fear into the hearts of most men, and yet his daughters have the poor man wrapped around their fingers.

Sure enough, we round the corner to the mouth of his study and find him sitting at his desk in the center of the massive room, scanning a stack of documents. He's aged slightly, the lines around his mouth growing more pronounced. But with his blond hair hanging loose around his shoulders and dark eyes narrowed in concentration, he's no less formidable than the man I remember. Looking at him, I'd assume he's hard at work if it weren't for the hint of pink fabric peeking from behind his chair.

"Is Aljona with you?" Ellen asks though her raised eyebrow reveals that she's spied the same telling clue I have.

Sighing, Mischa sets his papers aside and steeples his fingers. His brows draw together, enhancing the harsh planes of his face and the effect is admittedly intimidating. Most people only ever see this man, but as his gaze falls over the girl in my arms, his jaw twitches slightly, betraying a rare hint of softness no one could deny. As his eyes cut up to mine, he winks.

"Aljona would like to initiate a peace treaty," he says to Marnie, his voice booming, accent heavy. "Will you hear her terms, Marnie?"

"No!" Marnie grumbles from my chest. "I don't want stupid terms! I want my doll—"

"It was wrong of you to take her doll," Mischa says over her, but a gentle edge lessens his otherwise stern tone. "And it was wrong of her to kick you." He inclines his head, directing his voice to anyone who just so happens to be hiding behind him. "You both acted inappropriately. Therefore, the only way I can see to settle this matter is..." He throws his hands into the air with a sigh of defeat. "I will buy you two new dolls, and you can keep them separate—"

"Mischa!" Ellen shakes her head. From the firm set of her shoulders, I suspect this is just another battle in a longstanding war between them. "You can't keep spoiling them. They'll never learn." Hands on her hips, she raises her voice, "I propose a punishment of no dessert for the both of you."

"No!" With a cry of protest, Marnie wiggles from my arms. At the same time, another girl pokes her head from behind Mischa's chair, scrambling to her feet. Straight brown hair and the fact that she's nearly a foot taller sets her apart from her sister.

"But Mama!" they whine in unison.

"But Mama," Mischa intones with a pained grimace. "Can we not have both punishment and peace?"

He reaches into his pocket and withdraws two brightly colored items that make the girls squeal and crowd him, jumping in excitement.

Ellen scoffs. "Sweets?"

Mischa doesn't seem to catch the disapproval in her tone. "Apologize to your mother, both of you," he demands, unnervingly stern once more.

"We're sorry," the girls sing in unison with twin smiles, the picture of sweetness.

Mischa can't resist, sporting a grin to match. "Now, Mama…" He bats his eyes imploringly, drawing giggles from his cohorts. "One little treat?"

Ellen rolls her eyes. "It doesn't matter what I say. You'll just sneak it to them anyway—but still no dessert."

With their current goodies—two lollipops—the girls don't seem to mind.

"Mine's bigger," Aljona, the older of the two at the age of five, declares, shoving her lollipop into her mouth. She takes off with Marnie, nearly four, right on her heels.

"Not, uh!"

"I'll make sure they don't kill each other," Ivan says before huffing after his siblings. "As payment, I want four lollies, Papa," he calls back.

Mischa chuckles with pride as he watches them go. When he finally returns his attention to his wife, his eyes fall to her stomach rather than her disapproving stare. "How did I do?" he asks innocently.

Crossing her arms, Ellen shrugs. "Better than last time. At least you plied them with candy and not piles of toys. They will drain you dry if you let them. You need to learn to tell them no."

He shrugs indignantly. "I can tell them no—"

"And mean it," Ellen corrects, sliding a hand down to her belly. "Let's hope you practice in time for the next one. Speaking of children, aren't you even going to welcome your oldest home?"

Mischa looks up sharply, breaking into a full beaming grin. "You!" Lurching to his feet, he circles his desk in mere seconds. "What are you doing here early?"

I'm in his arms before I can even explain.

"She snuck in," Ellen says. "Her plane got in early, and Evgeni apparently forgot to call ahead. She's already seen the dress."

"About that..." Mischa pulls back, his face uncharacteristically red. "It's a small gathering, Mouse—"

"Tell her the truth," Ellen goads. "She won't be any less angry when she finds out."

"So...it's more like a ball," he admits with a sheepish grin that undercuts his hardened exterior a second time. His eyes sparkle, and it's painfully apparent how much this event means to him. "Your debutante ball. It's time you were presented to the world for who you are, Willow Stepanova. Especially so all those rich fuckers at the conservatory know that you aren't some random fling."

I wince but force a smile rather than confess that—as far as the men at the conservatory go—no man has expressed interest in me at all, as a fling or otherwise.

"And to share how proud we are of you," Ellen says, gently rephrasing his words. "I tried to keep it casual, but Mischa spared no expense. You'd be surprised by how well he's done. He even designed the centerpieces—"

"Creative investments," Mischa corrects. His calculating frown resembles that of a brooding tactician more than any party planner. "Investments into your future. Hell, even some of those high society bastards will be there."

I can hear the pride in his voice but guilt grips my chest. It must show on my face as well, because Ellen turns to me, brushing her fingers along my cheek.

"What's wrong, darling?"

"She's probably exhausted," Mischa says, returning to his desk. "Go get some rest before the girls decide to demand a year's worth of play from you. But first…" Much as he had with the sweets, he turns around to reveal yet another surprise balanced on his calloused palm—a polished wooden box. "A little present to celebrate your birthday."

"One of many," Ellen corrects with a conspiratorial smile.

He lifts the lid, and I swallow hard at the sight of what lurks beneath it on a bed of blue velvet—a string of pearls finer than anything I've ever owned. I can't take my eyes off them.

"My daughter, the pianist," Mischa says, chuckling in amusement at my expression. He lifts the pearls and returns to me, holding the strand between his fingers. "I must admit that's something I never thought I'd say."

"We are proud of you," Ellen murmurs. Stepping behind me, she lifts my hair from my neck as Mischa secures the necklace around it.

I look down, watching the delicate pearls settle against my collar. In so many ways, my transformation feels complete. Safiya Mangenello is dead and gone. Willow Stepanova stands in her place. And yet, I can't ignore the tiny voice in my head whispering...

For how long?

"Now, get some rest." Mischa shoos me off with a wave of his hand. "And you, wife—" he glares at Ellen. "Tell me how we ensure this next one isn't a girl."

I slip into the hall, trailing one hand along the worn, though ornate wallpaper while the other fiddles with the pearls around my neck. Lost in thought, I nearly trip over Eli, crouched within a doorway a few paces from the study. Coincidentally, just within eavesdropping distance.

"What's wrong with you?" he demands, rising to his feet.

I shake my head to indicate nothing, but he frowns, honing his gaze on my face. I have to resist the urge to turn away, revealing the lie for what it is. I'd forgotten how perceptive he can be, even at his age. No one else can read me like he can.

"You've been weird since you got back," he declares, crossing his arms over his chest. "And you're taking this whole party thing well. Any other time, you'd raise hell if Aunt Ellen tried to make you wear a fancy dress."

I feel my eyes widen, and his cheeks redden, negating some of his maturity. "I can say hell," he mutters, glancing nervously over his shoulder. "Sometimes."

I shrug and continue down the hall. Anyone else would accept the gesture as an end to the conversation—but not Eli. Stubbornly, he's right on my heels.

"It's not nothing," he argues as if reading my mind. "The last time Aunt Ellen bought you a dress, you avoided her for two days."

A rebellious act that feels so childish now. Maybe it's the year I've spent away that's reshaped my mindset? Those spoiled, pampered artists corrupted my more practical ways. Gone is the girl who used to play in the mud and eschew the thought of any dresses.

The real world taught her the true cost of freedom. Life is all an act requiring a fitting costume, like any role in a performance would. To belong to this sheltered realm, you follow its few, hallowed rules. You don't fracture the simple, pretty melody you're required to uphold, and your life can be just as beautiful.

Why resist that?

I never have to worry that my tuition will be paid. Protected from the horrors of the world, I have a bodyguard assigned to me at all times. While I was away, Mischa arranged for a hairdresser on-call for performances. My clothing is tailored to my measurements, and the place I call home is an ancestral manor with miles of land to its name.

My future will consist of traveling with the most accomplished musicians before some rich man snags me as his wife, all with my father's permission...

Liar, a part of me hisses. The sighting of Donatello just reinforces the opposite reality—Mischa isn't my father. Ellen isn't my mother, and for all their love and kindness, I am not their daughter.

I wasn't Donatello's, either.

My real parents abandoned me at the mercy of a monster who couldn't even do me the courtesy of devouring me himself. He threw me away and never looked back.

I squeeze my eyes shut against the memories. When I reopen them, I'm in my room again, standing before the bed. I finger the dress still lying here, snatching handfuls of the fabric. Maybe it's the color that softens me to it? Or that it's so similar to the dress I'd been meant to wear when Mischa first acquired me.

This arrangement of fabric symbolizes the twisted full circle my life has become—I'm the heiress of an empire that would have chewed me up and spit me back out.

"You can't ignore me, Will."

Eli's here as well, I find, watching me from the doorway. "You've been quiet, too," he admonishes.

I feign surprise and point to my mouth.

He rolls his eyes, unamused. "You know what I mean." He raises his hands, letting his fingers contort. *You just stood there and let them talk around you. You never let anyone talk around you.*

I shouldn't be surprised that he's improved so much with signing despite me being away. Knowing him, he's been practicing.

I've grown up, I sign back.

He shakes his head, still motioning with his hands. *No. Something happened. I know it. What's wrong? Did something happen at that stupid school?*

No. I insist, turning to stare from the nearest window rather than face him directly.

An education overseas gave me an even more insular upbringing, and while music isn't an exciting profession, it's safe. Much like the most carefully composed concerto, it's beautiful, formed of predictable notes, and contained order. You can stray from the rules only so far and still create something incredible.

Music healed me from hate.

Or perhaps it's become more of a Band-Aid in some ways—one I'm terrified to rip off.

I can't be that scared, angry little girl again.

I won't let even his memory steal my life from me a second time. Shaking my head, I banish him only to discover that Eli's still watching me.

Will you be at the party? I ask, changing the subject. *I can ask Mischa to make an exception.*

"It's not him I'm worried about," Eli grumbles out loud, wrinkling his button nose. "Come with me?"

Grateful for the change in subject, I follow him into the hall and into the wing opposite this one where Ellen, Mischa, and the children stay.

"Mama?" Eli calls as we near a suite of rooms. We've barely rounded the corner when a slender woman with long dark hair coiled into a braid appears at the other end of the hall. Anna. A shapeless brown dress helps her to almost blend into the wood-paneled walls. It's her quiet beauty that gives away her resemblance to Ellen, her half-sister. Otherwise, they're as opposite as night and day.

"There you are, darling," she calls, sighing in relief. "Oh, and Willow! I didn't know you were home so soon. Welcome back."

She steps forward to throw her slender arms around me. While she's distracted, Eli chooses this moment to pounce.

"Do you think I could stay up late tomorrow night, Mama?" he asks. "Willow wants me at her party. Please?" He's as shameless as Aljona or Marnie, batting his eyelashes charmingly with a grin to match.

Anna bites her lower lip. "I don't know, darling…" Hesitantly, she runs her fingers through his hair, eventually returning his smile. "I'll think about it."

He throws his arms around her with unbridled joy. "Thank you!"

She kisses his cheek, smoothing his hair one final time. "I suspect you two have a lot to catch up on," she says, winking at me. "I'll let you enjoy your time."

The moment she's out of view, I turn to Eli, signing, *You were worried about her? She would give you the moon if you asked for it.*

He shrugs. "You know she doesn't like being around a lot of people."

He's right. She and Eli reside in the most secluded wing of the manor for a reason. Even during the years I lived here, I could count the interactions I've had with her alone on one hand, and rarely does she join events that aren't restricted to the family. After the death of her father, Ivan, two years ago, she's been even more reclusive.

I've heard Mischa and Ellen mention snippets of her past in hushed whispers; that she had been held captive for years by a rival family.

I've known her to be nothing but kind; however, it's obvious that Eli is her sole devotion. Anyone might think she was his biological mother. Once, a few years ago, I'd gathered up the nerve to ask him: *if Ellen is your mother, why do you call her "Aunt?"*

His answer, as always, portrayed a logic well beyond his young years. "Aunt Ellen doesn't need me as much," he said wistfully. "My mama does."

I didn't know what he meant then. Ellen needed him—anyone with eyes could see that. A lesser woman would have shunned Anna from his life, doing her best to assert herself in her natural role. But as selfless as she is, Ellen knew what he wanted, and was brave enough to make that sacrifice for him.

From Eli's perspective, the reasoning was more childish and, in some ways, tragic. Ellen had more than enough children with Mischa. Anna? She had none. In his analytical brain, that wasn't fair, so he rectified it as only a child could.

"Will?" He grabs my hand, his gaze more piercing than ever. "You zoned out again. Maybe you are tired? Playing music all day would make me want to sleep too." He smiles in that impish way his younger siblings have yet to master.

I roll my eyes and sign, *We can't all be soldiers like you.*

It's a strange thing for a boy to aspire to be—especially one with so much wealth and opportunity at his disposal. On the other hand, it's an obvious outcome to anyone who knows him. While he loves Anna and Ellen, he worships Mischa, a man who sneers at anything not involving fighting tactics or knives. Or at least he used to. It's strange what children can do to men like him. With Ivan, another dutiful mini-soldier, he was gentle but still stern.

But when Aljona was born, he barely raised his voice in her presence. And when Marnie came? He had the various displays of weapons hanging in his office quietly replaced with paintings.

It wasn't as if the girls made him softer, oh no.

Mischa guards his family jealously. The bigger it grows, the tighter his grip becomes on the world around us. God help the poor men who fall for Jona or Marnie.

Or me.

"I'm going to find the others," Eli declares, apparently bored with our reunion already. "Go get some sleep."

I watch him skip off, and a part of me throbs in a subtle, aching way. I miss the days when I could have raced off with him and wrestled in the dirt with the others. Our gap in ages never really mattered, until one day it did.

And it became more apparent than ever what an anomaly I am in this family. Like an off-note in an otherwise flawless aria. You don't notice it at first—perhaps one might assume it's part of the song. But the more you play the piece, the more pronounced that one note sounds.

Until it's all you can hear, grating above the rest.

Destroying the otherwise harmony.

5

WILLOW

I can't sleep for long. Restless, I start to wander the halls, scanning the shadows that drape the hallways and the occasional painting I pass. Judging from the quiet, everyone else is already asleep this time of night, leaving the manor an eerie shell of its daytime chaos. It feels so strange to be alone in the heart of such a bustling hive of activity.

Until suddenly, I'm not. A figure appears near the top of the grand staircase, his silhouette recognizable even in the dark. With a nod of his chin, he beckons me closer. "Mouse," he says, his old childhood nickname for me, given my obvious silence. "Come."

He descends the steps, leaving me to follow him into his study.

"I've had to learn pretty damn quick how to read your expressions," he declares, observing me from behind his desk. I doubt he's even gone to bed yet, considering he's still wearing his clothing from earlier. Sharp with intensity, his dark eyes scan my face. "You're thinking about something, and I doubt it has anything to do with a party," he gruffly surmises. "You and I never mince words, so tell me what's on your mind."

He's right, but I don't even know how to broach this topic. What to say. That I've been thinking too much of the past? Wanting answers I shouldn't pursue.

"I know that look," Mischa grumbles, apparently more perceptive than I've given him credit for. "You have the same look about you that Eli did when he asked me what happened to the bastard who sired him. It's only understandable; you're thinking about the past."

I swallow hard, caught off guard by the admission. Eli never once mentioned his biological father, at least not to me. Mischa has always been "Papa" in his world. As far as I know, his real father had been a monster who separated him from his own mother at birth.

"I'll tell you the same thing I told him," Mischa says gruffly. "I'll answer whatever questions you have, but I will not coddle you, and nothing I may say will ever change my love for you." His eyes shine in the dim glow cast by a sole lamp, and I feel a painful mixture of hope and dread crawl up my throat.

With a wave of his hand, he indicates the leather chair before his desk while he claims the one across from it.

"What is it you want to know?" he asks, folding his hands before him as I sit.

I feel my fingers twitch helplessly, unsure of where to start. Unlike Eli, signing is not his forte, so I reach for a slip of blank paper resting on his desk, and he hands me a pen.

Cautiously I write a single question—what do you know about me?

It's a question I've dreaded proposing for so long. I'm holding my breath in anticipation of his answer.

"About the man who sold you?" he wonders, cutting to the heart of the matter.

I wince. Hearing it out loud triggers a wave of emotions I didn't expect. Pain. Confusion. Sadness. Rage…

Donatello. Once upon a time, he could have been known only as the man I admired more than anyone else in the world. The man who labored to acknowledge my birthday every single year in lieu of my parents. Who swore to protect me.

All lies. He'll forever be regarded merely as the man who sold me.

I've never asked Mischa about him, because I never wanted to know just how much my new guardian might know about my past. About Donatello. And if he did know…

Why let him live so close to us, in a city just a car ride away? Why let him live at all? Why let him thrive?

The thoughts are vengeful and childish, but they fester no matter how hard I try to ignore them. Mischa loves me; I know he does —but an irrational sense of betrayal makes it harder to think clearly.

Because if he does care for me so much, then why hasn't he hunted down Donatello on his own? Why hasn't he punished the man who hurt me?

All I can see is his face. His smile, mocking me seven years later.

"Nicolai never told me his name," Mischa says, referring to another man I've strived to forget—Nicolai Baryshnikov, a slave trader, among other things. The same man he unwittingly rescued me from. "What do you remember?"

I lift the pen, pressing the nib to the page, but as the seconds pass, I can't bring myself to write anything more than a faint, hollow line. Shaking my head, I set the pen aside altogether.

"I won't tell you what to feel," Mischa says with a heavy sigh. "But maybe it's for the best that you don't remember."

He rises and approaches me. His hands settle over my shoulders, urging me to my feet, and I'm in his arms again, crushed to his chest.

"You are my daughter," he tells me. "Mine. No one will ever harm you. Never. Do you understand?"

I can only nod, burying my face against his shoulder the way I would when I was a child. My eyes burn, welling with tears I don't have the energy to fight back anymore. They spill down my cheeks unchecked as Mischa withdraws.

"Good girl," he praises, running his fingers through my hair. "Now go. Get some rest."

As I leave, an unexpected sense of relief loosens the tension in my shoulders I wasn't aware of until now. For whatever reason, his ignorance comforts me. It makes it easier to breathe and think ahead as a woman in my position should. Donatello Vanici is dead to me. Tomorrow, I'll be presented to the world as a Stepanova, and I wouldn't have it any other way.

I exit the study with my head held high and nearly run into a slim figure lurking beyond the doorway. Ellen. Her golden-brown hair streams loose down her shoulders, and a white nightgown sets her apart from the darkness around her.

"Willow? What are you doing up?" She strokes my cheeks, her smile strained. "I forgot to tell Mischa about the final arrangements for tomorrow," she says, slipping past me. "Goodnight."

I don't know what it is about her expression that makes me swallow in alarm.

Still, I start down the hall, but as murmuring voices catch my ear, I quietly circle back.

"You were eavesdropping," Mischa scolds, his voice easily reaching me as I falter just beyond the doorway.

"And you were lying," Ellen counters haughtily. "You lied to her. Why?"

"I don't know what you're talking about," Mischa says, but his tone gives him away. Ellen is the only one capable of wringing that gruff, raw baritone from him. Guilt.

"You've known the identity of the man who sold her for seven years," she declares. "In fact, you've been waging a campaign to keep him away from this area—and don't look at me like that. You aren't as secretive as you think when it comes to your business arrangements. Why didn't you tell her? I could understand if you thought she wasn't ready, but we decided together to tell Eli about his—"

"Because he's not dead," Mischa growls. "Eli? He is like you, able to square the past and leave it buried. Mouse? She is like me. I'm sure she remembers him. His name. Everything he did to her— but if he is not acknowledged out loud, he doesn't exist. She can go on living in peace. But if she knows he's still alive? Still breathing, walking, existing in this world. She won't ever let go.

Ever. I don't want that for her." His voice breaks, hoarse and hollow. A sudden thump alludes to him striking his desk with a clenched fist, and I imagine Ellen approaching him, wrapping her slender arms around him from behind.

"Tell me what is on your mind," she pleads.

"You once fantasized about a life of peace for us," he says. "And we have it. The children who aren't destined to be casualties in some senseless war. Children who can study music over hatred and fighting. So, if to maintain that peace, I have to lie, I will lie."

"She'll learn about him soon enough," Ellen says softly. "God forbid she runs into him. She's back until September. Don't tell me you plan to lock her away in a tower until then."

"I won't have to," Mischa snaps. "She'll have her pretty party and be distracted until her schooling resumes. She'll be safe. As for now? Donatello Vanici isn't welcome in my territory, and I've made that clear. If the motherfucker didn't own half the damn harbor, I could drive him from the city altogether. From the country. As it stands, I won't let him near her."

"I know you love her," Ellen says, her voice soothing. "But one day, she'll have to face her past."

"Not alone," Mischa declares. "Never alone. And only when she's ready to finally leave it behind."

They grow silent, though it could be the sound of my pulse drowning them out. It surges through my ears, deafening me as I return to my room. My thoughts are a maze of confusion.

Betrayal.

And grim resignation.

Mischa is right.

As long as my past lives, I can't.

6

WILLOW

Morning comes far too soon, and I rise from my bed, having barely slept. My head throbs as snippets of a nightmare still taunt me.

I had been there again. In the home I lived in before ever meeting Mischa, a beautiful manor every bit as storied as this one. Smaller in size but no less comforting, I can remember every inch of it so clearly it hurts.

In that home, I grew so much.

And in that home, I lost everything.

My present should be so much brighter. As if to taunt me, golden daylight streams in through my windows, warming my cheeks. Inside, however, I feel so cold. It's like my thoughts have turned to ice, jagged, and painful.

Maybe Mischa was right? Ignoring the past is the only way forward. As the faint smell of cooking food carries on the air, I'm willing to try.

I get dressed in a sweater and jeans for now, but my debutante dress awaits, hanging from the front of my wardrobe as a glaring reminder of what today signifies. For all intents and purposes, I am nineteen, finally a woman.

Supposedly, I should be freed from the bonds of my childhood...

But dangerous thoughts creep into the silence, countering that narrative. I can't help the comparison—would Donatello have spent as much on his version of my debutante ball? Would he have slaved over every detail and gushed with pride about his planning?

It stings to even imagine it. His smiling face. His sloppily wrapped gifts. The dress he'd design for me...

I don't know how long I've been lost in thought when my door opens and a kind face peeks from behind it.

"You're awake," Ellen says warily. Her blue eyes are unusually guarded, her gray day dress subdued. Is she aware of what I overheard last night? As her gaze fixates on the dress, I can't tell. She crosses to it, fingering a corner of the massive skirt. "I just wanted you to know that today is your day, and I'm so proud of you for humoring us. We know you hate parties. And dresses. And attention—"

I shake my head, cutting her off.

"Yes, but I just want you to know that we didn't plan this on a whim," she insists. "We've..."

She turns away, gazing through the gap in my white curtains to the view revealed beyond my bay windows. The vast stretch of the manor looms below, a yawning mass of emerald green lawns and sheltered forests. What does she see within such a realm?

Safety? Or another looming reality that makes her bite her lip and clasp her hands?

One look at the slim fingers symbolizes the violent start to her relationship with Mischa that most wouldn't expect when seeing them now. Rather than sporting a wedding ring as it should, the digit on her left hand itself ends abruptly at the knuckle, severed years ago.

"He's been worried, you know," she admits, her voice soft. "About what your proximity to him might do to your future. If doors might be slammed in your face, that otherwise wouldn't be. He knows he isn't perfect, but you and the other children… You mean the world to him. To give you what he thinks you deserve, he will do anything. I need you to know that. He loves you."

So he lies to me. I could assert as much, but I don't. Regardless, I'm startled by the anger building in my chest, so raw it hurts. I try choking it down and grit my teeth against it. Try to rationalize it away—he loves me, I know he does.

But so did Donatello.

"This means a lot to him," Ellen continues, still gazing from the window. "Think of this party as his way of trying to make amends and bridge the gap. He's even planning on wearing a suit. Can you imagine?" She laughs as I attempt to picture it— Mischa in anything other than fatigues or simplistic clothing.

Her amused grin lasts for only a second before she's frowning. "It's funny how things change. There was a time when I would have never imagined him plotting and scheming something other than revenge or retaliation…" She trails off and clears her throat. "Well, get some rest. I'll keep the children away for the day, and later, if you want, I can help you get dressed?"

I nod as she crosses to me and kisses my cheek. "Happy birthday, Willow."

I watch her go as more memories return, but these thankfully don't star Donatello. I can still remember the first day she and I met. Back then, we were nothing more than captives held at the mercy of one man we both love now.

Sometimes it feels like I'm dreaming. That one day I'll wake up, and I'll be that scared little girl again.

More often than not, I used to pray that day would come soon.

At least then, I'd stop dreading it.

7

WILLOW

The day slips away until it's evening before I know it. Night paints the world beyond my windows in hues of navy that serve as a backdrop to a swollen full moon. Already shuffled off to bed, the children's boisterous playing has been replaced with faint music and the bustle of footsteps from down below.

My heart pounds with every new sound to invade—the growing din of numerous voices, along with the musical clangs of silverware and delicate china. The swish of ivory silk as I spin before the mirror and try my best to smile. Ellen's soft gasp as she oversees me, her hands clasped in approval.

"What do you think?" she asks, already wearing her own frothy pink gown.

I observe my reflection in the glass without conveying an answer right away. A stranger looks back at me, her teeth bared in a seemingly painful expression. She looks far from a debutante— just a stone-faced pretender. Large brown eyes stare blankly, and

I can't even tell what she might be feeling. Happiness? Contentment? Terror?

I look away from her, eyeing the skirt billowing out around me. Gratitude thickens my throat, and all I can do is finger a section of intricate lace over and over. I've never worn a dress like this. Even for my recitals.

"You look so beautiful," Ellen murmurs. She smooths her hands along my hair, brushing the tresses from my face, but with her next to me, the contrast between us is stark. I barely come to her shoulder, gangly and gaunt with cheekbones that are far too prominent. In comparison, she's willowy and lithe, her beauty unmarred even by the jagged scar on her left cheek, fully displayed with her hair swept into an elegant coil.

I could be self-deprecating if I wanted to, drawing on the few descriptions of myself I've heard from various colleagues while training in Vienna. I'm pretty, they say, but far too serious. My looks alone aren't enticing enough for most of my classmates to broach a conversation with me. According to some, my father may even be a mobster, explaining my need for security and seemingly unlimited funds.

Physically, at least, my nose is longer than Ellen's and blunter. With my thin lips, even my best smile is no comparison to her charming grin. I used to wish she really were my mother. That I was as calm as her. As quiet and strong. Mischa's name alone could make grown men piss themselves, but one word from her could restrain him like nothing else.

In some ways, their relationship is inconceivable. A man with such a capacity for violence, shouldn't be capable of love. A woman so gentle should be unable to tame a monster.

Their love is comparable to the most complex concertos involving a wide range of instruments to perform—intricate and intimidating, but undeniably perfect when played. Some might compare their union to a fairy tale.

Or a curse. If my life has taught me nothing else, it is that peace is fragile, and when it ends—and it always does end—the resulting chaos renders the happier times nothing more than a weapon. One that cuts into your thoughts with every waking moment, subverting any attempt to suppress it. Stubbornly, the past resists, blaring through your thoughts like a shout growing louder by the second. Louder and louder still, until it drowns out everything else.

Donatello.

Donatello.

Donatello!

"You look so surly tonight," Ellen scolds, pinching my cheek. "Is it the style? I can try a different look."

I blink and realize that she's already arranged my hair. A long plait loops around my skull, forming an elegant coif similar to hers.

It's perfect, I sign, and her relieved grin only enhances the gentle grace cast by her dress. I don't resist as she smooths the gown over my waist, adjusting the fit. With an appreciative sigh, she stands back.

"You're a woman now," she says wistfully. "It feels like just yesterday when you and Eli would play hide and seek for hours, and when Mischa would braid your hair. Do you remember? With Ivan already in school, the girls will follow before I know it." She cradles her belly. "At least I have one more to savor. Now shall we?"

I start to follow her, entering the hallway. An admirer is already there, wearing a casual shirt and jeans. "You look nice, Aunt Ellen," he chirps.

"Thank you, Eli darling." Ellen ruffles his hair before shooting me a knowing glance. "I'll see you downstairs."

As she leaves, Eli steps forward, his lips pursed. "Mama didn't want me to stay up late," he says to me with a sigh. "She wanted me to tell you happy birthday, though, and give you this." He hands me a beautifully wrapped box.

I open it carefully, and my eyes widen at what I discover inside of it—a delicate pair of gold earrings.

They're beautiful, I sign before placing them on my nightstand.

"They're okay," he says with a mischievous grin while taking something from his pocket. "But here is my present. Before you ask, Mischa said I can have it," he explains, holding a small knife on the flat of his palm. "I carved it myself. Do you like it?"

Recognition runs through me as I take in the dagger's familiar shape. It's the same one I used to practice with as a child, running drills to the point of exhaustion under Mischa's discretion. I rub my finger over the polished leather hilt, feeling my heart swell with emotion. Etched there in gold is a single name—Mouse.

"You can use it to stab those rich guys if they get on your nerves," Eli suggests with solemn seriousness. "Papa said I can tell you to 'kick anyone's ass who doesn't treat you right.'"

I reach out, placing my hand over his cheek. With his knife in my grasp, that taunting voice in my head vanishes. I can think again, and I feel so childish for letting the negative thoughts take over in the first place.

"Don't get sappy on me," he scolds, dodging my touch, but his smile is so infectious I'm grinning back. "Now go to your fancy party. I scoped it out, and I bet you'll have to use that knife pretty soon."

I raise an eyebrow, though I doubt he's exaggerating. Nervous energy rides the air, sending my heartbeat racing. Excited butterflies take flight in my stomach, and I sneak one last look at myself in the mirror.

If I squint, I see less of that stone-faced girl from before. A woman instead takes her place. Willow Stepanova. Who might she meet at her own debutante ball?

I honestly have no idea as to the kind of men Mischa would invite. Rich and bold, as Eli claimed? Or a more dangerous breed?

"We should spy on them from the top," Eli offers, extending his arm to me. "That way, you can decide who to stab before you go down."

I gratefully hook my arm around his, letting him guide me down the hall. Even from here, the noise is deafening—murmuring voices and elegant music. Rather than approach the grand staircase, Eli and I creep to a rarely traveled wing that overlooks the grand hall.

The space itself is massive, crowned by an ornate vaulted ceiling. Marble flooring amplifies every sound in the spacious interior.

Two hallways on the upper level provide a more private position from which to observe those below.

"Wow," Eli exclaims, sneaking a look over the wooden railing.

I touch his shoulder in silent agreement, too awed to make my own remarks. The full extent of Mischa's planning is breathtaking. Garlands of roses hang from the ceiling along with ivory banners and delicate accents.

"Is that a smile?" Eli teases, wrinkling his nose. "You look pretty, by the way." He tugs on a section of my skirt. "Like a princess. Your knife looks nice too."

And maybe I should embrace that. I'm no longer the little Mouse Mischa rescued or the naïve child before that. I am Willow Stepanova, beloved member of a powerful family.

Mischa is right. The past has to stay dead and buried. I can move on and keep living. I won't let it drag me back.

Leaning over the banister, I take in the new world I'm entering. Already, a sizable number of attendees crowd the room, and I feel a burst of pride for Mischa. He's succeeded where most men fail in forging a new path for himself and for his family. He even stuffed his muscular bulk into a suit, proudly displaying Ellen on his arm.

I grin as I envision him attending one of my musical events in the future. The *mafiya* leader turned lover of music.

Suddenly, his expression hardens, setting my nerves on alert. Confused, I follow the line of his gaze to a man standing near a corner of the ballroom. An unwanted guest?

His back is to me at first, but then he turns.

And time crawls to a stop. As if in a daze, I vaguely note his strikingly tall figure first, before my eyes drift up to his dark brown hair. The firm line of his jaw next. It's like my brain knows to do anything it can to stall before I finally register the rest of his face…

That firm, stoic jaw.

Those eyes.

That smile.

Images slam into my skull one after the other. That same figure in another life. Memories swarm me of crawling onto his lap, relishing his attention. Running my tiny fingers over the expansive planes of his face and understanding, even at that young age, that he looked different than most. His eyes were a rich brown, his nose so stern he could seem more intimidating than thunderstorms—my biggest fear then—and yet a simple quirk of his mouth could transform him into the most comforting presence I'd ever known. Even Mischa can't muster the same level of playful softness.

But Mischa's love was never a lie.

Everything about my past with Donatello Vanici was. A brutal, terrifying, horrifying lie.

I blink rapidly, expecting him to disappear—but he doesn't. I pinch myself, willing him to vanish. My eyes burn but with every tear to fall, blurring my vision, he stubbornly remains.

Oblivious, he tilts his head, allowing the glow from a hanging chandelier to illuminate him in painfully stark detail. He's the man I remember from my childhood, only aged exactly seven years, dressed in a suit that strains against the bulk in his forearms. Dark stubble speckles his chin, and his eyes scan the room as watchful as ever.

Beside him stands another man I recognize despite him having grown several feet, sprouting into a near copy of his uncle. Vincenzo.

"Will?" Eli stage-whispers. "What's wrong?"

His voice snaps me back with a chilling realization that has me gripping the railing, in danger of pitching over it—this isn't a dream.

Or, even more terrifying—I've finally gone insane. Around me, the walls melt, forming a puddle that obscures everyone and everything but him. He's untouchable by the chaos, standing as tall as he did the day he dragged me before Nicolai Baryshnikov and left me for dead.

"Do what you will with her," he'd said. *"I don't care."*

I don't care...

And apparently, he hasn't, frolicking like a man without a care in the world, here to attend the birthday party of a girl he thinks he's never met. Does he assume that Willow Stepanova will be as easy to charm as Safiya Mangenello?

As I watch, he goes rigid, his eyes flashing. A vicious sense of triumph roots me in place. I hope he sees me. Notices me. Remembers me...

But without ever looking my way once, he heads for the exit of the ballroom, pulling Vincenzo after him.

I turn away so quickly I nearly trip over the skirt of my gown. There's no way down from here. I can only stagger forward, craning my neck for a view of the figure retreating toward the front of the house.

"Will, what's wrong?" Eli is already by my side, using his hand to steady me. "You look like you've seen a ghost or something."

But I have. There isn't any way to explain the truth to him.

My fingers are shaking too badly to form any coherent reply. It's too hot. The air is too thick. Suffocating.

"Is it the dress?" Eli asks, padding after me as I tear into the upstairs wing. "I'll get Aunt Ellen, and she can—"

I grab his hand, shaking my head no, though I barely register his worried expression. It's like the walls of this home fade, and I'm a child again, unable to see anything beyond the figure retreating from me. I can't even cry out.

All I can do is hate him.

Chase him.

Follow him to the boundaries of a slamming door and watch him leave. Again. I'm shaking as I reach the top of the staircase, waiting for him only to find the foyer devoid of anyone but my father's guards. Then I remember that it will take him minutes to reach this part of the house from the lower level.

"Will?" Eli tugs at my skirt. "What's wrong?"

My fingers are moving before I even realize what I'm signing, *I need you to do me a favor.*

He cocks his head. "What kind of favor?"

Cover for me. Surging past him, I cross the wing, entering my room in a rush. I set the knife aside, pacing circles as my mind races.

"What do you mean?" Eli demands, right on my heels. "Where are you going?"

It's the same question I'm asking myself. I don't know. I can't think…

It's like someone else possesses my body, making me claw at the fastenings of my gown Ellen had so lovingly done up. With sheer brute force, I unhook it enough to wrench myself free of the massive skirt. The fabric falls to the floor with a pathetic thud, resembling one of the many roses decorating the main hall.

"Hey!" From the corner of my eye, I see Eli turn his back to me, his neck beet red. "If you didn't like the dress, you could have told them before the party," he scolds.

I can't apologize. I'm too busy reaching for my closet. Throwing open the wooden doors, I rummage through the few items left hanging. I only brought a few things home from school—assorted shirts, skirts, and jeans. Apart from those items lurks one lone black dress at the very back of the cabinet.

My heart pangs as I grab it by the hanger. I wore it to the older Ivan's funeral with a sweater over the top for modesty—it was the only thing in the store that suited my height without requiring inches to be taken off the hem. On me, the dress came just past my knees.

Observing it now, it suits a far different purpose than mourning. It's tight enough to run in. Or stab someone while wearing it and obscure any bloodstains. In a sense, it's the polar opposite of the white dress I'd been given after being abandoned.

This…is a fitting dress to kill Donatello Vanici in.

Teeth bared, I slip it on, still wearing my new white heels.

Why? My brain is on autopilot, racing ahead too quickly for my body to keep up. I keep seeing him, his back to me. Leaving, always leaving…

But following him now would be foolish. Pointless. Unless…

I can find him alone. Unguarded.

To do what?

Silver on my dresser catches my eye, and I lunge for the object, testing my thumb over a sharpened edge. Eli's knife.

"Will…" His voice, trembling with alarm, grates on the anger, making me falter.

I turn to find him watching me, his blue eyes fathomless in the dark. "What are you doing?"

Guilt chokes me for the fear in his gaze. *I have to take care of something,* I sign to him. *Please, just cover for me.*

"Cover? How?"

A part of me knows this is wrong. My fingers are moving anyway. *Make a distraction.*

Pushing past him, I reenter the hall, heading for the staircase. A figure walks by, too perfectly timed to be real. I'm imagining him, storming past two guards stationed near the front door. In this hallucination, I hear him clearly. "We'll return to the hotel."

Rather than descend the main staircase, I skirt around to the servant's wing and out a door that leads to the side of the house. The fact that I run into no one is a testament to the scale of the party Mischa planned. It feels as though everyone, from the servants, to the security detail, is positioned outside to manage the flow of guests.

Only one car awaits out front now; however, its headlights painting the driveway gold against an ebony sky. I crouch behind a row of hedges, inching forward until I'm just paces from the manor's entrance. The car is close enough to touch, a black luxury model.

As if on cue, two men exit the front of the manor and approach the vehicle. The tallest of the pair gestures for the driver and hands him a large box that the man promptly brings to the trunk.

He opens the compartment, placing the box inside, and I don't know what possesses me to grab a rock from the lawn and throw it. The skittering noise draws the driver's attention, and he walks toward it just long enough for me to slip from between two hedges and climb inside the trunk entirely.

Admonishments run through my mind. There's no way no one saw me. What the hell am I doing?

When footsteps approach, I tense in anticipation, knowing I'll be caught.

But the lid slams shut instead, and the sudden darkness has the effect of a bucket of ice water being dumped over my head.

I'm in the same car as Donatello Vanici.

The knife is in my grasp, and I cling to it so tightly it hurts—but I don't drop it.

Instead, I channel another set of memories from my childhood. Mischa, shouting at me as we trained in the yard, his warnings unrelenting.

"Never let your guard down, Mouse! No matter how exhausted you are, you fight. You win. Now move!"

With his voice in my head, I feel a strength I've never experienced before, giving me the sense of mind to strain through the dark and get my bearings.

I'll trust this protector over the other two who failed me.

I'll take his words to heart.

I'll fight.

And I will win.

8

WILLOW

We don't travel far from the manor, though every passing second might as well be an eternity. In the dark quiet of the trunk, there is nothing to ground me but the endless motions of the vehicle and muffled snippets of noise. Eventually, a lone shred of logic seeps through the splintered thoughts circling my brain—we could be headed anywhere.

I can't hear any coherent conversation from inside the car—just murmured voices. One overpowers the other, deep and rich. My entire body stiffens in response to it, and I grit my teeth so hard my jaw aches.

He is so close…

He and Vincenzo, a boy I never thought I'd see again. The sight of him hurts the most. Beneath all the festering rage and hate, there is only pain when I think of how our relationship used to be. My Vinny. He is so tall now, embodying his uncle even in stature in a way he never could with his huge eyes and awkward glasses. Does he even remember the little Safy who used to follow him around with the devotion of a puppy?

Did he even care when Don tore that girl away from their world?

I feel strange. Lost. Empty. Like I've ripped off a mask I've been wearing for so long, I'd forgotten it wasn't my real face. Without it, I'm someone nameless devoid of a real identity. A waif with her blond hair falling from its elegant coil, draping her shoulders with random strands.

There is no order to my appearance. No retinue of security or staff to reinforce my supposed importance. Willow Stepanova is an untouchable idea in this moment, and though it hurts like hell to admit it…

I will never be her.

Safiya is growling, thirsting for revenge. That scared little girl from my past is scratching at the boundaries of my control, desperate to be unleashed. The longer I'm so close to these snippets from my past, the harder it becomes to restrain her.

I'm sweating with the effort, tightening my grip over the knife. Finally, the car slows to a stop, leaving me trembling in the aftermath. As if from underwater, I hear the doors opening and the slam of them closing again.

Soon my panting is the only noise to fill the silence. I can't tell if the driver is still nearby, waiting to retrieve the box placed here beside me. Jealousy is an irrational thing to feel, but it crawls through my chest as I make out the professionally wrapped gift. There are no flaws marring it like the presents Donatello once gave me—he didn't do this himself. So desperate to make an impression on Mischa's daughter, he procured only the best.

What gift would he think might impress such a girl?

I finger a corner and then rip at the glossy blue wrapping paper. Beneath is a white box, and inside it, a mirror bright enough to reflect what little light there is and reveal my shadowed reflection.

An inhuman creature stares back, her teeth bared in a feral snarl, her once elegantly styled hair a wild mess.

Finally, I hear a low whistle and then footsteps trailing away from the car. The driver?

I scour the inside of the trunk until I find a release that opens it. Cautiously, I lift the lid, blinking as my eyes adjust to a dim source of light coming from above. From what I can tell, I'm in a garage. Rows of luxurious vehicles are parked beside this one. Through a row of windows, I can make out what seems to be an office where several men mill about.

My heart races as I rise to my knees. Slowly, I slip one foot from the trunk, bracing it against the pavement before I leave the vehicle entirely. Straining to keep out of view, I lower the lid as much as I can without slamming it closed.

Low to the ground, I inch my way forward, scanning the area for any hint of an exit. But there are too many, and a parade of vehicles streams in and out. I don't see Donatello anywhere. With no other options, I stand and approach the office, tugging the remainder of my hair loose. The knife, I tuck within my bra between my breasts, praying that the fall of the material obscures its shape.

"Hey, what are you doing here?" a man demands, calling from the doorway. I flinch as he takes one look at me. Whatever he sees makes him clear his throat, and some of the suspicion in his gaze softens. "Are you lost?"

Relieved, I nod, and he inclines his head toward a silver elevator on the other end of the garage. Above it is a sign reading: *To the Grande Hotel Lobby.* That explains the suit he wears—a crisp, black ensemble nearly identical to the style worn by the other men in the room. It must be a uniform for the drivers hired by the hotel.

"Guest services are that way," he says.

I take a step in that direction, only to turn to him and start to sign. It's random nonsense, but he doesn't know that, flushing pink with confusion.

"I'm sorry," he admits with a pained grimace. "I don't understand sign language."

I mime for a pen and paper, and he ushers me into the office and hands me both. Crouched over a desk, I embody every bit of what I learned about being rich from my classmates. There is a dichotomy to it one must learn to master. It isn't enough to be rude; you have to be delicate as well. There's an art to knowing how to simper and smile with an air of superiority. When to sneer and when to bat your lashes.

In short, you perform no differently than when playing an instrument.

I lost my card key, I write. *My uncle is staying at the hotel, and we got separated. Can you tell me what room we're in, please?*

"You haven't tried the front desk?" He eyes me warily and sighs when I shake my head. "Name?"

My hand trembles so badly I can barely form the letters. In the end, I press down hard enough that the nib of the pen tears through the page.

Reading the name, the man raises an eyebrow. "Donatello Vanici?"

"I drove him tonight," another man pitches in from across the room. Seated at a desk with his feet propped on the edge, he eyes me with a raised eyebrow and shrugs. "He hired full service, and there's a package I was supposed to deliver for him tonight. I could take her up."

I don't mind. Thank you, I scribble.

With a grunt of acknowledgment, the man rises to his feet. "Wait here, Miss."

He leaves the office to enter the garage, and sweat drips down the back of my neck as I wait.

Eventually, he returns with a questioning frown and an unwrapped gift box tucked beneath his arm. "Damn kids," he grumbles, tugging at the gray tie accenting his black suit. "Someone went through the trunk."

"I'll check the cameras while you write a report," the man near the door grumbles. "Just make sure nothing's stolen. That's the last thing we fucking need around here."

"Quit your bitching," the man with the gift snarls. "Let me take her up first." He jerks his head for me to follow, and I nearly trip in my haste to keep pace.

Together, we enter the elevator, and the man swipes a badge before selecting a floor just a few numbers down from the highest level. Within minutes, the doors open onto a lush hallway accented by blood-red carpet and wood-paneled walls polished to shine.

The driver shuffles forward to a room a few paces down and swipes the card to let me inside.

"Your uncle, huh?" he wonders, inspecting me with a curious expression. "Look, if either of you needs a ride in the future, here is my private card. I'm looking to trade up, if you know what I mean. The pay here is shit." He rummages through his coat and withdraws a plain business card. "If the ride is for you, text this number. You know how to text?"

He grunts when I nod.

"Good. Text this number with your name and where to pick you up, no questions asked. And don't forget to tell your uncle, if he's hiring. Oh, and tell him happy birthday for me." He hands me the present and leaves.

I can't seem to move other than to slip his card where I hid my knife. Or turn away from the surprisingly modest space. My first coherent thought is that the air doesn't smell like him, too crisp and clean.

Apparently, I wasn't the first to find a way in here, either. A cake rests on the king-sized bed, along with small, square items wrapped in shiny silver packaging.

It's so anticlimactic in a sense.

He should be sprawled in a massive penthouse, reveling in his money, unbothered by any skeletons in his past.

But this arena is as fitting as any to finally face him after all this time. Squaring my shoulders, I step inside, closing the door behind me. I drop the present near the entrance and find myself inching toward a row of windows overlooking a view of the busy waterfront.

We must be in the heart of the city. Several skyscrapers surround this building. The nearest one is close enough for me to make out various people exposed by gaps in curtains or blinds. They live their lives regardless, oblivious to being on display.

On a floor roughly equal to this one, I catch a man who seems to be staring intently in this direction. The second I spot him, he shifts out of view.

And I turn away, withdrawing my dagger from its hiding place.

For the first time, I feel a pang of guilt for leaving Mischa and Ellen to wonder where I am.

But after tonight, I'll finally be able to live among them with no more crippling uncertainty.

No more pain.

After tonight, I'll finally be free to become someone else and leave Safiya Mangenello behind for good.

I'll silence Donatello Vanici's memory, one way or another.

DON

*V*inny, my sweet, cunning boy. He has taste after all—the little bastard went all out when picking his present for me. She's perfect—a pretty, innocent-looking piece of ass every bit as beautiful as any pampered heiress.

Her dark eyes watch me, so fucking wide. Endless. I'm too drunk to be poetic about it, but if I weren't, I'd describe her in the sexiest terms that get a man's cock throbbing. Mine, at least.

Beautiful.

Dangerous.

Unsettling.

Psychotic.

She has that knife raised high before I even have the sense to pivot out of her reach. Undeterred, she swipes for me anyway, her eyes blazing, teeth bared.

Laughing, I grab her wrist, and she recoils, stumbling into a sideboard in her haste to wrench away from me.

"You aren't a professional," I deduce, sizing her up with a glance. Disappointment melds with the effects of my last whiskey, and my shoulders slump in defeat. So much for my good boy sending a naughty toy my way. "Sexually or otherwise," I suspect, sounding like a child denied a treat. "Not a part of my gift, it seems."

What a damn shame.

A second glance makes it more obvious that she's no whore. She's far too slight for one, no hint of muscle in sight. Her skin is paler than the style these days, and her hair looks to be a natural shade in between blond and brown—no hint of highlights or some shit most escorts adorn themselves with. But her hands give her away —slim, pale, struggling to grip the knife she holds.

She's no assassin, either.

"Revenge, is it?" I ask as she whirls to face me, blade drawn. "Which loved one of yours did I kill? A beloved daddy? A brother? It can't be your mother," I add, easily parrying her next attempt to slash my throat. "I don't kill women."

Her eyes flash at that, and she lunges again, flailing more wildly with her blade.

"So, your mother then," I deduce while twisting on my heel to avoid her attack. Unguarded, she doesn't even try to stop me from gripping her waist, tugging her against me. It's only as her eyes meet mine for a split-second that I realize I've fucked up.

Pain lances through my side, drawing a hiss as I buck out of her range. Shit. I don't even have to look down to know she got me. I can feel the blood already starting to pool beneath this godforsaken suit. Fuck it. What a way to end the night. Hissing in irritation, I swipe at the wound without bothering to inspect it in full.

"So, you are trained, after all," I rasp. "Fuck, playing games, then."

I snatch a handful of her hair, using the grip for leverage to shove her away. Only when I let go, do I realize how rough I've been. She's so thin that in theory, she could go right through the wall. At the last minute, she catches herself with her free hand, already spinning to come at me again.

Even as I brace myself for her next blow, I'm impressed. Someone trained her well.

But her skill eliminates about ten potential motherfuckers off the list of who her employer—or avenged family member—might be. None of those sons of bitches would ever have the balls to train a woman.

"So, I offended your mother," I say, trying and failing to maintain eye contact. Her gaze is a viper, darting around the room in search of an exit. I barely manage to shift my stance enough to keep her from lunging for the door. "Did I fuck her?" I ask, raking my gaze over her body from head to toe. "Don't tell me you're my long-lost daughter."

It's sick, but as my eyes fall over the small breasts peeking beneath the neckline of her dress, I pray to God she's not. Though, fuck. At least then, I'd have a daughter to carry on my legacy in addition to Vin.

Her cheeks flush with fury at the suggestion, her chest heaving. Wrong answer.

"Did I fuck you?" I sound as skeptical as I feel, and the answer seems to be a definitive no. I would remember her. Those eyes. Those lips. Her smell—one inhale and I'm high on the stench —roses.

"Did I hurt you?" I ask, noting the shift in my pitch. I sound damn near genuine. "If I did fuck you and never call, trust me— put the knife down, and I will be more than willing to make it up to you. I was probably drunk."

Very, *very* drunk, I decide as my gaze descends her shapely legs. Piss drunk. Vin had probably snuck something into my drink as a prank—it wouldn't be the first time. His way of trying to convince me to stay sober.

But her eyes narrow, and more color floods her cheeks. Rather than peg her issue, I've insulted her.

And she comes for me again, eyes blazing.

For a heartbeat, she transforms into someone else. Someone even smaller, scrawnier, her honey-colored hair in pigtails, her expression so feral she resembled a stray mutt more than a little girl.

I'm almost startled into saying her name out loud. Almost…

But she's dead. I know because I hand-delivered her to her killer.

Fire slices through the meat of my cheek, drawing my attention to an outstretched pale hand lashing through the air. The little bitch is quick, reaching me before I have the chance to block. She lands a good punch to my chest, already maneuvering her knife to go again.

Grunting, I ram my shoulder into her side, knocking her off balance. Before she can recover, I fist my fingers through that mass of hair, noticing just how damn thick it is. Soft too. Perfect for gripping. Pulling.

To test that theory, I use a handful of it to shove her onto the bed face down and pin her in place, jabbing my knee against the small of her back. I'm not gentle—she should gasp at least. Cry out.

But she doesn't make a sound. Strange. I'm used to the theatrics that tend to color these situations. The screaming. The monologues. The listing of grievances and shouting.

She isn't the first person I've found in my room willing to kill me. Not by a long shot.

Even as she struggles, grappling at the bedsheets with nails drawn, she doesn't say a word. Doesn't make a sound. It's strangely…hot.

A series of thoughts flit across my mind—sick, twisted shit belonging to the old Don. The fucker who would relish in slipping his hand beneath her dress, palming that sweet, ripe little ass and seeing how silent she'd be then.

My hand is already moving, fingering the hem as her limbs quiver just beyond my reach. Groaning, I form a fist and brace it against the mattress beside her instead. As if to mock me, I catch a handful of condoms. The cake, I discover, is already smashed on the floor, having been knocked off the bed.

So much for Vin's present.

"Who do you work for?" I demand of the woman.

She attempts to lift her knife in lieu of giving me an answer. With a sigh, I snatch her wrist, bending it back just shy of painful. She has to go still or risk injuring it. Her eyes cut up to mine, burning so hot it's like they're on fucking fire.

"Tell me, and I'll let you go."

She bares her teeth, desperately trying to buck me off.

I rip the knife from her grasp, eyeing it from end to tip. It's a custom blade, one of damn good quality. Too good to be wasted on a murder, where common sense would dictate it'd have to be tossed or destroyed afterward. No, this has to be personal.

I inspect the blade's leather hilt while running my finger over it for any clue. All I find is a scribbled engraved message in what looks like a child's handwriting.

"Mouse?" I say, reading the inscription out loud. "That some kind of nickname?" When she doesn't answer, I trace the curve of her squirming hip up the length of her back and wind up looking straight into those fiery eyes. "No. You aren't a mouse," I tell her. "I think you're more like a wicked little kitty. A tiger. Huh, *tigre*?"

She rears up as far as she can with her arm still in my grasp. I recognize how her cheeks hollow, but I don't try to avoid the glob of spit she lobs my way. It lands on the corner of my fancy lapel, relegating this suit as yet another casualty of this night.

"If Vin sent you, after all, I wouldn't blame him," I tell the woman, scanning her face for any hint of recognition of the name. She gives me nothing but more perfectly white teeth. Those eyes blaze even hotter, and it doesn't take much of an imagination to guess the insults flying around the inside of that pretty skull.

She can join the club of people I've disappointed.

"So maybe I did try to set him up with some spoiled little bitch. All I want is for the bastard to turn out better than me," I say. "Is that so wrong?"

In so many ways, he already has. Over twenty without a felony to his name. No blood on his hands to speak of. Apart from a pistol for protection, I never even taught the bastard how to shoot a weapon. A real weapon.

And yet my first choice for his father-in-law would be one of the most infamous gun runners this side of hell.

"I want him to be protected," I say in my defense, flicking the knife into the air and catching it by the handle. "Like I never was. I want the kind of security for him that can be provided only by a good name. A name people fear."

And if a side benefit to that happened to be forming an alliance with a powerful family in the process, then so be it.

"I'd do anything for him," I rasp to the silent form flailing beneath me. "I couldn't love him more even if he were my biological son. He is my son. Besides, it's not like I'm asking him to draw blood or enter the Stepanov business. Just—" I break off at the same exact moment the little tiger goes limp.

"Stepanov," I repeat the name deliberately, scouring her body for a reaction. This time, I catch it in slow motion—her entire body tenses. Though she tries to turn away from me, I don't miss how those eyes go wide as her teeth skewer her bottom lip between them. Hard.

"Did Mischa Stepanov send you?" Frankly, I'm asking the question hypothetically more than anything—not that she gives me an answer. Frowning, I wrack my brain, trying to remember if I really had done something to accidentally offend my deadliest rival. More than crashing his little party. More than with just my reputation.

Something egregious enough for him to send a woman after me, wielding a knife etched with the word *Mouse.*

It sounds insane enough in my head that I don't bother entertaining it out loud. So I laugh instead. If Mischa wanted me dead, I know enough of his reputation to have full confidence that he'd do it himself.

She must know him somehow, I deduce as she turns away from me, clawing at the mattress.

"Is he your next target, little *tigre*?" I wonder. My lip quirks at the thought of it—her slender form tangling with a brute like Mischa. But the amusement dies when I picture her dead in the aftermath. Mutilated. In pieces.

Some men don't need rumors to inspire terror in their wake. Not when they leave a body of evidence behind. Mischa Stepanov's body of evidence is terrifying even to those in this business with a mountain of bodies piled in their closets.

To men like me. I wouldn't wish his wrath on my worst enemy.

Not even this snarling, feisty little *tigre*.

She kicks out with her legs, forcing me to apply more pressure to my knee to keep her down. The motion brings me closer to her, and I fully take advantage of this new perspective. Every time she flexes her thighs, a warm sliver of bare skin becomes exposed, brushing the back of my extended leg.

Heat I haven't felt in a long time flares, forcing me to grit my teeth against it. And as if sensing the reaction, she goes limp again, refusing to move a muscle in defiance.

"I can tell you one thing," I say, releasing her arm in favor of stroking through that mane of hair. She tries swiping at my hand with both of hers, but from this angle, she can't reach.

And I have the lion's share of exploration. From her hair, down to her throat. From that slender column of flesh, down to the top of her spine and a defined, muscular little shoulder.

Once again, I was wrong—she's toned as hell, but her overall size helps to disguise the actual strength coiled in the lithe little body.

Strength that she hones in a vicious buck of her hips that nearly succeeds in dislodging me. Keeping her down requires more effort. I'm gritting my teeth, sensing a bead of sweat form on my temple.

For all this exertion, we might as well be fucking.

I adjust my weight to keep her restrained, and an ominous ripping sound issues from my sleeve. Sure enough, the entire goddamn suit gives way next with a metallic ping of a button flying off, landing on the floor. I have no choice but to shrug it off and toss it aside. I snatch at the shirt as well when the damn thing constrains my movements. Using one hand, I rip at the buttons until some of the pressure loosens.

"I'm not going to hurt you," I tell the woman. "Stop resisting, and I'll turn you over to the hotel authorities. They'll probably let you go with a slap on the wrist. Trust me, that's the upside offer. Sorry to put a damper on your little revenge plot, but I'd rather not die today…"

I trail off as her eyes find mine again. So damn piercing. Though she still hasn't said a word, it's like I can clearly hear her voice echoing in my head. Sexy in cadence, shouting obscenities.

"You know," I say in between pants. "It's usually after we fuck that a woman tries to stab me."

In another burst of strength, she contorts her hips, using her slightness to her advantage enough to skirt my knee and flip onto her side. I barely manage to pin her by the shoulders, easily maneuvering my weight on top of her. Skilled or not, she can't fight pure gravity. I'm too damn heavy for her to resist.

And she's so damn small. It's almost too easy to have her immobile, my knees trapping her legs, my weight balanced over her narrow hips. Of all the thoughts to enter my mind, one of sheer practicality takes the cake—if we were fucking, she'd have to be on top. Otherwise, I'd crush her in this position. Break her.

But even now, she's still resisting. Still fighting, her teeth bared, eyes darting around the room, anywhere but me. I don't know what makes me brush my thumb against her chin. She contorts her neck and nearly takes the appendage off, snapping with her teeth.

Our eyes meet, and maybe that was my goal all along. They're amazing, those fucking eyes. In a world where men only make eye contact to intimidate, women to seduce, grifters to lie. It's been a long damn time since anyone has looked at me. Stared without a damn for who I am or what I might do.

To her, I'm not Donatello Vanici, a black-hearted son of a bitch with a past too chilling to escape. Or maybe I am. The way she rages silently, her chest heaving, cheeks flushed, eyes narrowing. Her reaction confirms my previous hunch—this is personal.

But not to avenge someone else.

"What the hell did I do to you, little *tigre?*" I murmur, stroking her cheek again though she recoils so violently a troubling cracking sound issues from her neck. The fact that she's still trying to kick me assuages my worries of any serious injury.

But her reaction proves it.

"I can assure you that whoever you're after, it isn't me. I have never harmed a woman."

Physically at least. Emotional distress could be debated by a handful of scorned lovers, but that isn't her grudge. Now more than before, I'm sure of it—I would have remembered her, drunk, drugged, or not. Those eyes. This scent. That pouty, stubborn pink mouth. I would have recalled this lay. Her size especially. I've never met a woman so delicate, and—judging by the grunt I choke out as her knee slams dangerously close to its intended target—so fierce.

A part of me rails at the decision before I even let her go and stand from the bed. She scrambles into a sitting position, racing to adjust her askew dress. Her heavy breathing alone reveals how exhausted she truly is. That and the fact that she doesn't come for me automatically. So, much like her newly christened namesake, she sizes me up, hunting for a weak point to pounce on.

And there are plenty. Keeping her in my peripheral view, I risk glancing down and hiss in irritation. She nicked me good with her knife, causing a splotch of blood that ruins this shirt and ensures Vin will get to collect on his bet. I managed to rip the top buttons on it, leaving it open and gaping, exposing part of my chest.

"Goddamn it," I snarl, fingering the flopping lapel. "The one damn time I try to keep the son of a bitch intact…" I trail off, fixing my attention on the cause of the destruction.

Before my eyes, the little *tigre* transforms. Her eyes widen in alarm, fixated on my chest. Out of guilt for nicking me? No. I brush my hand over my left pec, and I know what has her attention.

A topic that not even a sexy little hellcat will ever get the chance to defile. I turn my back to her, forsaking the stupidity out of sheer, pathetic pride. Absently, my fingers trace the contours of a marking I've memorized every inch of by heart. My reason for being who I am now. For leaving the old Don behind.

This name is everything I stand for as a new man. A new person. Despite how drunk I get, or how many men like Mischa Stepanov shun me, never will I let myself forget it. I may have failed her when it mattered, but she'll always haunt me. Always.

I will never escape her.

"You can go," I snap to the woman on the bed. Suddenly, playing games with a hellcat isn't so appealing. There's a part of me that will always crave the thrill of the fight. Then there is the man who just wants to rest. To watch Vin marry some spoiled little *mafiya* bitch and live his happily ever after. Everything I've bled and fought for, the horrible shit I've done…

All of it will be worth it for that one moment. It will.

Impatient, I wait for the sound of footsteps. For the door to slam. I give her ample time before I whirl around to find her still crouched on the bed, her eyes like saucers, staring at me as though I'm a ghost. Or a monster. Some horrible mixture in between the two.

And my exhausted fucking brain… It toys with an impossibility too foolish to seriously entertain even for a second. Considering it at all makes me no better than a goddamn masochist. For over seven damn years, I've avoided poking this wound.

Until tonight. Vin's already scraped the surface of the scar by saying her name.

So why not stick a knife in it.

My jaw aches as I pry my lips apart. I know before I say the name that it's useless to suspect this woman could be her. Still, I torture myself. "Safiya?"

An image of her, blurred and distorted after years of suppressing her memory, appears in my mind. A cherub face. Eyes the color of amber. A sweetness unmatched by even the most cheerful incarnation of Pollyanna. She used to love that stupid book. Relished in finding the good in anything, even in the monsters who surrounded her and the parents who, by their actions, condemned her to death. The little girl I sold. The innocent life I ruined. The flame that ignited the creature I've become today.

Safiya Mangenello. Her life is a cross around my neck, my burden to carry until I die. And this woman isn't her. There's none of that sweetness, that innocent, pure joy. None of that yearning to please or her gift for sowing peace.

The Safiya I knew would never wield a blade against someone. Not her, the girl who cradled dying birds in her hands and wished only to play in the mud. It was her gentle spirit that made her so easy to mold and manipulate at will.

It made it even easier to kill her.

"Safiya Mangenello," I repeat hoarsely, watching the woman's face for any shred of acknowledgment. Her lips are pursed, her expression carefully controlled. But she can't hide a subtle flinching. While not Safiya herself, she's heard that name before.

Whoever hired her must have fed it to her. As an example of why I deserve to die? Or maybe as part of some elaborate trick. Pretend to be Safiya. Even imitate her mute nature to get inside my head and make me lower my guard.

There is just one flaw with that plan. Safiya couldn't scream, even if she wanted to. This woman will.

I adjust my grip on the knife, suppressing the tendril of unease warning me to stop. Let her go. Ignore this slight.

But Vin's not here. Without his calming influence, it's easier to entertain the icy thoughts for longer than I normally would. Fuck, I swear I literally see red, flashing across my vision for a split second. From the window? I look over, but apart from the lights in a nearby building, I see no such color.

My fucking head… I didn't drink enough, it seems. Old Don lurks beneath the confines of my fragile sanity, growling like a goddamn animal.

To be fair, she could have gone after me, and I wouldn't care. My life. My reputation. My livelihood. Anything or anyone but my family—what little of it remains, alive or otherwise.

Olivia and our child.

Vincenzo.

Safiya.

They are the few aspects of my life I've deemed off-limits. No one will ever sully them before me.

"Did he tell you to say it?" I demand, gripping the blade so tightly it shakes. "The bastard who hired you? Huh? Did he tell you to pretend to be a mute little girl in some sick, fucking way to get inside my head? Answer me!"

She doesn't. Her eyes remain fixed on my chest, but her expression slips. For a heartbeat, she isn't a tiger anymore. Just a woman, pale, trembling in the shadow of someone more than twice her size.

That look feeds the darkness inside me like a match striking tinder. Crueler fantasies come to life on the edge of my consciousness. I could easily crush her throat in my fist if I wanted to. Pin her down. Prove my point by making her scream… My fingers flex at the thought, and I can't stop myself from taking a step toward her. Then another.

I reach out, but in the end, I grab my jacket, tugging it on despite the loose sleeve.

"Safiya Mangenello couldn't plead for her life," I confess, facing the woman once more. I can't help the way I flinch as the words leave my mouth—that fact has haunted me every waking moment since I betrayed her. "But you will. Tell me who hired you—"

She lurches to her feet in such a display of grace; I almost forget my hate. This pain… As elegant as a dancer, she races toward me, her gaze on my face, her beautiful features displaying pure terror.

I'm too startled to react like I should. I halfheartedly lift the knife, but her hands, soft and outstretched, slam into me first. She's not strong enough to push me down outright—and yet I let her, using the momentum to dive to the floor.

It's something in her eyes, those dark, fucking intense eyes. I can hear her voice again, as if she shouted into my ear, though she never makes an actual sound. *Get down!*

I only have enough sense of mind to curl my arm around her waist, pulling her with me. We barely hit the floor before I have her beneath me, shielding her body as the world explodes. My neck prickles, stung by spraying material. The sound of broken glass shatters the quiet, along with a low, telltale buzz that precedes an explosion of noise in the corner of the room.

"Fuck!"

In addition to finding a beautiful assassin in my room, it's been a while since someone's taken a shot at me, let alone a sniper. I rock onto my knees, staying low to the ground. Only as my gaze falls over the woman do I entertain the possibility that she could be a part of this attempt. Distract me while the shooter takes his aim.

Even as the suspicion enters my mind, her tiny hands grip my forearms, her eyes scanning the room with that tiger-like intensity.

"Stay down," I tell her, watching her stiffen as my mouth brushes her ear. "On my lead, we head for the door. Got it?"

Her mouth tightens, but she nods without meeting my gaze directly.

Tearing my attention from her, I try to take stock of the situation as quickly as possible. The shooter must have aimed twice. One initial shot shattered the window, and another took a chunk out of the wardrobe in the corner of the room. Through the fractured glass, I can only make out the darkened landscape and the nearest row of buildings. One's close enough to be the shooter's nest, and a flicker of movement in a window draws my notice.

"Got you, you sick fuck," I hiss. Keeping close to the ground, I lurch for the door, dragging the girl by her arm. She's quick, keeping pace on her hands and knees—but she runs into me as I stop short with a grim realization.

To open the door, I have to reach for the handle and risk entering the shooter's line of sight. I could always grab the gun from the closet safe, but there's no way I'd have a shot from here —not to mention that any move puts the woman at risk. I eye her and consider the most reckless of solutions—taking the risk anyway, long enough for her to escape.

I tighten my grip on her arm, prepared to shove her back—but already footsteps are racing down the hall.

"Boss?" a familiar voice rings out. I recognize the gruff baritone as belonging to Javier, my personal guard. "Is everything okay in there—"

"Be careful," I warn. "Open the door but keep cover. Sniper."

The handle turns, and the door opens just wide enough for me to shove the girl through. A whizzing noise hums past my ear as wood goes flying.

"Fuck!"

The second the girl moves, I follow her, slamming the door behind me. Lurching to my feet, I discover the other two guards on my detail already running to meet me.

"Send a team to comb the building northeast from here," I demand. "I think I saw the son of a bitch on the same floor with a view facing mine."

One of the men takes off while I turn to Javier. "Where is Vin?"

As if on cue, the door down the hall opens, and Vin sticks his head out from behind it, looking half asleep. "Where's the party?" he demands. His gaze goes to the woman still in my grasp, and he raises an eyebrow. "Though it looks like you've been having more than enough fun on your own—"

"Get your shit," I tell him, peering into his suite. The curtains are drawn shut, obscuring the view of any would-be shooter positioned outside. "We need to go now."

"What are you…?" Finally, he seems to notice the hole in my door. And the blood on my shirt.

"Holy shit!" He ducks into his room, presumably getting dressed.

"Sir," Javier says. "I have a team scouting the perimeter, and Lionel will bring around the car to the garage."

"Who do you think it could be?" Vin demands, staggering from the room while wrestling his foot into a shoe. "The Salvatores?"

"Could be," I say with a nod. "The sniper, at least." I turn to the woman and tighten my grip on her arm just as she tries to slip from my grasp. From the corner of my eye, I catch Vin staring at her, but there's no conspiratorial glance shared between them. Vin has a shit poker face, but in his expression, I see nothing but genuine interest as he scans the woman's thin frame.

I grit my teeth, caught off guard by the irritation that flares. Apart from her attempt on my life, I have no claim to her. Though, on second thought, I do. The mystery she presents regarding Safiya's memory is mine alone to explore.

In whatever way I chose. By coming to me, she sealed her fate. I'm entitled to her—at least to making her talk. And I fully intend to.

"So, what now? Were you hit?" Vin demands, turning to me. He slips his hand into his suit pocket, and I feel a sense of pride. The boy is already prepared to fight, future doctor or not.

Not that I plan for him to ever pull a trigger.

"I'm fine, but now I need to get you out of here. You—" I incline my head to the other guard. "Take Vincenzo to the countryside villa." One of my new properties purchased after I secured the port. "Javier—" I turn to find the man still issuing orders into a headset. "You come with me. We'll go separate routes in case we're followed—"

"That's stupid," Vin argues, still fastening his pants. "I should be with you."

"The shooter came after me," I point out. "You'll be safer on your own."

"On my own," he says, eyeing the woman pointedly.

But I don't have time to explain. "We need to move. We'll meet up at the villa."

When he hesitates, I approach him and throw my free arm around his shoulders. Lowering my mouth to his ear, I say, "Me getting a bullet through the head isn't the same as you getting one through yours. Trust me on this." This is no time for fucking bravado—I let him hear how my voice breaks. I mean every word. "Do this for me, my boy. Please."

He scoffs, rolling his eyes. "Fine. But next time, I want a companion like yours." He nods to the girl, and for a second, I consider letting her go with him. Then I remember her prowess with a knife.

My grip on her wrist tightens even more, and I sense her tug, attempting to resist. But for whatever reason, she doesn't scream. Doesn't shout. Doesn't kick me or utilize her nails—yet.

Again, that pesky, dangerous suspicion creeps in. Could she be Safiya? Perhaps. Or just a damn good double, hired and armed with a knowledge of the girl's medical history.

Either way, I don't let her go, dragging her down the hall after Javier.

"I have two cars ready, sir," he explains as Vin and the other guard depart in the opposite direction. "The authorities have already been contacted. Those on your payroll will form a perimeter escort."

"Any word on the shooter?"

He shakes his head as we enter the stairwell. "Not yet, sir. But we —damn it." He stops short, his hand on his headset. Wide with alarm, his eyes cut toward me. "I've gotten word that a group of men has entered the hotel. Not Salvatore from what my men can tell. I'm not sure if they are hostile, either."

"Who?" I ask, recognizing the way he's parsing his words. He's beating around the bush for a reason.

"They are Stepanov's men," he says bluntly. "I don't know if it's coincidence or—"

"I just prostrated myself before the bastard and kissed his ring," I say, frowning. "He has no stake in my feud with Salvatore—" At least none that I know of. "Could it be unrelated?"

"I don't know, sir," Javier says, continuing down the steps. "However, I suggest we move. Now."

I start after him and nearly have my arm wrenched out of its socket. I turn to find the girl gripping the banister so tightly her knuckles are white, her heels practically digging into the floor. Again, it's like I can read in her eyes everything she doesn't say out loud.

She's terrified. Is Stepanov who she works for? Though why the man would go through the trouble of digging into my past and taunting me with Safiya's memory, I don't know. Or maybe Mischa is another unwilling bastard on her hit list? He may be somewhat reformed now, but I've been out of the game far longer, though that doesn't seem to matter to her.

I could let her go.

Track her later and cut my losses.

Or I could throw my arm around her waist, catching her off guard and wrench her off her feet. She's so slight, it's almost too easy to throw her over my shoulder. Her fists land harmlessly over my back, but even now, she doesn't scream. Doesn't make a goddam sound apart from the frantic pace of her breathing.

The unwelcome suspicion bites even deeper, but I ignore it, pushing everything from my mind but the need to move.

"Put extra detail on Vin," I command Javier as I draw up to his side. We're nearing an emergency exit, hopefully near the garage. "If all hell breaks loose, he takes priority. I don't care what the fuck happens; you save him over me. Do you understand?"

"Yes, sir," the man replies, though his frown reveals his thoughts on that plan. "Master Vincenzo will take a majority of the detail."

"Good."

I'd rather take a Salvatore bullet myself than risk Vin coming anywhere close to danger. Though hell, I did escort him right into the home of the ultimate devil.

Mischa Stepanov's name has come up tonight more often than not.

And an ominous feeling in my gut warns that I may not like wherever these clues lead.

10

WILLOW

I'm lost within another waking nightmare, but pinching myself does little to wake me up. Each vicious stabbing of my nails against my wrist just reinforces the grim reality I can't escape.

Over and over, my own brain mocks me with the images—watching Donatello Vanici come within seconds of death—a fitting end he deserves—but rather than let it happen…

I reacted in a way I will never understand.

I should have killed him.

I came so close…

The worst fact to reconcile is that I can't even explain it rationally. Fear wasn't what held me back. Weakness either—and if so, all I had to do was sit back as a telltale red dot appeared over his chest. Ironically, he was the reason I recognized the target for what it was. When Vinny and I would play with water guns in the summer heat, he would affix tiny lasers to our weapons with tape to heighten the fun. I clearly remember turning my firearm on him more than once, aiming my light over his smiling face before pulling the trigger and drenching him.

I could have let him die.

Why didn't I? Rather than come up with an answer, my brain is too busy scouring the past. A million lessons circle my mind, each one uttered in Mischa's gruff baritone. *"Never let your guard down,"* he would insist until his voice grew hoarse. *"Always aim to kill. Focus, Mouse! Focus! Focus!"*

And yet, I failed. My quarry sits unharmed across from me in the back of a black armored car driven by his guard, and all I can do is stare at him.

At his chest.

While covered by his shirt now, the image of the bared, tanned flesh beneath is seared into my memory. Some of the scars I remember him sporting, even back then. The silvery straight line along his collar that he swore resulted from him being stabbed as a teenager. Those ropey, circular patches across his pecs he would always refuse to explain.

He's gotten even more injuries since then—but one new set of scars startled me the most. It was a name, tattooed there in ink so scarlet it could have been blood.

The name of a girl he sold to a monster. His little Safy. His beloved adopted sister. It isn't awe or sentiment that has rendered me speechless since I first glimpsed it. It's rage. Anger so all-encompassing my brain cannot comprehend it.

My mind goes blank as my chest tightens with every breath I take. My eyes burn with the threat of tears that never fall—but I'm beyond sobbing.

The bastard had the nerve to mourn me. To act as if saying my name caused him pain. To act as though he cared. A different woman might be fooled, but I will never forget his face the day he led me to Nicolai Baryshnikov like a lamb to slaughter. I will never forget his steely, ice-cold expression, or the words he said to me before turning his back and leaving me to die.

"Do what you will with her. I don't care…"

Years later, armed with the knowledge that living within Mischa's orbit endowed me, I know now how dramatic a statement that was. How pathetic. How cowardly.

And now he mourns me as a martyr, a fallen innocent whose name he bears out of some twisted sense of guilt. But he has no right.

No amount of regret can bring that Safiya back.

And killing him won't avenge what has been done to me. I know that now. He deserves more. A pain worse than death. Pain like that of a child sold to be a slave.

Some aspects of those early days in Nicolai's care are too dark to relive even after all of these years. To survive, I had to suppress those memories and focus everything I had on survival. Time in Mischa's family healed some of those wounds; I can't deny that.

But just by being here, in Donatello's orbit, all of those old injuries feel ripped open and raw. The pain distracts me from everything—like common sense.

Up close, he looks the same, as strange as it is to acknowledge. My imagination has transformed him, distorting his features, and making it easier to picture him as a creature befitting of his sins. However, his hair, though slightly longer, is still thick, neatly trimmed. His skin still clings to hues of gold and his eyes…

They're the same eyes that have haunted me relentlessly all this time. Watchful, quickly shifting from charming to stern, to—whenever Vincenzo's safety is called into question—terrifying.

Losing me didn't change him. Didn't humble or harden him. He just went on, the same old Donatello.

He lived without me.

But I've thrived without him.

You are a Stepanova, I tell myself, pinching a sliver of my wrist. *You are the daughter of a lion. You are protected. You are loved…*

"I know who you are," Donatello growls. His sly grin glimpsed in the semi-darkness throws my reassurances into question. "Antonio Salvatore hired you," he declares, his voice smug with conviction. I vaguely recognize the name from our shared past—the one he cursed to hell and back after Olivia died, sounding crazed as he did so. "The bastard dug into my past and told you how to act. How to look. You are convincing, *tigre*, but I am not fooled. Tell me your real name. Though, trust me when I say I would prefer to pry it out of you."

I shiver, hating the raw note in his voice—stubbornly, my brain instantly defines it—pain and anguish. Like he cares. Like the little girl he referenced matters to him at all. When she doesn't. I didn't.

So, I meet his gaze and do nothing. Eye contact with him is a different animal from years ago, when I had to crane my neck back just to look at him adoringly. I had viewed him only as Don, then. My savior. My protector. In a violent world, neglected by my parents, I knew he would always be there for me. Save me.

Love me.

My love for him was easy to shed after barely a week in Nicolai's custody. But the hate? That remains, festering inside me, coloring the way I sit, hunched away from him. The way I breathe, my nostrils flaring, chest heaving. I think the hate has permeated my entire being so thoroughly he can smell it on me.

He sits forward, inhaling audibly, his eyes narrowing and widening in quick succession. Cocking his head, he furrows his brows. "Are you Safiya?" The question comes in Italian, and I barely manage to keep my expression composed.

How long has it been since someone has spoken to me directly in my mother tongue? Too long to count, though I've studied it as well as I can on my own, narrating old fairy tales to myself in the language. But hearing him speak it is a twisted, callous reminder of everything I've lost.

His punctuation is crisp, musical in delivery. With three words, he taunts me. Three little words.

Still, I give him nothing.

He sighs, sitting back in his seat, crossing and uncrossing his legs. "No," he says, deciding on an answer for himself. "You are not her. Safiya was sweet. *Delicata.* A little dove. You, seem to be a vicious little snake."

I clench my jaw—I can't help it—and by doing so, I fall right into his trap. His eyes gleam in triumph, and he sits forward again, tucking a fist beneath his chin.

"You understand me, don't you?" he murmurs. All along, he's been speaking in our native language, mocking me with this relic of my past. It hurts to realize that I don't understand him fully. My brain struggles with some of his pronunciation. But his expression clearly conveys his meaning, adding context to every word. Every syllable.

"Tell me your name, little *tigre*," he says softly, switching to English. "Say it, and I will let you go. I know Antonio sent you. You reek of his meddling, and I believe you are his type—" He looks me over and chuckles. "Too sexy and probably too damn young."

His tone implies a double meaning to that insinuation, and heat floods my cheeks. Amused, he chuckles.

"What lies did he feed you about me for you to bare your fangs, little *tigre*?" He eyes his side, and I feel a flush of guilt mixed with pride. I stabbed him. But in the process, I lost my knife, breaking another one of Mischa's prized rules—always cherish your weapon.

It's in his pocket, and he brushes his hand over the telltale lump in the fabric as if to taunt me. "He must have told you something horrific enough for you to look at me the way you do. So vicious. Like you want to do more than sink your claws into me."

He's right. I want to kill him. But my original plans for revenge are already growing and expanding. Having a knife in his chest isn't good enough. No. He deserves something far worse.

"Tell me your name," he goads, reaching out to stroke my cheek.

I start to cringe from him, but recognition hits me like a punch, locking me in place. His hands are calloused from years of hard labor, and my traitorous body grows hot, remembering this aspect of him so clearly. He used to tell me stories of the days he would work in his father's repair shop, doing whatever odd jobs he could to help his family stay afloat. That business acumen pushed him to excel in any enterprise he undertook, even the criminal ones.

I'd been so naïve to his true nature back then. To me, Donny was God. The man who sheltered me from my parents' instability, giving me respite, welcoming me into his small, makeshift family. He had a wife then, Olivia, and a little baby boy. To be honest, he transformed into a stranger days before taking me to Nicolai. If I had to pinpoint the moment he changed, it would have been the day his wife and son died.

The light in his eyes vanished overnight, and the warmth in his voice grew cold. In theory, what he did to me should have hardened him more, completing his descent into madness. But here he is, more like the old Donny, the figure in my memories.

But then his eyes darken, scanning my face. "Safiya..." He inhales sharply as if just saying the name pains him, and I sit straighter, steeling myself against whatever he might say.

"She had an illness as a baby," he explains, seemingly oblivious to how I jump. "Afterward, she developed aphasia. She was mute, you see. Never said a damn word in her life. Though your boss must have told you that. But it was more than a coy little silence." He sits forward even more, practically frozen mid lunge. Something in his expression changes, darkening his gaze, making his shadow loom taller. "She couldn't cry out when afraid. She couldn't whimper. She couldn't scream. When in pain, she couldn't even gasp in alarm like you or I can. It is a silence unmaintainable by anyone without her affliction. And when you scream for me, little *tigre*, I will know for sure that your ruse is a hoax. So I suggest you come clean now."

A shudder runs through me. This tone I also recognize from my memories. The voice I used to overhear him utilize during heated conversations with the men in his employ. The voice I heard the day Olivia died.

The voice of the Donatello who struck fear into the hearts of his enemies.

Do I fear him now? The answer comes to me easily. No.

I meet his gaze and hold it until he's the one forced to turn away. Just when I think I've won, those cold eyes return to mine, glinting with a renewed intensity.

"Javier?" he snarls toward the driver's seat. The tinted window in the partition separating the back of the vehicle from the front lowers.

"Yes, sir?" the driver responds, a man with short black hair, olive skin, and a serious expression that renders him the polar opposite of my playful Evgeni.

"Has Vin made it to the villa?"

"Almost, sir. They have so far been unbothered by any attacks."

"Good." Returning his attention to me, Donatello raises an eyebrow in a way that makes my breathing hitch. "Send word to them not to wait. We'll be taking a detour."

"Oh?"

"I'm in the mood for a drive. Take us to Havienna."

My eyes widen, and he nods, stroking his chin.

"You recognize that name, eh *tigre?*" He reaches for me again, fingering a lock of my hair. "I'm sure your employer told you all about that. But how much will his money be worth when I'm through with you?" Switching effortlessly to Italian, he murmurs, "Tell me your name, little hellcat. I don't think you'll like what lies in store for you if you don't."

He fits the part of intimidating captor; I will give him that. His body is practically balanced on his knees, his eyes boring into my own, his tone a lethal whisper. At the back of my mind, I think I should feel some ounce of alarm.

But I don't. I feel nothing.

Donatello Vanici cannot hurt me any more than he already has.

I'd bet my life on that.

11

WILLOW

Within minutes, he grows bored of me and returns to his previous position, slumped against his seat, his gaze focused on the window. Alarm makes me stiffen, and I cut my eyes to the door, wishing I had the energy to wrench it open and leave. I prefer the anger. The threatening side of him is easier to withstand.

Because when his eyes soften… Something in his expression now recalls those old, peaceful days when I would curl up by his side with a book while he pored over ledgers or business documents. Little had I known what his true work entailed.

In my ignorance, I only knew that I enjoyed being beside him, sneaking glances at his stern, focused face while he'd been too distracted to notice. No matter how lost in the details of his empire he became, he would always humor my presence. Always.

His large hand would absently stroke through my hair in acknowledgment, and I can still recall the feeling of calm that used to come over me. A feeling I haven't been able to ever achieve since.

God, I used to live in such awe of this man.

Now, without the lens of childhood to distort him, all I see is a cruel bastard no different than any other in this twisted war of men. But Mischa doesn't clothe himself in the blood of dead children by way of armor.

"It must be exhausting to be so angry with me," he taunts, leaning his head back against his seat. He lets his eyes fall shut, an act that betrays just how little he fears me.

A smart woman would lunge for the knife. Instead, I lower my gaze to the strip of flesh bared by his ruined shirt and can't seem to do anything more than stare. My fingers twitch, my teeth grinding together as I imagine his reasoning for having that name tattooed there. For sympathy? Pity?

It certainly can't be out of guilt. He had weeks to find me before Mischa Stepanov entered Nicolai's that fateful day—but he never came.

I don't even realize I'm moving until it's too late. My fingers twitch in the still air, reaching across the distance between us, grappling for the lapel of his tailored suit jacket. It's expensive judging from the fabric's softness—a world apart from the simplistic clothing he used to wear.

But he still smells like tobacco. Like old, expensive cigars and musk. Like fresh air and rain. My lungs greedily fill with his scent, comparing it to those old dangerous memories. My throat tightens at the threat of them, and I wrench my hand away just as he stirs, opening his eyes.

Rather than react in alarm, he snatches my wrist, running his thumb along the back of my hand as if testing the flesh for any hint of my identity. These smooth, manicured hands obscure so much of who I really am. His frown deepens.

"You are not Safiya," he says coldly. But then he raises his free hand, tugging his shirt aside, revealing the planes of his chest and the letters scrawled across it in scarlet ink. Tightening his grip on me, he forces me to touch the curve of the S. The A next, which curves around the outline of his pec. The f...

"Do you want to hear what I did to her?" he asks, though there is no pride in his voice. Just exhaustion that matches the wrinkles etched into the flesh around his eyes. "I lied to her," he tells me, forcing my fingers to trace the path of the I. "I told her I would always protect her, though I knew then that I couldn't. I wouldn't. I sacrificed her love to my hate, and at the time... I didn't regret it. You know what they call me, *tigre*? The men who hired you and the others. *Il Mostro*." He switches to Italian, using his free hand to stroke my cheek. I don't know why I let him. Why I'm so riveted by the flesh beneath my fingertips. Up close, it's easy to tell that this tattoo wasn't done carefully like Mischa's many adornments. With every new child, he has their name added to a tally on his back, his way of marking his growing family.

Those carefully inked designs are nothing like this. Raw, jagged lines. Smeared ink as though something other than a professional instrument made the initial incision. And I can picture exactly what from my own experience with the weapon—a knife. A small one, wickedly sharp, utilized crudely to form the final creation inch by inch. To stain the skin, the creator had to use raw ink, rubbing it into the open wounds for no other reason than to cause pain. Agony. Horrified, I realize that this isn't a tattoo.

It's a punishment.

"You're disgusted," he murmurs, dragging the pad of his thumb to the corner of my mouth. My reaction doesn't seem to bother him. If anything, he relishes in my discomfort, swiping his tongue along his lower lip in satisfaction. "Aren't you, little *tigre*? Horrified by what I've done. Your boss fed you a lie, didn't he? That you could stick your little knife through my chest. Kill me. Avenge whatever wrong you think I've done against you. But he was wrong." He laughs and presses down on my lip to expose my clenched teeth. "You couldn't kill me, even if you wanted to. I've been dead for a long damn time. You really want to hurt me? Tell me your name. End this game for good. Kill any hope I may have that you could be…"

His hand falls from my face, but his grip on my wrist doesn't relent, forcing me to feel where a crudely shaped letter y ends, roughly over his heart.

"You are not Safiya," he tells me, applying so much pressure my nail is driven into his skin. "Say one little word and prove that to me. That will do the job better than any knife, *tigre*. Because Safiya? I didn't kill her with my own two hands—that would have been too easy. No. I had to see the look on her face when I delivered her into the arms of a twisted, sick son of a bitch. I had to watch her cry for me, unable to make a sound. She couldn't scream even if she wanted."

He shoves me back so hard I slam against the leather seat cushions. Hunched over, he tears at his hair with both hands, but his expression is anything but anguished. He smiles, teeth bared, eyes flashing with a maniacal gleam.

And for the first time, I feel my heart clench in a way that could be out of fear.

"I knew what would happen to her," he says, laughing softly more to himself than to me. "I knew. And I told myself it was worth it, *tigre*. Her pain, her death, her lost innocence would all be worth it. Because if I could do that to her—" He breaks off, his eyes on his hands as he lowers them before him. "I could do anything. I could survive anything, and I have. I've survived. But if you are Safiya… Everything I've suffered would have been for nothing. So, tell me your name."

I jump at the growl concealed in those final words. It's not a command, but a plea. A poor man begging to be put out of his misery.

When I don't grant his wish, his nostrils flare, cheeks flushing red. "What is your name—"

The mechanical whir of the partition lowering renders him silent, and the driver calls from the front seat. "Sir?"

"What is it?"

"We've arrived."

Dread forms a rock, sinking to the pit of my stomach. Arrived. That word has more connotations to it than I think the poor driver is aware of. Even before I sneak a glimpse from the window, I know he made good on his threat.

To bring me here. The place that had been my haven long before Mischa's manor. The place where my life was ripped apart by the very man seated across from me.

"Welcome home, imposter Safiya," he tells me, wrenching open the door to the back seat, ushering in a burst of cold air, damp with a drizzle of rain. "Get out."

I can't move. My gaze is riveted on the looming manor house. It's been over seven years since I saw it last, but in so many ways, it seems like I've never left. The darkness obscures any signs of age that might mar the stone structure, but the faint moonlight enhances its old beauty to a painful degree. The lawns have since become overgrown and wild, though the same curved stone path leads to the main entrance—a large double door, painted red, nearly swallowed by a swath of creeping vines.

"Come," Donatello commands, exiting the car first. Before I can react, his hand lashes out, snagging my wrist, dragging me after him.

I dig my heels in, twisting to free myself from his grasp—but he's persistent, snatching me by my waist and lifting me off my feet entirely.

"Don't tell me you aren't enjoying your homecoming," he snarls, ruthlessly mounting the front entrance to the house.

Memories come in a flood, drowning me in remnants of the past. Living here with him. My old room, adorned with pretty pink wallpaper. The study where he used to work. The spacious backyard and the fountain I used to play in. The hallways where Vin and I would waste hours over games of hide and seek.

My eyes burn, and no amount of blinking can keep the tears at bay. They descend in a torrent, and I lash out at the only target within reach. Him. I kick wildly, hoping to strike his chest. My fists hammer at his back before I try clawing at his forearms instead.

Unperturbed, he adjusts his grip on me to kick open the front door, stepping inside.

And in a mocking twist of fate, I'm home again, in the arms of the man who threw me away. His laugh forms a haunting bridge to the past as he sets me down and drags me further inside.

It's dark, and a cloying layer of dust drifts on the air, making me cough. Despite the thick shadows, it's obvious that some level of care has gone into maintaining the property. Donatello grapples at the wall, and scattered lights come to life, bathing everything in an orange glow.

I go numb, struck by agonizing recognition.

The hallway—though less furnished—looks the same. Still, emerald green, accenting the wooden staircase leading to the upper level. I can make out the doorway to his study from here, bathed in the glow of moonlight.

And whatever my expression reveals makes Donatello release me as if stung. Swallowing hard, he backs away, blinking rapidly. Anguish washes over his face for a heartbeat before something cold hardens his expression, darkening his eyes and tightening the line of his mouth.

He grabs my arm again, this time brutally enough to hurt. Whirling on his heel, he tears toward the study almost too quickly for me to follow. I trip in his wake, forced to brace my free hand against the wall for balance. On my way through the doorway, a series of marks catch at my fingertips. Tiny little cuts etched into the wood.

I don't have to look to imagine the small handwriting accompanying each one. Names. Don. Olivia. Vinny. Safy.

"Look at me." Wrenching me forward, Donatello shoves me into a leather chair positioned before a massive oak desk. His desk, coated in a layer of dust. His bookshelves remain, as do the paintings he'd had hanging even back then.

One, in particular, greets me now, looming on the wall behind him. The self-portrait of a little girl, painstakingly crafted with a mixture of finger paints and crayons. I'd insisted on him putting it right there.

So he would never be alone.

I would always be with him.

"Look at me, little *tigre*." He crouches before me, bracing his hands on either armrest, trapping me in place. "You are not her." He scoffs at the prospect even as his trembling fingers find the ball of my chin. He touches me. Snatches his hand away. Grips me tightly, shoving my head back against the leather.

His eyes rake over me mercilessly. From my scalp, down to my heaving chest. His jaw twitches, his breathing audibly unsteady. Heavy. Rasping.

"You can't be her…" To prove it, he grinds his thumb down the length of my cheek as if the bone structure alone is evidence enough. A dangerous possibility creeps into my thoughts. Did he ever stop to picture how his Safiya might look seven years after his betrayal? Did he imagine some weak, broken, mournful creature?

Anyone but me. I am not broken, holding his gaze even as tears blur my vision. I am not some sniffling little victim.

But he is still that man. That brooding, expressive Donatello. Even now, the look on his face robs me of the anger I've held onto. He should be shocked at the sight of me. Alarmed. Repentant. Fearful.

This man…

He's hateful, his eyes blazing as his nail catches the corner of my mouth with a searing sting.

"Tell me your name," he bellows. "Now. Tell me your fucking name!"

His eyes are unfocused, cutting lower to my throat. Without warning, he hooks his fingers beneath the thin straps of my dress, wrenching them down my shoulders before I even have the sense to stop him. I'm at the mercy of the cool air and his unyielding gaze, assaulted by both at once. My hands jerk in a vain attempt to shield myself, but the look in his eyes freezes me in place.

He shows me no mercy, eyeing my womanly body smugly as though the curves prove his next words true.

"You cannot be Safiya."

Not the little stick of a girl he knew. His *cucciola*, his puppy, lovesick with devotion. In his mind, she never grew up.

His trembling finger continues his inspection, tracing my collarbone, and I flinch, my thoughts colliding. This isn't how it's supposed to go.

"You can't be Safiya," he says, laughing coldly to himself. "I wouldn't want to fuck you if you were."

To him, it's perfect logic, emboldening him to cup my breast in the palm of his hand. Callously, he drags his thumb across my nipple, laughing harder as I stiffen.

"Ah, no, little *tigre*… Your game is up," he declares, his smile breathtaking, wide with relief. "That girl meant the world to me. I'd know her…"

And yet he condemned her to a fate worse than death. He swallows hard at the realization, and his next stroke is harsher, making me jump. I can't take my eyes off of him as he boldly gropes a part of me no other man has touched.

My brain tortures me with flashbacks of the man he used to be. Of us. Back when I was a useful toy to him. A silent little spy. No man has ever looked at me the way he does now.

Like I'm prey.

"No," he growls, clenching his fingers around the globe of flesh in his grasp. "Tell me your name. Now. Tell me." He lowers his mouth to my ear, letting his gruff rasp drip against the lobe. "Though it's too late. I've already seen through your ruse. My little Safiya wouldn't endure this treatment. Not from me."

From him. The man she loved so innocently. Her protector. Her Donatello.

His touch would make her cringe. Resist. Fight. It would be wrong to endure the heat of his palm. To inhale his scent and remain still.

Still enough for him to press forward, muscling his bulk between my thighs, utilizing his weight like a battering ram.

"No, little *tigre*," he murmurs, letting his lips graze my jaw. "You almost had me fooled." He repeats it ceaselessly, as if hearing it out loud reassures him where his eyes do not. He doesn't take them off me, peering into me with increasing confusion.

My lips part as his thumb rasps over my nipple. Again. Harder. Harsher. A sharp inhalation catches in my throat, the sound alarmingly loud in the quiet.

"Don't tell me this arouses you, *tigre*," he scolds. His opposite fingers sink into my hair, fisting a handful to lock me in place. "You like it rough?" He flexes his fingers, teasing me with the tips of each nail.

My heart races, surging, pounding against my ribcage. That faint taste of fear grows more potent. Run, a part of me warns. My brain issues a string of commands to my paralyzed limbs, but they don't budge.

"Your employer must have paid well to acquire someone so determined. You have grit; I will tell you that," he says, withdrawing his hand to stroke my other breast. The light touch proceeds the moment he catches the entire globe in a grip so tight my teeth chatter. "What was the deal, huh? You seduce me if you couldn't kill me?" He chuckles and withdraws his hand, using the tip of a finger to caress over my nipple so intimately my cheeks flush.

It's the surrealness that addles my senses, sending my thoughts into turmoil. Before my eyes, this man melds into an amalgamation of the caring figure who used to tuck me in at night. And a creature eyeing me with an emotion that makes my breathing hitch. It's the way Mischa looks at his wife in the shelter of darkness when he thinks they're alone and concern for the children no longer tempers his actions.

Hunger. Fire. Lust.

"You're blushing, *tigre*," Donatello warns, tilting his head so he can better observe my mouth. "Tell me your name. You've excelled at your act until now. Give me your name."

He clamps down on my breast and tugs, pulling me toward him. Heat floods my belly. Disgust…

"Perhaps you don't want our game to end?" he suggests, running his tongue along his lower lip. Switching to Italian, he says, "Tell me your name. I'd fuck you senseless if that's what you want. Just give me your name."

Anger flashes through his gaze at my silence. He palms the armrests again, and the furniture creaks as he leans forward, bringing his nose within a hair's width of mine.

"Perhaps your aim is to drive me insane?" he wonders, letting his breath baste my cheek. "Fuck. It breaks my heart to tell you this, *tigre*, but I'm already there. I lost my mind years ago. You think to torment me? I live in torment."

His large hands move to my waist, grasping at the skirt of my dress. Grunting, he tugs. Cold air assaults the flesh of my stomach before I even process what he's done—rip my dress open, baring my front fully to him.

His irises look blacker in the dim lighting, adding a harshness to his features the man in my memories lacked. He's a stranger, hunched over me. A stranger who smells like home and feels so familiar my body is a slave to the contours of his fingers, unable to sense the danger in them my brain is all too aware of.

His hands find my hips, so large they nearly overlap as he lifts me from the chair and shoves me onto the desk nearby. Limp, I fall back, forced to stare up at him, still trying to reconcile this man with the specter who has haunted me all this time.

Donatello, the man whose face I used to fall asleep picturing while imagining all the ways I'd kill him. Get my revenge. Make him regret leaving me. Forgetting me. Erasing me.

In this moment, those childish fantasies die. The little girl who conjured them is forced to grow up, faced with the ravages of time.

"Now, this is a skill I'm sure your employer won't approve of," he scolds, fanning out his fingers over my waist. The touch distracts me from his words, and I shiver as his thumbs toy with the waistband of my panties, threatening to slip beneath the thin lace.

"Pity," he continues in a harsh tone that doesn't match the unsteadiness apparent in his trembling fingertips. "How can someone like you feel pity for a poor bastard like me? Don't deny it. It's written all over your face. You may hold your tongue, but your eyes..." He inhales sharply as if tasting the word, relishing the flavor of it. My eyes. He might as well be drooling over my soul. "Those eyes give you away. I see you clearly. In every way, I see you."

He sounds so earnest. He truly believes that, every word... While the truth's twisted irony grows the longer he lets his touch linger over me. The more he looks. I think it's the inherent wrongness that leaves me so riveted despite the indecency.

He sees me, his Safiya, right beneath his nose. Maybe he never really knew me. Never really cared.

Something in his gaze shifts as if he's reading my mind, and he shakes his head.

"No. No! You don't look at me like that." He curls his fingers around the waistband of my panties in cruel retaliation for insulting him. "Like I'm the one toying with you, when you... You provoke me in the worst way. A lesser man would kill you for desecrating what you've tried to."

He brings one hand to my throat, toying with the thrum of my pulse. His thumb finds a spot Mischa taught me to recognize—a vital artery. He presses down directly over it, hard. Harder...

"Would anyone even care if I killed you?" he wonders in a cruel whisper. I brace myself as he lowers his weight over me, hovers his mouth above where his thumb still lies. "You are at my mercy. Tell me your name, and I'll let you go. Or gasp. Whimper. Anything to prove it. I'm begging you. I'll get on my knees if that's what you fucking want." He chuckles madly at the thought of it. He sounds mad. Earnest. A man at his wits' end with nothing to lose. "Prove to me you are not Safiya. Or... Prove to me you are her."

He frowns as if he doesn't even understand the question leaving his mouth. He tilts his head, his breath hot on my cheek, his hips pressed hard against mine, dominating the space between my legs.

"My Safiya wasn't a fighter," he says near the hollow of my throat, still pressing so hard I feel lightheaded. "She loved me like... She loved me—" His voice breaks, triggering an unexpected pain lancing through my chest. It builds and builds, spreading up my spine, setting my eyes on fire.

"She loved me," he insists. "And do you know what I did to her? What I let happen to her? My Safiya? My sweet girl..."

Lace rasps against my hips, ruthlessly dragged over the tops of my thighs. I remember how to move, lurching against him, swatting at his hands.

"I sold her." His eyes are unfocused, staring into space beyond me as his strength easily overpowers what little resistance I muster. He cinches a fistful of my panties and tugs. Fabric tears, making my stomach lurch before cool air replaces the thin barrier, and there's nothing to shield me as his touch roams. He palms my thigh, and I go rigid again, my thoughts spiraling.

"I offered her on a silver platter to men who would tear her apart." His voice goes hoarse with dread. Guilt. Agony. "I let them hurt her. God knows what they did to her." His mouth finds the crook of my shoulder as his hand inches higher. Higher.

I pummel him, trying to clamp my thighs against the intrusion.

He doesn't even flinch, so lost inside his own memories, I doubt he can feel anything. "I killed her in so many ways, *tigre*," he whispers into my flesh, sounding like a broken man, a world apart from the ruthless finger prodding between my legs.

My lips part, my breathing harsh on the air. It's an impulse I haven't done in years. Try to scream…

My nails dig into the flesh of his forearm as he brushes his thumb against me. Soft. Harder, forcing my flesh to conform to the pressure. Fire ignites my cheeks. I know what happens between a man and a woman. I am well aware of the physical act my parents so obviously enjoy.

But rumors, or my classmates, or what snippets of romance I glimpsed in books made it sound so blasé. So simple.

This is punishing. Relinquishing your body to another. Feeling them force their way inside despite the sheer limitations screaming that it's unnatural. They could never fit. Even a finger is too much. Too big.

"Ah… *Sì*," Donatello declares in triumph. "You may hold your tongue, for you are not Safiya," he states, drawing back so suddenly my head swims. "Count your blessings on that. I may be a fool. I may harbor pathetic hopes of her bestowing her forgiveness upon me from beyond the grave—but I am not that naïve." He steps back, adjusting his askew suit jacket. Cold, his eyes sweep over me. "Go back to your employer, whoever he may be. Tell him that you failed. But know this…"

He starts for the door and pauses over the threshold, his back to me.

"Come after me again, and I won't show the same restraint. Believe whatever lies your master fed you about me, but understand one thing, *tigre*. I am still *Il Mostro*. Attack me all you want, but if you ever insult the memory of my family again? I will kill you. With my bare hands, I will kill you. Slowly. Sloppily. I'll have you praying to the devil himself for mercy before I'm through."

He leaves, shutting off the light as he goes.

12

DON

By the time Javier and I reach the villa, it's mid-morning, and Vin has the nerve to come skipping down the main staircase as I stagger into the foyer.

"You look like shit," he declares while looking sufficiently bright-eyed and fucking bushy-tailed. "Where is your little friend?" He cranes his neck to peer beyond me, as if expecting the blond to come in through the front door.

I push past him in search of a couch to lie on, ignoring the question.

Where is the puzzling little *tigre*? Hopefully, on her way back to her master, sufficiently convinced to leave me in peace.

Peace…

That's the name I've given to this hollowed state of being. Peace. *Peace.* I scoff out loud, feeling my upper lip quirk as I slump onto a leather chaise in the drawing room. As a relatively new property, it's sparsely furnished with whatever the previous owners left behind.

"Looks like someone didn't get any sleep last night," Vin remarks from the doorway. I can practically hear his smirk. But, like always, he's too kind-hearted for his own good. Already, he's crossing to the large windows, drawing the curtains shut to block out the sunlight. "I wouldn't either," he adds from over his shoulder. "Because of sex, hopefully. Or the pain—there's blood on your shirt, Don, and your cheek is scratched. You sure you're okay?"

"I'm fine, smartass," I grumble, letting my eyes shut. Behind them is a wealth of misery, waiting to follow me into my dreams. Safiya, her face blurred by years of neglect, her memory faded and worn. And an older, beautiful blond, her dark eyes taunting me with the threat of a reality too painful to imagine.

Too tempting to resist.

My Safiya back from the grave, willing to put me out of my misery for good. I'd suffer whatever revenge she'd bring my way. Anything. I'd suffer anything for her.

But as my little virgin *tigre* proved, my hopes are futile, as fragile as a hymen straining against my fingertip. I will admit that it was a shock, a welcome bitch slap to my senses. I'd almost fallen for her scheme…

She wasn't Safiya.

But she was different. I can't stop myself from flexing the finger I'd had inside her, recalling that tight warmth. My brain is a sick fucking thing, conjuring dangerous realities where they shouldn't exist. Like that, my would-be assassin was a virgin, so tight I doubt she'd had a man touch her before, let alone fuck her. And her smell...

My forefinger is in my mouth before I know it, and I groan at the remnants of her taste. Sweet. Ripe. My cock stirs, and I regret leaving her there, though perhaps it's for the best. I've kept Havienna in my possession for too damn long. Soiled by the memory of the imposter Safiya, it's about damn time I burned it to the ground and let those ashes fade into dust.

I need to let her memory do the same.

Finally, I need to let my sweet girl go.

"I'll leave you alone to relive your night," Vin taunts, his footsteps tracking his retreat into the hall. "That cut looks nasty, though. When you wake up, hopefully, you'll be in a good enough mood to let me apply some First Aid—"

"Vincenzo." I lift my head as much as I can, straining my eyes to make him out through the dark. My side does sting like a bitch, but any treatment will have to wait. "I want you to pack your things. I'm sending you back to London."

"Why?"

"I've changed my mind. A gangster's daughter is not good enough for you. You deserve to struggle through medical school a lowly bachelor and find some sweet nurse to marry," I rasp, letting my head fall back against the cushions. As I stare up at the ceiling, I think I'm trying to convince myself of this course of action more than him. "Who needs a Stepanov name when you have mine?"

And I'll do whatever it takes to forge enough of a reputation that the mere whisper of the name Vanici will guard him well enough even in the afterlife. God himself wouldn't dare touch him. I owe him that much.

"I've thought about transferring here," he says, catching me off guard. *Here,* where the schools aren't anywhere near as prestigious as the one he attends. And damn it, the boy is so damn sensitive I suspect that's his real motive without having to hear his explanation. He thinks I can't afford his shiny new future.

Either that, or he's more concerned by my burgeoning vice than he's let on.

"No," I growl. "You're getting your ass back to London even if I have to kick you there myself."

"I'm not a little boy, Don."

"You're not," I agree. "But you are my boy. Mine to protect, even if my love is overbearing in nature. You are all I have. So, let me spoil you to my heart's content as any good Papa should. You're staying at that fucking school."

"I know, I know," he says in a tone that betrays he's rolling his eyes. "I'm your sole heir, burdened with the weight of redeeming your fearsome, gruesome reputation, dear uncle."

"And you will," I say in agreement. "I have no doubt about that."

I may have failed Safiya, but Vincenzo will salvage this sordid legacy. He'll live well into old age, find a good loyal wife, and spawn multiple children. He will know the peace denied to me.

So help me, God, he will know it.

"Goodnight, Don," he says, closing the door to the room after him. "Try to get some sleep, and we'll discuss this when you're sane and less fixated on mulling over your eternal torment."

I choke out a laugh. "Smartass."

In the silence he leaves behind, the specters return. Olivia. Little Nico. Safiya…

"I'm sorry," I tell her, reaching out for her ghostly figure. "I'm so sorry, my little Safy."

She fades without an ounce of mercy.

Not that I deserve it.

For what I did to her, I deserve the pitiful conclusion no doubt awaiting me at the end of this miserable life.

And I'm ready for it.

A commotion of noise and chaos snaps me awake. Alarmed, I reach into my jacket for a weapon before I realize several defining realities. One, I didn't think to arm myself before sleeping—a testament to just how badly the little *tigre* assassin has shaken my resolve.

Two, if the figure storming into the room I'm in now were my enemy, I'd most likely already be dead—and their first course of business wouldn't be to wrench open the blinds, ushering in a painful stream of white-hot daylight.

"Son of a bitch." I shield my eyes with the back of my hand, struggling to regain my bearings. Judging from the headache pounding through my skull, I'm long overdue for my morning shot of whiskey. "What the hell—"

"Have you lost your goddamn mind?"

"Fabio?" I lower my hand and strain my burning eyes through a sea of white light. Sure enough, the accountant is the one glaring down on me from the center of the room. One look at his face, and I know the brutal wake-up call is the least of my worries. "What's wrong?"

"You tell me," he croaks. His hands are shaking, tearing at his graying hair as he starts to pace. "What the fuck, Donatello? What the actual hell? I put my life on the line. For you! My literal neck on the chopping block, and you do something like this—"

"If you care to explain what it is that I've done, I'd be more than happy to apologize," I grouse. It takes nearly everything I have in me just to get the words out.

Damn, I feel beyond hungover. Beaten. Wrecked. I could chalk it up to a near-death experience, but that only touches the surface of what truly ails me. Sleep was a poor refuge from her. That face. Those eyes. Not quite wide and innocent like little Safy's. Colder. Harder, shaped by unmistakable hatred and rage.

She couldn't be Safiya…

But she haunted me nonetheless. I see her still, daring me to make her talk. Taunting me with her silence as Fabio rants and raves around her.

"…know you have a suicidal, self-destructive streak," the man growls, and I reluctantly attempt to focus on his ramblings. "But this? Even the mere thought of it is so insane I knew I had to ask you directly. You wouldn't be that foolish. Not with this."

I incline my head toward him, wincing as pain stabs through my skull. "With what?"

He stops short, frowning as he realizes he never exactly told me what it is I'm accused of. It must be bad, I suspect.

So bad that the calm, collected Fabio has lost his cool.

"Willow Stepanova," he says, scanning my face intently as if to see how I'll react to the name. "Her family is in an uproar."

He pauses as if expecting a reaction from me. Groaning, I swipe at my jaw and shrug. "Let me guess. She didn't enjoy her party?"

"No," he rasps. "She went missing last night. Mischa has his whole damn entourage out looking for her."

Alarm cuts through the fog in my brain, and I sit forward, trying to picture who would dare rip away the man's daughter right from under his nose.

"Do they know for sure that she was taken?"

"Not yet," Fabio says, still eyeing me sternly. "But there are rumors, Don. Rumors that claim you were seen at your hotel with a woman who suspiciously matches the girl's description."

I scoff. "I never even met the woman! You were there when I was unceremoniously thrown out on my ass."

"Yes." He nods, his eyes wide. "I was there, Don, when Mischa Stepanov insulted you. I was there when you left. But I wasn't there when you supposedly dragged an unwilling blond from your hotel room in the middle of the night. I wasn't there for that."

My brow furrows. "That's a rather interesting retelling of it. Especially considering a sniper tried to kill me in said hotel room and I was 'dragging' said woman to safety."

"My God." His face falls. "Are you serious?"

"Dead serious. I want intel run on Antonio Salvatore," I say, curling a fist. "If the bastard came after me directly, he won't get to make the same mistake twice. He's always been a jealous son of a bitch. I bet he's pissed that I won the port deal over him. I've heard he's been trying to buy a share for years—"

"Noted," Fabio says over me. "But first things first, tell me more about that woman. Like why you were with her in the first place. A whore? A fling? What did she look like?"

"She looked…" Blond and slender with haunting cat-like eyes. "She looked like a woman who waved a knife in my face; that's what she looked like."

Fabio strokes his chin. "You and your entanglements."

As though I'm accosted by murderous women daily.

"This… This was personal," I say. "I took the woman so we could have a nice long discussion about why it is unpolite to dredge up someone's past."

"So, you spoke to her?" Fabio sighs and staggers to a nearby chair, collapsing onto it. "Thank God. If you had a conversation with her, then that settles it. It wasn't her."

I raise an eyebrow, confused by the leap in logic. "How so?"

He shoots me a strange look. "It's not common knowledge, but Mischa's daughter is mute. Can't say a damn word. Some kind of trauma from when she was young and… Don?"

"Describe her," I croak, sensing the blood drain from my face. "His daughter. What does she look like?"

"Blond. Pretty. Smaller than you'd expect for a girl of nineteen. God, don't look at me like that. Tell me it wasn't her."

"She tried to kill me," I croak, lurching to my feet. "She tried… With a knife!"

And if, by some horrible twist of fate, the little *tigre* had been Willow Stepanova, why would she want me dead?

"Don't look at me like that," I snap. "I never even met the girl!"

"You need to fix this," Fabio demands. "Where is she now?" He scans the room as if expecting a woman to come jumping out of the closet.

"I left her," I say.

"Where?"

"Havien—a property I own in the countryside." There's no need to bring up Safiya or my old home and the suspicions that might arise in him. I taught the girl a lesson, nothing more.

He nods, raking his fingers through his hair. "Okay. You were attacked. You took her to safety and left her in a countryside villa safe and sound. Right? Tell me you didn't touch her."

The look on my face makes him hunch over, cupping his hand against his mouth. "I'm going to be fucking sick—"

"It has to be a misunderstanding," I insist. "Why would Mischa's daughter want to kill me?"

"Forget his daughter! What about the man himself? If I heard the rumors about you, then I'm sure he already has as well. It doesn't look good for you, Donatello, even if what you say is true."

His tone sends an ominous sense of dread through my stomach. Turning to the doorway, I call out, "Javier?"

The bodyguard appears there within seconds. "Yes, sir?"

"Where is Vin?"

The man frowns at my tone. "He went into the city—"

"Bring him back and get him on a plane," I say, pushing past him. "Now. And get me into contact with Mischa's people. Offer whatever assistance he needs to find the girl."

"While you get your ass to that villa and make sure your little knife girl isn't the daughter of the most powerful man in the city," Fabio snarls. "And if she is, you get on your knees and do whatever it takes to fix this. Whatever it takes."

"It wasn't her," I snap. But I was more convinced in the case of her being Safiya. As for Willow? *She's mute*, Fabio said. *Can't say a damn word...*

But Willow's birthday was supposedly just the other day— Safiya's was several months ago. I try to cling to that small shred of reinforcement, but it surprisingly doesn't soothe the unease brewing in my gut any.

"Let's pray she's hiding out with some lover, and her father will find her decently scandalized like any rich, well-bred girl," Fabio warns, coming up to my shoulder. "Because if she isn't..."

The answer doesn't need to be voiced out loud.

If the girl was Willow Stepanova, I might have signed my own death warrant.

And Vin's.

13

WILLOW

*H*e left me once to a much worse fate…

And I survived. I endured. I went on to thrive in a new world he could only dream of me living. His betrayal hurt me, but I stayed standing.

Watching him leave this time shatters the pathetic barrier I spent seven years building. Those lies I told myself. The scenario I fed myself, the fantasy promising that I'd find him again as I am now, and put a knife through his chest. As he lay gasping, I'd stare into those glinting eyes until they went dark for good. He would see my face in his dying moments and realize with a cold sense of finality who I am. What he did.

I'd finally be able to let him go.

The man in that fantasy was cruel and heartless but resigned to his fate. He'd always see me coming.

In reality, this Donatello is a stranger—an unpredictable one at that. Tormented, haunted, anguished. He keeps the name of a dead girl slashed into his chest as a constant reminder. He mourns her jealously. He's martyred her.

But when faced with her specter, he crumbles into denial. More than that. He was so damn convinced I wasn't her. Because his perfect, precious Safiya was a saint. Someone he loved enough to threaten murder at anyone who dares challenge her memory.

He loved her.

And he let her die.

Why?

Why?

It's the confusion that barrels into me in a brutal, relentless assault. It leaves me gasping, clawing at the dusty wooden floor in search of stability. An answer. Clarity.

Why?

The walls of this place laugh at me and all those childish whims I've clung to. Reality is as cruel as a searching hand, prodding into one's deepest depths. There is no hiding from it. No escape.

Donatello didn't even recognize me—not because he had forgotten his Safiya. I just don't match the horror he conjured for her. His innocent little Safy's suffering isn't comparable to my own. Even after he threw me away, my pain isn't good enough to impress him.

He can't even recognize the scars of the wounds he inflicted.

Because in his mind? They aren't gruesome enough.

I'd laugh if I had the voice to. Scream. Find a new knife and stab him again, and again and again until he saw me. Really saw me.

I am his monster.

Mischa's grace changes nothing. Donatello ruined me far beyond any physical violation. He teased me with what love could be and ripped it away.

But Mischa and Ellen have shown me what love is. It is brutal, violent affection. The tears fall as I recall all the ways they've protected me without question.

How do I repay them?

I can't even be their perfect, accomplished Willow Stepanova.

I will always be Safiya Mangenello. Unwanted, rejected, repulsive little Safiya, undeserving of Don's love even then. And now, I can't even live up to his memory of her.

I don't know how long I lie here. Minutes? Hours?

As if from miles away, I hear the sound of approaching footsteps, but I can't move. I can't even lift my head to see just who is rushing toward me.

Because I know in my heart that whoever they are isn't him. He left me again, truly left me. The little girl in Nicolai's manor at least got an explanation. *I don't care…*

This time, I get nothing but comparisons to a dead girl who no longer exists.

Even now, I'm not good enough for him.

I never was.

"I think it's her," a voice calls, distinctly male but unfamiliar. His steps race toward me, and warm fingers brush the hair from my face. "God, it is her. Send word to Mischa. Fuck…"

The horror in his voice triggers a wave of confusion until I realize I'm curled on the floor beside the desk, my face coated in dust. I don't have my knife anymore, just a crumpled business card clenched in my fist though I don't even remember grabbing it. My dress hangs off of me, my panties discarded nearby, my knees clamped together, my face damp with tears, eyes squeezed shut.

And the blood. *His* blood—I can feel every smeared drop, drying on my skin.

"She doesn't seem injured," the man nearby says, his voice wavering with relief. "From what I can tell, at least."

I can't move to reassure him, or the other worried voices that erupt nearby.

I can't move at all.

"Here," another man demands, "put this on her. Cover her up now, you idiot!"

Soft fabric drapes me. A coat?

"Are you okay, Ms. Stepanova?" the first man asks. "Can you hear me?"

"She's in shock," someone else declares. "We need to get her home."

I'm a little doll again, callously thrown away, but I lack the rage that infected Safiya in the aftermath of Donatello's betrayal. I don't fight the man who bundles me into his arms and rushes me into a waiting van. I don't bite at the fingers that gently wipe the grime from my face. I can't even process the voice urging assurances into my ear.

"You'll be okay, Ms. Willow. You're safe."

Without Donatello, I have never felt safe. If anything, I've rebelled against any feeling of stability or peace. I always held out hope for him, even out of hatred. He would see me. Acknowledge me. Let Safiya finally die avenged.

But Donatello never loved that girl I used to be. He couldn't even see her shadow standing before him years later.

Only one man has ever upheld his promise to keep me. Protect me.

I don't feel anything until I finally open my eyes and see him, standing on the steps of our family home. The van barely comes to a stop before I lunge for the door and scramble out of it. I run to him, but he's already halfway to me, wrapping me in his arms so fiercely he takes me off my feet.

I break. The tears I've kept in until now spill down my cheeks. My shoulders shake, wracked with sobs I can't voice.

But Mischa holds me tight, crushed against his chest.

"I've got you," he says, his mouth buried in my hair. "I've got you. You're home now. You're home. I've got you..."

14

DON

The girl isn't at Havienna when I arrive, Fabio in tow—but someone was. Someone strong enough to break through the front door. In the dust, several sets of footsteps allude to the presence of more than one person. All men, judging from the size. They primarily lead into the study with individual groups advancing further into the house. But fairly quickly, they must have left.

Taking the girl with them.

"She might have called her employer," I suggest out loud.

Fabio doesn't seem convinced. "There are at least five sets of tracks here," he deduces. "That's more than enough for a private team. Like one of the many Mischa has in his employ. I need to confer with my contacts, but if he's miraculously found his daughter within the past few hours, then we know."

Know what? That the little *tigre* who tried to kill me was really the daughter of a Russian mobster. *The* Russian mobster. A literal princess in her own right with no reason to want me dead.

At least none I dare entertain. Swallowing hard, I direct a question toward Fabio, "You said she's a mute?"

He nods absently, manipulating his cell phone. "Much isn't known about why. The man isn't exactly known for his openness when it comes to his family. She is a musician, so I guess she can hear."

Like Safiya, stricken as an infant with an infection that left her hearing intact but prevented her from ever speaking. In all other aspects, she was no different than any other girl. She could read. Write. Draw. Play.

It was easy to forget her silence, when she was more than boisterous enough to make up for her lack of speech. The barrier was never a hindrance between us—I only had to look at her face and know exactly what was on her mischievous little mind.

And her final expression is all I see whenever I close my eyes. The features have faded with time, but that tormented stare remains. The pain. The anguish. The betrayal.

"I can't get a signal out in this fucking godforsaken…" Hissing, Fabio heads for the foyer. "I'm going to go see if I can get better service out by the car. Though honestly, we should be heading back. Even if you didn't take the Stepanova girl, someone did. And someone tried to kill you as well." Wincing, he stoops to stroke his thigh and sighs. "My knee is acting up the way it does before shit hits the fan."

He storms from the house, and I should follow him. I don't know what keeps me here, standing motionless in the center of this study.

I left this place the day I sold Safiya. I couldn't bear to step one foot through the door and wander these halls without hearing her echoing footsteps. I couldn't imagine sitting at this desk without having her sneak in to curl onto the floor beside me. Living here without her was out of the question.

After all this time, it's still the damn same, stocked with what furniture I didn't bother to salvage or sell. Books still line the shelves, old business tomes mainly, but even now, a few titles catch my eye. Her old favorites.

I'm drawn to one in particular, and my hand shakes as I wrench it from a thick layer of dust and observe the cover in the fading daylight.

Pollyanna. It was her favorite. I think she strove to fashion herself in the same way, hopeful and optimistic in the face of strife. My happy girl.

The pain of her memory feels sharper now more than ever. A constant throbbing in my gut, made worse by the marks I spy scraped into the dust on the floor. The rough outline of a small body is visible over by the chair. Someone bigger than Safiya but still diminutive and slight.

A woman too feisty, too fierce to be even a *mafiya Pahkan's* daughter.

"Donatello."

I turn to find Fabio standing in the doorway once more. One look at his face and my heart stops.

"Willow Stepanova was returned to her family earlier today," he says hoarsely.

"Thank god," I say, laughing with genuine relief.

But Fab isn't smiling.

"What's wrong?"

"She was found half-naked, covered in blood," he croaks, his expression a cross between disbelief and horror. "Her clothes ripped from her body. Her underwear in pieces. I shouldn't have to tell you where, should I?"

"Son of a bitch…" The room spins, and I collapse into the leather chair, rubbing at my temples. "She couldn't be—"

"Correction, she is," Fabio hisses, crossing toward me, his face red. "You kidnapped Mischa Stepanov's daughter. You dragged her away from the city and raped her in your derelict family home—"

"I did not!" I bellow. "I barely touched her."

He shrugs with a callousness I've rarely seen in him. "That's what it looks like. And who do you think Mischa is likely to believe? You? The bastard he can't even be bothered to grant an audience with despite you pining for it for years? Or his daughter's torn clothing. His men found her, you think he won't believe them? You've been waiting for death for a long time, Donatello. I think you're about to get your wish."

"Let him come for me," I growl, still rubbing at my throbbing temples. Reality tempers my bravado a bit, and desperate hope is all I have to cling to. This is a dream. A nightmare. Any minute I'll wake up to Vin taunting me about having hidden my whiskey. Still, I play along, scoffing at Fabio's insinuation. "I can handle Mischa."

It's a lie, but only in the context of loss vs. gain. Mischa has far more at stake than I do—but what I do have worth protecting is too great to risk.

"Vincenzo!" I lurch into motion at the thought of him, rising to my feet. "I need him safe—"

"I've already suggested your men move him to another location," Fabio says, and I sway with relief. I'd hug him if the man didn't look liable to slap me. "But this is deep shit, Don. I can't help you. Fuck, I shouldn't even be seen with you."

"So enduring your friendship and loyalty is, Fabio."

"Don't give me that shit," he snarls, digging through his breast pocket for an item that makes my eyes widen in shock. "Don't look at me like that, either."

He proceeds to prop a cigarette between his two fingers. He withdraws a gold lighter as well and ignites the end, inhaling deeply. It's been over a decade since I've seen him reduced to this.

"It will take more than your alcoholism to explain this shit away," he adds, starting to pace. "You're lucky I'm still standing here. And if you want to fix this, I can help you. But I want honesty. You mentioned that she tried to kill you, if I believe your little story. So what did you do after, huh? Enact your revenge?"

"No!" Gritting my teeth, I storm away from him and brace my hands against the desk. Contrary to his snide remark, I remember every fucking second of last night. All of it. "I'm telling you, I didn't fuck her. I barely touched her."

"So, what did happen, then?"

"I…" After sleep and in a somewhat clearer mental state, I know how crazy the truth sounds. Insanity. A madman's paranoia.

"Now isn't the time to play coy, Donatello. For the love of God!"

"Alright! I thought… I thought she was pretending to be Safiya."

"Shit," Fabio says as understanding dawns over his expression. "She's mute. And the girl was… I didn't even stop to think of that."

I nod, scowling. "I thought Salvatore or some other twisted cunt hired her to get to me. If she couldn't kill me, then her aim was to torment me. Make me relive that guilt—"

"When in reality, she was the poor daughter of a fucking psychopath. For all we know, she could be simpleminded." In horror, Fabio hunches over again. His face pales, and he truly looks on the verge of vomiting. To console himself, he takes another hit of nicotine and exhales harshly.

As dramatic a display as it is, I can't blame him. I've worked so damn hard to cultivate peace for Vin's sake. In one cruel twist of fate, have I fucked up everything?

Or was that her aim all along? The sneaky blond with the fiery eyes. What the hell did I do to her?

"I think your best chance is to request a meeting," Fabio says, rising to his full height. "Now. As soon as possible. Request a meeting with Mischa. Explain your past. Prove you didn't harm the girl."

"And what?" I demand. "He'll take me at my word and send me on my way with a kiss? I couldn't even get an audience with a bastard to form a truce over the fucking harbor."

"But that was a formality," Fabio warns, his tone cold. "This? This is life or death, Donatello. This is no game. For Vin's sake, I suggest you prostrate yourself before the man and plead for mercy. Trust me, you do not want a war with Stepanov. The man is ruthless, and he has enough money to not only kill you—but ruin your name and anyone associated with it forever. The only doctor Vincenzo will ever be is the kind who uses his fancy degree to keep him warm at night while begging on the street for spare change."

I flinch at the imagery and slam my fist against the desk so hard my knuckles crack.

"You know I'm right," Fabio says.

And he is. Mischa is a force to be reckoned with.

But so was I. Once.

I know the heartlessness required to build a name attached to a fearsome reputation. I know what it takes for a man to cut off his humanity. I know the lengths such a man must go through to purge his soul.

Even now, Mischa does not frighten me.

But if the man takes it in his head that I did harm his family and decides to retaliate, Vincenzo won't be spared regardless of my guilt. It's the thought of him that makes me sigh, resigned.

"Do it," I say, spinning to face Fabio. I lift my hands in defeat like a child accepting his punishment. "Call a meeting. Whatever the terms, I'll uphold them. I only ask that the man hold his fire until we can speak face to face. Secure Vincenzo's safety in the meantime. As for Mischa? I'll meet him anywhere as long as he keeps this between the two of us."

"Good," Fabio says, already racing from the house. "Very good."

So is the price of a future. For Vincenzo, I'd pay anything. Give anything.

I've already failed Safiya.

I won't fail my son.

15

WILLOW

Death has been a permanent fixture in my life, the one constant that even Mischa's carefully constructed haven can't fully eradicate. When Ivan—Mischa's long-term mentor and the grandfather of his children—died suddenly of a heart attack, a pall had fallen over the house unlike any other sadness to come before it. Time seemed to stop, and this cheerful, private world was forced to accommodate the harsh, grim reality if only for a moment.

The child's laughter had quieted. The bright, cheery colors had been slowly replaced with black accents of mourning, and a picture of Ivan dominated a space in the drawing room where it still resides.

For all his protectiveness, there is only so much Mischa can shelter his family from.

And to anyone who might not know better, the house reeks of mourning. Hushed voices sound muffled from behind my bedroom door. Gone are the typical shrieks and laughter of the children playing. Any movement throughout the manor now is done softly enough so as not to disturb even the mice hiding in the rafters.

Or the one in this bed. Lying here, I eye the ceiling, recalling the past seven years I've spent in this home as Willow and the playful Mouse. I used to pine for Havienna and its sturdy walls, but this place is my true home, even if I've only ever felt like a stranger. An outcast struggling to fit in where I don't belong.

My spacious room holds so many more memories than the tiny, modest one I left behind. I picked out the wooden bed frame myself under Ellen's direction. Eli and I used to take turns squeezing under this sturdy piece of furniture to hide during our games of hide and seek. Mischa himself helped me paint the walls a soft shade of beige to make the space my own.

There wasn't a day I spent away at school when I didn't wish I could be back in this very spot.

But now a shadow looms above me, casting a pall that even the bright colors of my room can't overcome. It stretches across the ceiling, growing darker with every minute to pass by. Soon, I see a face lurking within the darkness, his eyes cold and watchful, eyeing me dismissively.

You are not Safiya…

"Willow?" A quiet knock on the door ushers in a slight figure who crosses my room with soft, cautious footsteps. I sense her approach my nightstand, and a dull thud alludes to her placing something there. The smell of food tickles my nose, though I don't bother to lift my head and see the meal for myself. "Darling?"

The mattress barely dips beneath Ellen's weight as she presumably sits beside me. Soft, her fingers run through my hair, parting the strands. At the back of my mind, I know the silence is cruel. I can't imagine what she and Mischa might be thinking after the state I returned to them in.

I know it's wrong to give them not even an ounce of reassurance.

And yet…

I can't move.

"You need to eat," she says gently. "I've brought your favorites. I even managed to get a hold of that jam you like. The one with the strawberries. Willow?"

She sits with me in silence for a while, continuously petting my hair before finally, with a sigh, she stands.

"I'll just leave it here," she says.

She's barely left before a heavier set of footsteps advance toward my room, resonating determination. This visitor doesn't knock, boldly opening my door and approaching my bed without waiting for an invitation. I can recognize him by the sound of his heavy breathing alone.

The mattress sinks beneath his weight, and I expect a loud, bellowing command to follow.

Anything but a sigh, deeper than Ellen's.

A small commotion of tinkling silverware draws my notice. I don't turn to see what he does, but a minute later, something appears before me, dangled inches from my nose. It's square, beige, and slathered in a red, jelly-like substance.

"Take a bite," Mischa urges tiredly. "Just one. You can give me that much."

His tone tugs at some inner part of me I can't resist.

"That's it," he praises as I raise my hand, accepting a piece of toast slathered with jam. I sample a pathetically small bite, barely registering the taste.

"Another while you're at it," he says, refusing to take the bread when I offer it back. "If I could bribe you to eat the whole damn thing, I would."

Despite everything, a smile tugs on my mouth. I try to resist it, but Mischa's thumb appears from above to softly brush my nose.

"A few dollars could get you to do anything," he taunts. "God, help me the day I can no longer goad the girls with treats."

And I remember. Money was the language to bond us. When I was younger, he used to slip me coins in exchange for chores or favors. If only a bribe were enough to change things now—but no amount of currency can erase the crushing pain lingering in my chest. Donatello's return was just the final straw to compound a deeper question that's haunted me for longer than I care to admit.

Mischa knows me only as Willow, his little Mouse.

But who is that woman, really?

"Look at me," Mischa demands, his voice a shadow of its usual baritone.

I pull myself upright, registering the details I hadn't before. It's late in the day, my second being back. Or is it the third?

"That's it," Mischa murmurs as I finally turn to face him.

He props his thumb beneath my chin, lifting it.

I've never seen him look so…old. Wrinkles enhance the haggardness of his appearance. Bloodshot eyes reveal that he hasn't slept, and dark blond stubble coats his chin, marking days without shaving.

But as he watches me swallow, some of the tension in his expression loosens. He sighs again.

"I think I will bribe you," he says, drawing his hand away. "Whatever you want, it's yours. Just eat for me."

He lifts the tray Ellen left for me and settles it over my lap. I scan the items, desiring nothing. More bread, vegetable soup, and a ham sandwich carefully constructed with extra tomatoes and no crusts.

He watches me sample each item, and when I finish, he ruffles my hair. The shape of his mouth could be called a smile if it weren't so tormented.

"I have tried never to coddled you," he says, his voice gruff. "You deserve this honesty, even if it hurts."

But he struggles to voice it, and full minutes pass before he finally cups my cheek, urging me to face him again.

Fathomlessly dark, his eyes scour mine, seeing into my skull without requiring the aid of any sign language. "Did he hurt you?" he demands. I sense the tension in his fingers that he struggled to keep from his voice. They shake. His throat twitches around a hard swallow.

For me, I sense. He's tempering his anger, his rage, all for me.

I reach out, brushing my finger along the blond stubble on his jaw. It clenches against me, and he sighs in relief.

"He asked to meet with me," he says. No name, but none is required. Only one man might make him glare so icily.

Donatello.

"If you don't allow it, I won't." His expression makes me shiver despite his obvious restraint. A man like Mischa can only suppress his fury for so long before it seeps into his gaze, promising vengeance. "You say the word, and I will rain hell down on him. You say the word, and I will kill him. Do you understand me?"

I do. Much as I used to fantasize as a scorned little girl, Donatello Vanici's life is in the palm of my hand.

All it would take is one frown. One nod. One nuanced reaction he could interpret as permission.

In pursuit of such a thing, he tilts my face against his palm, inspecting my expression. Whatever he sees in my face makes him nod and swipe his hand across his mouth as if he has to physically remove the fearsome scowl forming. Gradually, his lips flatten into a hard line, and he nods.

"Alright." He smooths the hair from my face and reaches for a glass cup filled with water resting on the meal tray. "For you, I will show this restraint. Only for you. Now drink."

He brings the cup to my mouth without giving me the chance to refuse. Dutifully, I down every last drop of liquid, and he ruffles my hair, cracking another faint smile. But then it fades, replaced by a more serious expression.

"Your mother wants me to convince you to let the doctor examine you."

When I shake my head, he grabs my hand, bringing it to his chest.

"Please," he says in a tone I've never heard from him. "Do this for me, please. If he hurt you... Let me protect you, Willow. Give me this one thing."

Let a doctor examine me. He'll find nothing, but maybe that's the point. I've been so wrapped in myself; I haven't stopped to think about what my parents must be feeling. Their pain.

Their fear.

Extending it any longer would be cruel.

So I nod.

"Good girl." I'm in his arms before I know it, crushed against his chest as he shoves the tray aside. I don't resist the embrace. He feels so different from Donatello even as he had back then.

Don was warm and light, his laughter infectious.

Mischa is solid, rigid, but unyielding. A brick wall that won't crumble easily. A permanent fixture I'm not afraid to trust, relaxing into his grip.

"I know he hurt you," he says, smoothing his hand over my hair. "I do not know how, but I will make him pay. You say the word, and I will."

He tilts my face to meet him, inspecting my expression.

Slowly, he nods again. "Fine. You let the doctor examine you, and I will hear what the motherfucker has to say for himself. Deal?"

I nod, but I find myself leaning into him again, pressing my cheek against his shoulder.

And he doesn't let me go.

16

DON

*M*eeting Mischa Stepanov, unarmed and on his terms, is one thing.

Looking the part of a fucking sycophantic patsy while doing so is another. I couldn't stand to face myself in the mirror before leaving the house, but I'm sure I look every bit as ridiculous as I feel. This emerald, piece of shit jacket was Fabio's idea, and already I'm tugging at the collar, feeling my body strain against the confines of the cotton. To be fair, I figure no designer in the world constructed a suit specifically with this type of meeting in mind. Groveling before a *mafiya* leader in the hopes of convincing him that I didn't violate his daughter. *Fuck,* what a mess.

A glass of whiskey couldn't soothe my nerves.

Deep down, I'm partly convinced it's all a trap. I'll walk into this neutral territory and find a bullet lodged in my skull before I can even utter a greeting. Hell, I'd deserve it for being stupid enough to fall for it.

That fate would be a fitting end, all things considered. Once again, little Safiya is smirking at me from the grave. Once again, because of her, I've stumbled, jeopardizing everything I've strived to create for myself. I will never outlast her memory.

I feel her presence now more than ever, haunting me down the narrow hall of Fabio's downtown offices in the heart of the city. Its location makes it difficult to ambush. With Fabio's connections to the governor, no man would dare mount an attack on him directly.

It's as figuratively safe as a mother's bosom, but I'm not naïve enough to trust in it completely. Mischa isn't known for his strict adherence to the typical rules of engagement, be them explicit or otherwise. The man made his mark by clawing at every bit of his sizeable empire that wasn't handed to him out of fear. He waged a bloody war against an oil magnate he believed wronged his family, and as the rumors go, his own wife was once his captive, brutalized and scarred for his amusement.

As cold a thought as it is, I have to wonder if the man truly even cares about his daughter's supposed predicament out of love? Or just anger at what it looks like on the surface? Another man dared to defile what is his, leveling a slight no true leader could ever let go unchallenged.

Though, even I can admit another man wouldn't show this level of restraint. Antonio Salvatore would have already tried to tear me to pieces were one of his daughters found in the same state.

And what a state it was. The blond, fiery-eyed *tigre* who just so happens to be mute. What grudge could she have against me?

My brain dances around the answer. It could be the whiskey in my system, or sheer twisted logic, but the more I mull over her, the more solutions come to mind. Like the fact that Mischa

Stepanov is the type of man to run in the same circles as Nicolai Baryshnikov, a well-known money lender to the Russian mob. Could Mischa have a fetish for children and procured a girl for himself? My Safiya, raised as his own?

No. I shake my head, laughing at the possibility. My black heart might get some peace from the ending, but it's too much like a fairy tale to ever be real.

Isn't it?

Lost in thought, I tug on my tie, and I barely register a man's voice, addressing me from up ahead.

"You're properly dressed at least," Fabio remarks from the doorway of his private office. As agreed, a Stepanov agent lurks at the other end of the corridor, while my men, including Javier, have to wait outside of the building.

"You play this right, and you can smooth this over," Fabio warns, opening the door. "You can wait in here."

His office is empty apart from two leather chairs placed directly across from each other, out of range from any of the large windows showcasing a view of the city.

"At least my kennel is well furnished," I grouse halfheartedly. As agreed, I'm expected to wait on the man like a naughty child called to a headmaster's office. Patiently, I must anticipate my punishment.

"Don't fuck this up, Donatello," Fabio warns. "But I know you won't. If there is one thing you care about, it's family."

He's right.

And he's wrong. Safiya Mangenello is proof alone as to the opposite. I'm a selfish fuck, and I always have been. But Vin isn't like me.

"How long until he shows up?" I ask Fabio as I enter the office and take a seat facing him.

He shrugs, smoothing his hands down the front of his own suit. In a crisp navy blue, he cuts a stern figure befitting any neutral party. "Whenever he fucking feels like it. You're lucky he even agreed to this."

"And his daughter? How is she?"

"You probably have a better idea of that than I do," he says ominously. "Seeing as how you claim you didn't touch her."

"I said I didn't rape her," I clarify. "And I didn't drag her kicking and screaming into my room either. She came at me. Besides, I'm still not even convinced the girl I was with is Willow Stepanova. Attacking an unarmed man with a knife doesn't sound like the actions of some innocent, sweet little pianist, daughter of a *mafiya* lord or not."

But it's starting to sound more and more like the actions of a spurned daughter, alright—just not Mischa's. Gritting my teeth, I glower from the window and try to refocus on what matters. Making it through this meeting with my hide intact, for one. Doing whatever it takes to keep Vin out of any potential feud.

In short—be on my best goddamn behavior.

"Well, let's be sure before the man comes, why don't we?" Fabio reaches into his pocket and withdraws a folded slip of paper. A photograph.

And the woman staring up from the glossy surface renders me silent.

"So, it *was* her, you son of a bitch," Fabio snarls, shoving the picture into my hand. "God damn it, Don! I got that picture from her fucking school files. Look innocent and sweet enough for you?"

And by God, she does. Pale as snow, hair like spun gold, eyes that soul-sucking shade of brown. She cleans up nice, the little *tigre*, her hair in a neat bun and a starched white blouse in lieu of a low-cut dress—but even as she smiles, I'd recognize that stern tilt to her mouth anywhere.

"I don't understand," I blurt out loud, swiping my finger across that beautiful face.

Fabio laughs. "You fucked up, Don," he says, fishing yet another cigarette from his pocket. He lights it up and inhales deeply, flicking the ash into the base of a nearby potted plant. "To be honest, you were probably drunk. I wouldn't blame you if you were, but now you need to make this right. Wait for Mischa; I don't care if it takes him a fucking week to show. You wait for him, and you make this right. Understood?"

I hiss out a sigh of agreement. "Yes, Mama. I'll be a good boy."

Fabio jabs the lit butt of his cigarette toward me and nods. "I'm going to hold you to that, Don. As for addressing Mischa, do you remember what terms to use?"

Now I really feel like a scolded schoolboy. "That outfit of his likes to refer to their leaders as *Pakhan*."

"Good," Fabio says. "I suggest you practice your pronunciation as we wait."

Trailing a cloud of smoke in his wake, he leaves the room, slamming the door behind him.

I slump into the chair, still eyeing the picture in my grasp. With the pad of my thumb, I trace the pouty line of the woman's mouth, imagining it curled into a snarl, those eyes filled with hate.

"What the hell did I do to you, little *tigre*?" I murmur.

But the potential answer is too insane to consider seriously. I swat it away for as long as I can before it unfurls in my mind regardless.

Safiya Mangenello, all grown up, somehow rescued from her fate by a man with a reputation fearsome enough to strike terror into the devil himself. It sounds too surreal. Too much of a fantasy. Not to mention that even if Safiya did survive, her birthday would have been months ago, not days.

And if Mischa *did* get a hold of the girl, then it was probably with an aim in mind more sinister than adoption. Nicolai Brayshnikov certainly isn't known for fostering a nurturing environment for children or women.

Regardless, Mischa bought her, and despite how impossible it seems to believe…

His Willow could be my Safiya.

After seven years, the tables have finally turned. With Mischa on her side, my girl has the power to destroy me.

And Hell…I can't blame her if she did.

17

DON

*N*early three hours pass before I sense the mood in the entire building shift. The place falls silent as if someone flipped a switch. Any chatter drifting from the hallway dies instantly. Hell, no one so much as coughs.

Footsteps approach next, and Fabio opens the door, followed by another man who needs no introduction.

Mischa Stepanov has been a boogeyman for so damn long that meeting him in person, I'm struck by the fact that he is just another man. A tall one, his blond hair hanging loose around his shoulders, his dark eyes cold.

He wears a pair of faded green combat fatigues, eschewing the suit and tie dress code Fabio insisted on. With a sweep of his gaze, he sizes me up without extending his hand in a customary greeting.

"*Pakhan*," I say, rising to my feet. Hands in my pockets, I don't know what to do other than incline my head in respect. "Thank you for meeting me like this—"

"The only reason my boot isn't on your throat is because my daughter asked me not to kill you," he says, his accent so thick the pronunciation gives his words an ominous twist.

I grit my teeth just to trap a stupid question in my throat where it belongs. *Did she ask verbally?* That alone would disprove the theory of her being Safiya.

And assuage my guilt.

I still can't reconcile the obvious. The way she reacted to the girl's name. The mere fact that she seemed very intent on driving a knife through my chest. No other reason fits unless I drunkenly laid with the man's daughter at some party within the past year —and given that she's been supposedly sequestered at a prestigious conservatory, I doubt that.

Not to mention I know for a fact she's a virgin.

"I figured you would be begging by now," Mischa remarks with a scoff. He takes a step, and Fabio lurches as if he means to throw himself between us.

"Shall we sit?" he asks, ever the stickler for protocol. "Please, allow me to—"

"On your knees," Mischa says over him, his gaze boring into mine. "Rushing to explain why my daughter was found on your fucking property. Naked. Alone. Covered in blood."

Fabio cringes at the mental image. So do I.

"It was my blood," I clarify, swiping my finger across my cheek. Days later, the scratch left by *tigre* has scabbed over into a thin, scarlet slash. "She attacked me." Though I don't have a right to be fucking defensive. Given how Fabio glances at me sharply, I suspect he's thinking along the same lines. "What happened was a misunderstanding," I add more softly. "I didn't touch her."

Mischa's eyes narrow, but devoid from them is the rage I figure most fathers would show if they truly believed another man violated their daughter.

"You know that," I suspect out loud. "I didn't force myself on her."

"We both know that there are other ways to force yourself on a woman other than with your cock," he growls, his upper lip curling from his teeth. "If that is your excuse, I'm unimpressed. And I heard that you were supposed to be the wordsmith."

It's a low blow—a dig to my past that dredges up old memories. Like the creative ways I used to describe the many methods I might use to kill a man.

Before enacting them out one by one.

To his face.

With Fabio in the corner of my eye, it's easier than expected to choke down the insult and keep calm. "There isn't a poetic way to describe one's innocence," I say. "Maybe you should question why your daughter came into my room alone?"

It's the wrong thing to say.

He starts forward, his hands in fists, a muscle in his jaw prominent. "Are you implying what I think you are?"

"I'm only stating the truth," I say. But for some reason, the rest won't leave my throat—*that she came at me with a knife. That she might be Safiya. That I sold her as a child and left her for dead.*

"You know what I think would clear up this misunderstanding?" Mischa suggests. "You prove your sincerity."

I swallow hard at his tone. Whatever the man may be thinking is obscured by his stoic expression. To find out his aims, I have to use my balls and ask. "How so?"

He smiles cruelly, and I doubt a simple verbal plea is what he has in mind. "You forfeit your holdings on the harbor to me—"

"That sounds like blackmail," I snap, unable to restrain my tone this time. Anger rips through me, and I have to breathe in through my nose just to keep my vision clear. Vin, I think, curling my fists so hard my nails dig into my palms. Think of Vin. Think of Vin…

"We should put this in writing," Fabio suggests, moving toward his desk. His tone is businesslike, but he grimaces as he fishes out a pen. Even in his rush to please both sides, he knows an unreasonable ask when he hears it.

"Why would you even want the harbor?" I demand, facing Mischa. "Considering you've spurned my every attempt to form an alliance when it comes to securing it."

"An alliance?" he questions, palming his chin. "Or a mercy to prop up what little holdings you have left? When it comes to doing business, I only enter agreements with men I trust. Not only will you forfeit your holdings. Afterward, you leave the city, and you stay away. If you ever come near my daughter again, I have every right to kill you. We both know why."

It's a blunt insinuation. One that makes me wonder just how much he knows of his supposed daughter's past. Going off the look in his eye? Everything.

And it all makes sense.

"You've been hostile to me for some time, Mischa," I say. "I've always wondered why. Most men who show me such avoidance aren't shy about their reasons."

"Most men have a code," he counters. "Lines they refuse to cross."

Like selling little girls to men like Nicolai Baryshnikov. He doesn't say it out loud.

He doesn't have to.

"From what I've heard, some men might consider your code looser than most," I snap. "For instance, I don't think most men meet their wives the way you met yours."

I certainly didn't. I would have gladly run a knife through my chest before ever laying a hand on Olivia. Mischa's wife was not so lucky, it seems.

An eyebrow raised, the man laughs. "And most men don't discard the children in their care the way I heard some chose to."

There is no mistaking it now. He knows. Just how much?

"Whatever happened between your daughter and me is in the past," I say. "I didn't hurt her."

"And yet here you are, aiming to make amends," he points out, gesturing to the space around us. "Or do you wish to compound your insult?"

By rubbing it in his face.

By spurning his gross extortion.

By spitting on the hand of the man who sees himself as the king of this shadow empire.

I want to. I do.

But I would be condemning Vin to a lifetime of fighting.

"Take the harbor," I say, dropping all pretense. I turn to the window, eyeing the glistening waters of the bay in the distance. I let the sight ground me, picturing Vin superimposed over the image. His life is worth more than property. More than anything.

"You leave my family alone," I add. "I'll keep my distance from yours. I don't want a war with you."

"If you ever come near my daughter again, I will kill you myself. You leave me the harbor, you leave the city by the week's end, and I'll be expecting a generous donation to my daughter's conservatory in Vienna to cement your contrition. Of your own volition, of course. You have a week to make the necessary arrangements, as well as to vacate any property you have within twenty miles—"

"And leave it to you?" I hiss, whirling to face him.

His eyes gleam. "Out of the kindness of your heart for any trouble you may have caused. I'm glad we cleared up this misunderstanding."

"I don't need a week," I snap to Fabio, who's hunched over his desk, pen in hand. "Give me until tomorrow. I'll be out of this fucking city. I hope your daughter enjoys the peace."

"She will," Mischa growls. "And you will never see her again."

He turns on his heel and storms from the room.

"That was…better than expected," Fabio says faintly, his eyes on the doorway.

"Fuck me. Just get it over with," I snarl. "Do it. I cede my hold on the harbor. Have my things removed from the hotel. And get Vincenzo on a goddamn plane."

I turn to the nearest section of the wall and form a fist, slamming it knuckles first mere inches from a painting of a scenic landscape only Fabio would find soothing. To me, it's a fucking taunt. I've spent so long clawing at pieces of land for myself only to see it ripped away in an instant.

"I'll overlook that," Fabio says. "But trust me, Don. You're doing the right thing."

"By rolling over like a whipped dog?" I hiss, inspecting my throbbing, reddened knuckles. The hand isn't broken, not that I care. I curl it again, landing another blow. Another.

"By choosing peace," he corrects calmly over the racket. "By choosing Vincenzo. Don't worry. I'll make all of the arrangements. You go cool off—preferably without another blond of questionable heritage."

I push past him, leaving the building in time to catch Mischa entering a car out front, flanked by his retinue.

As angry as I am, I know Fabio is right. I dodged a bullet.

And whether she truly is alive or not, Safiya got her pound of flesh.

May she finally rest in fucking peace.

18

DON

I leave Fabio's office and head to my own across town with the enthusiasm of a spanked child. So much for my grand, triumphant homecoming—it's already become an unceremonious exile.

I've barely owned the property for six months, and already it's out of my control. I might as well clean it out myself while Mama Fab tidies up my bad boy messes. *Fuck.* With every passing second, the reality sinks in—and damn, is it grim.

I've just given away almost everything I own to Mischa Stepanov without so much as a fight to show for it. The harbor. My holdings. My pride.

The last thing is the hardest loss to reconcile. That icy impulse deep within me stirs to life, aching to be indulged more than ever. The man I used to be would never tolerate that bullshit treatment from anyone.

Least of all, a man cocky enough to twist the knife when he has a rival cornered with his back against the wall. Not that I would have shown any more mercy.

All because of her. Even if the little bitch was Safiya... *Is Safiya...*

My thoughts trail off as I slump against the back seat of my car, my head in my hands. Rubbing at my temples, I drop the anger and taste the guilt lurking underneath. It's a bitter pill to swallow.

If Willow is Safiya, she could demand so much more from me. So much more.

I'm too much of a coward to try and imagine what she's been through. What she's seen. Though, isn't it obvious? The kind of pain and horror so intense that seven years later, she comes after me with a knife.

"Sir?" Javier calls from the driver's seat.

I lift my head and find that we're pulling into the parking lot by my office—but that isn't what has Javier so alarmed. Another car is already here, parked in the space beside mine. I don't recognize the model, but only two types of bastards would drive something so goddamn flashy—a blood-red sports car with gaudy gold trim.

The first being a blind, tasteless fucker with too much money to spend.

Or Antonio Salvatore.

"Call for backup," I snarl to Javier. At the same time, I stoop to reach under the seat and drag a black case from beneath it. With a grim shudder, I can only appreciate the fact that the little *tigre* didn't notice this cache while she sat in this very spot. I open the latch and withdraw a handgun. It's already loaded, and I tuck the weapon into my pocket, returning the case to its spot.

"Should we leave, sir?" Javier questions.

"Hell no," I call back. I'm already shoving my door open, climbing from the car. "Just keep the engine running and get another team over here."

"You think he's here for an ambush?" he questions, fiddling with the headset affixed to his ear.

I laugh. "I don't fucking care if he is. But if I kill him, I'll need the body disposed of quick, *so get another team over here.*"

I slam the door and start forward, finding my office already unlocked. It's a small building, staffed by a lone janitor I haven't gotten the chance to know too well. From what I recall of the man—older with a limp on his right side—he might be the type capable of being threatened into opening up the place. Sure enough, I enter the small lobby where a secretary would sit on a normal business day and find it empty.

Inside my office proper, a man lounges in the chair behind my desk, reclined to its fullest position. Dressed in a cream suit every bit as tacky as his car, he has his feet propped on top of the polished surface, leaving a trail of mud inches from my nameplate.

"I hear you've been naughty, Donny," he says, steepling his fingers. So many gold rings are stacked on each one that I'm surprised the sunlight glinting off the bling doesn't blind him. "Very naughty indeed." His eyes gleam, staring from a face that's seen the end of a fist too many damn times—mine especially. His crooked nose disrupts the polished, rich aura he desperately tries to exude. While his black hair may be coifed and his fancy jewelry 18 carats, at his core, he's still the same punk ass he's always been. Once I even called him a friend.

Antonio Salvatore.

"You have five seconds." I don't bother explaining any more than that. I reach into my pocket and grab my gun, withdrawing it.

Salvatore chuckles. "Relax, Donny. I'm here on business." He nods to the view beyond my window—a postcard-perfect snapshot of the waterfront. From here, a man could easily position himself to control the flow of goods that keep the world running smoothly—or this city at least. "Nice position here you've carved out for yourself," Antonio remarks with undisguised greed. "It would be a damn shame to give it all away. Especially to a cunt like Mischa Stepanov."

"I don't do 'business,' with men who try to have me killed," I snarl, hunting his expression for any hint of a reaction. The bastard was always good at his poker face, despite failing at everything else. He doesn't even flinch.

"Don't tell me you've had a hard time, Donatello," he simpers, raising a black eyebrow.

I grit my teeth. I could always kick him out, but he's here for a reason. Rat's like Salvatore do nothing without putting their own self-interest first. So why come to me and risk pissing off someone way higher on the totem pole?

"If I'm not mistaken, you were at the home of said cunt just a few days ago, sniffing around his daughter," I point out.

He smiles and shrugs. "A man's gotta eat. As much as it pains me to admit, Mischa runs this fucking city—and with the harbor, no one will be able to stand in his way. That just doesn't sound fair, does it?"

"Spare me the dramatics," I hiss, feeling my eyes narrow. At a glance, the fucker appears to be alone—but I doubt that. Given my recent brush with a certain sniper, I make sure to take a step back, putting myself beyond the window's range. "Tell me why I shouldn't shoot you. Don't doubt me when I say I've been dreaming about it."

God knows I have. If I were still the sort of man who kept a hit list in his back pocket, Antonio would be at the top of the list.

"Still so paranoid," he remarks. "You were always looking for enemies among friends. Though after what happened to your wife…any man would be rattled. Olivia was a beautiful woman."

I grit my teeth, recognizing the bait for what it is. With his lip quirked, the man watches me for an ounce of a reaction he can pounce on.

I meet his gaze instead and question—not for the first time—how I ever once called this bastard a brother.

"Olivia was beautiful, and she loved me," I say coldly. "No matter how many jealous bastards sniffed after her, she never strayed. Few men can say the same about their wives."

Salvatore's smirk flattens. "It's a shame what happened to her."

He doesn't even try to conceal the verbal knife this time. What happened? Someone gunned her and my newborn son down in our own fucking home. Various excuses had floated around then to explain the attack, but I know the real reason—someone wanted to hurt me. Killing Olivia was the best way to do that. The bastards thought I would crumble.

But I didn't, did I?

Facing Salvatore, I say, "Only a pussy would target a helpless woman and her child."

"Then it's a damn good thing you punished her murderers," he replies, returning his gaze to the window. "What a shame about Gino, though. You treated the man like family. Especially his little girl—it's a shame about what happened to her as well. What was her name again? Sofia? To die so young."

I flinch, and like any snake, Salvatore stirs at the reaction, flicking his tongue along his lower lip as if tasting the blood in the air.

"What the fuck do you want?" I demand.

With a sigh, he sets his feet on the floor and sits forward, leaning over my desk as if he owns it. "I want you to give your share of the harbor to me. I will deal with Mischa. The bastard cannot contest it as long as you make a legal trade. If he tries to draw blood over it, I have the *famiglia* at my back, and our allies are numerous. He wouldn't dare challenge it."

"No," I say. "But funnily enough, my safety doesn't seem to be included in that little plan."

I have to laugh, though, am I surprised by the half-baked scheme? No. Salvatore was always a covetous piece of shit, wanting what he couldn't have—namely everything I did. My position. My influence. My wife.

But to come here and ask me directly to piss off the *mafiya* on his say so? The man must have grown quite the pair of balls since our time under the elder Giovanni Rossi.

"Of course, you would be protected, old friend," he insists. "I'd love to welcome you back into the fold."

And have me groveling at his feet instead of at Mischa's.

"Get the fuck out," I snarl, dropping all pretense. I lift the gun and finger the trigger, wishing more than anything that I had the impulse to pull it. Maybe without my morning shot of whiskey…

As it stands, I need a reason to, not that I'd have to look too far. "Now. House rules say you're trespassing. I'd have every right to kill you."

"No need for threats." He stands, dusting off his slacks. "I will leave. But I wouldn't be surprised if Mischa finds himself unable to uphold his end of your little bargain—don't look so surprised, Donatello. The entire world knows of how you violated his daughter like the pig you are. But I suggest you think carefully —" He snickers as I take a step toward him, curling a fist. "Join me now, transfer the harbor rights to me, and you may see the glory you once achieved again. The offer won't last forever."

My trigger finger twitches with alarming resolve. Maybe that whiskey wasn't enough, after all? I can feel the icy coldness at the back of my skull, urging me to give in. Teach this sick fuck a lesson…

Shaking my head, I ignore it. "Leave."

He does.

And I slump into my chair, wondering just what the smug son of a bitch was hinting at.

Something well beyond my trouble with Mischa. Could Salvatore be planning to make his own play? If he were behind the attempt on my life, I wouldn't put it past the fucker to aim a little higher.

The only reason I haven't killed him—despite having no proof that he was behind the attack on Olivia—is because though nowhere near the height of their power, the *famiglia* is still a force to contend with this side of Hell's Gambit.

And if Salvatore is making a play for Mischa's throne, then even I can admit that a hell of a war is in store.

Should I do the good thing and warn Stepanov of what danger might be headed his way? After all, Salvatore is one to play dirty, preferring to break his target from within. Sounding the alarm would be the good, neighborly course of action.

Fuck that. I lean into my seat, prop my feet on my desk, and fish through a drawer for a cigar.

I may not trust my intuition much, but what is it telling me to do now?

Sit back and watch the fucking world burn.

As long as Vin is safe, I really don't give a damn who wins either way.

19

WILLOW

Mischa may have left me alone for the rest of yesterday, but his visit seems to serve as a signal to the others. It's barely dawn, but already a commotion outside of my door breaks the heavy silence I've been living in for at least three days—a tiny, girlish cry followed by a louder, boyish shushing.

"Be quiet," said boy declares, most likely Ivan, utilizing his bossiest tone. "You'll wake up Mama and Papa."

"She stepped on my foot!" a girl declares indignantly. "I'm telling Mama."

"Not uh, Jona," another girl counters. "You're such a baby."

"Uh-oh," Ivan mutters as louder, sterner footsteps approach. "Here comes Mama—"

"I told you, my darlings," Ellen says gently. "Willow needs rest. Leave her be. Why don't you play outside?"

"Is she sick?" one of the girls asks.

"Jona said Willow is dying!"

"She's not dying, my sweet," Ellen replies. "She just needs rest. Out to play. All of you."

As the children scamper off, whining their disapproval, a knock gently sounds on my door.

"Willow?" The door opens, and Ellen pokes her head from behind it. Her tense expression softens once she sees me sitting up, facing her this time. Warily, she takes a step forward. She's already dressed, her hair swept back into a neat braid draped over her shoulder. "How are you feeling?"

I shrug, and she advances with more confidence. The second she's close enough, she strokes her hand through my hair, tilting my face toward hers. A beautiful grin shapes her mouth, obscuring the concern visible in her gaze. I don't know what Mischa has told her; all I sense from her in this moment is genuine warmth. "Eli and I are going into town for some of those flowers you like. Do you want to come?"

I suck in a breath at the invitation. While their relationship may be far different from that of most mothers and sons, they do have their small traditions that have carried on even while I've been gone. Once a week, they go to the market, just the two of them. For her to invite me means more than a simple outing.

Heart in my throat, I scan her beautiful features, and guilt strikes me with unexpected force. All this time, I think I've been resisting it—her simple affection. But like Mischa's, I know it's genuine.

I shake my head but brush my fingers over hers reassuringly. Her smile widens.

"Get some rest, darling." After placing a kiss on my forehead, she withdraws, cradling her swollen belly with the flat of her hand. "Enjoy the quiet while you can. It won't be long now."

I smile in return and watch her go. It seems like my door barely has the chance to close before a smaller figure appears in the gap, watching me with huge, guarded eyes.

He says nothing, but I can sense why. My heart constricts as I remember the state I left him in—one he obviously hasn't forgotten. He may be able to read me better than anyone, but I can read him just as well.

I lift my fingers, watching them shake in the air before I find the nerve to finally sign, *I'm sorry.*

He blinks and turns away, shrugging his small shoulders. Like Ellen, he's dressed, ready to go.

Cautiously I stand and cross over to him. He doesn't move an inch, not even as I sink to my knees and pull him into my arms. This position makes it painfully apparent that we're almost the same height. He has to lean down just to return the embrace.

"I didn't want to tell," he confesses against my shoulder in a voice I've never heard him use before, faint and hoarse. My eyes burn, but I let the tears fall. He deserves that much.

"I didn't," he insists. "But Papa was so mad... Where did you go?"

I cradle his cheek against my palm and shake my head. One day I'll tell him, I swear it to myself. As it stands, all I can do is squeeze him, appreciating his love more than ever. I was so selfish to take him for granted—to take them all for granted.

Donatello can only damage what I'm willing to let him desecrate.

And he will have no more of me.

"Are you okay?" Eli asks once I finally loosen my hold enough for him to pull away. He scans my face intently but whatever he finds makes him press his lips together, unconvinced.

I'm fine, I sign. *Now go get me my flowers. I want the best ones.*

A wary smile alights his face, wrinkling his cherub nose. "I'll bring you some candy, too," he declares.

I nod and sign, *My favorite, of course.*

He beams. "You got it. A chocolate chunk bar."

"Eli, darling?" Ellen calls from down the hall. "Are you ready?"

"Coming!"

As he scampers off, I cross to my wardrobe and withdraw a simple shirt and jeans. I shower, get dressed, brush my hair, and when I leave my room, the hallway is surprisingly empty.

It doesn't take me long to sense where the other occupants are. Boisterous noises drift from below; excited murmurs and girlish shrieks draw me into the drawing room. I hover near the doorway, peering at the scene taking place within.

"And then what, Papa?" Aljona demands, bouncing on Mischa's lap as he sits on a leather chair positioned by the fireplace.

Marnie stands behind him, somehow having wedged herself between his back and the chair. Her position makes for the perfect perch from which to studiously braid pieces of his long hair. Across the room, Ivan lounges on the couch, his nose seemingly buried in one of his books. More often than not, his attention drifts to the tale Mischa is telling.

"And then, the prince found his princess," the man declares, his voice deep and booming. "She had already escaped the villain on her own, rescuing another princess while she was at it."

The girls exclaim in awe, clamoring for more.

"And then what happened, Papa? Did they get married? Huh?"

In disgust, Ivan mutters from under his breath, "That would be boring."

Chuckling, Mischa rushes to appease his audience. "And then…" He trails off, his dark eyes cutting in my direction. "It seems we have another listener who wants to join in. Should we let her?"

The girls turn toward me in confusion and squeal with delight.

"Willow!" In a flurry of flying pigtails and pink skirts, they rush to me, each one claiming a side of my waist.

"We thought you were dead," Marnie declares solemnly, her amber eyes wide.

"Are you feeling better?" Aljona asks, prodding my hip with a tiny finger.

I place my hands on their heads and nod, allowing them to drag me over to where Mischa is.

"Come sit!" they command.

Obediently, I claim a seat beside Ivan, drawing my knees up to my chin. Taking his eyes from his book, he meets my gaze with a rare, impish grin.

"Now, where was I?" Mischa asks, folding his hands over his lap.

"The princess!" Marnie declares, reclaiming her perch behind him.

Aljona crawls onto an armrest and cups his jaw in both hands. "Tell it right this time," she warns sternly. "It has to have a happy ending. And no monsters—" she glares at Ivan, who I assume from his innocent shrug was the culprit of what apparently derailed their last story time.

"Alright," Mischa concedes with a nod. "Now, the princess—"

"Sir?" The stern voice cuts the cheerful mood like a knife. Sporting an expression no less serious, Evgeni appears in the doorway. One look at his posture—and the telltale bulging in the pocket of his suit where his hand rests—sends alarm surging down my spine. Instantly, the girls fall silent, and even Ivan sits up, his expression puzzled.

Mischa's eyes narrow before he quashes the expression beneath a blank mask. "What is it?" he demands. I know firsthand how hard he's strived to maintain the boundary between the sheltered safety his children appreciate and the world beyond them.

With his jaw clenched in determination, Evgeni shatters that façade by crossing to him, his head lowered in respect. Going off his pained grimace, I suspect he is well aware of the norms he's breaking with every step. Whatever he has to say must be well worth risking his employer's ire.

"I apologize, sir. But..." Near Mischa's ear, he murmurs something the makes Mischa lurch upright so suddenly, he dislodges Marnie and nearly knocks Aljona off the chair altogether.

He spins to catch her a heartbeat before disaster, but brings her to me, lowering her into my arms.

"Papa? What's wrong?" She tries tugging at his hand, but he gently pulls away.

"You stay here." The order is as bracing as a slap in comparison to his previous playful baritone. Without another word, he turns, leaving the room with Evgeni on his heels.

I rise to my feet, thoroughly shaken. In all my years of knowing him, I can't name a single time he's ever shown this side of himself to his children. Not the caring father, but the cold *mafiya* leader striding with purpose. If I had to guess, only a handful of subjects would ever be the cause of this disruption.

The safety of his family being paramount among them.

I start after him, but Aljona grips me tight. "Don't go!"

"It's okay," Ivan says. Dutifully, he sets his book aside and takes Aljona's hand. Marnie races to him, and he wraps his free arm around her shoulders, holding both of his sisters protectively.

"I'll watch them," he declares with a brave nod. "I can do it."

Reluctantly, I leave them there, approaching the foyer. Dread pools in the pit of my stomach with every step I take. A cruel flashback taunts me—a moment seven years ago, when another man left a similar play session in horror. We had been at the beach, and I can still remember the day so clearly.

Vin and I were frolicking in the water while Don watched protectively from the shore. Suddenly, he received a call that made him take off, leaving us to the care of a bodyguard. It was only hours later that we learned the tragic reason as to why.

I have to blink back the memory, returning to the present. I'm in the foyer, facing the front of the house. The main doors are wide open, swinging aimlessly in a slight wind. At the base of the front steps, Mischa stands, watching the road, Evgeni beside him.

"They're approaching now, sir," the bodyguard warns.

I can hear the metallic clang of the gates opening in the distance, followed by shouting. The alarmed cries only seem to grow louder. More men stream from various corners of the property as if in some eerie, coordinated display.

They stop short near the road, and at the end of the driveway, a van appears, speeding toward the house. I vaguely recognize it as one of the family vehicles, but it's instantly apparent that something is wrong. A jagged crack slashes through the windshield, and shards of glass glitter over the lawn, falling at random from all four main windows. In a violent spray of dirt and gravel, it sways on and off the road before skidding to a stop in a bed of roses. The door to the front seat opens, and the driver staggers out.

Her slender shape sets her apart from the usual men Mischa employs. Horrified, I recognize her pale face, contorted in pain. Ellen.

I don't even register moving before I'm already running across the lawn on bare feet.

With a roar, Mischa barrels past me, gathering her into his arms. She resists the embrace, reaching for the mangled body of the van.

"Eli…" Her voice is a faint shadow of its usual cadence as if it's taking everything in her just to speak. Blood paints a startling bright path from her forehead down to her shoulder, staining her yellow dress.

Whatever pain she's in doesn't deter her from her sole focus. Persistent, she reaches for him, oblivious to Mischa. "Eli," she murmurs, her eyelids fluttering. "Eli…"

One of the men wrenches open the door to the back seat, and my knees buckle at the scene awaiting within. Blood paints the tanned leather in a vicious spray. Amid the carnage, slumped on his side is a figure so small, so pale…

I barely recognize him.

My mouth opens for a soundless scream. I can't hear. My pulse surges through my eardrums too fiercely, drowning out everything else. I reach for him, swaying on my feet. Only when Evgeni climbs in beside him and feels along his neck can I breathe again.

"He's alive," the man says. Easily, he lifts the boy into his arms and carries him out onto the lawn. What the light reveals churns my stomach even more. He may be alive, but his right arm is twisted at an unnatural angle, drenched in blood from the shoulder down.

"Fuck," Mischa rasps. His eyes dart helplessly from his wife to his son. I've never seen him like this—paralyzed.

"We need to get him to a hospital," Evgeni deduces. Turning to another man, he snarls, "Bring another car around! Now!"

"Is he alright?" Ellen demands, clawing desperately at Mischa's forearm. She's too weak to lift her head enough to see the boy for herself, no matter how hard she tries. "Please, is he alright?"

Even as she speaks, Mischa swears and drops to his knees, cradling her against him. He snatches a handful of her skirt, and I realize why. Ellen's whiter than snow in his arms—I've never seen the color drain from anyone's face so quickly. Not all of the blood staining the fabric comes from her forehead. A glaring amount streaks her legs, and a growing stain paints the fabric near her waist.

"Stay with me, Rose," Mischa pleads, stroking her cheeks as her eyes finally shut.

"The car is arriving, sir," Evgeni calls.

In a coordinated effort, at least six guards carefully arrange Ellen and Eli into the back of a different van, and Mischa takes the front seat.

"They were attacked on the road," I hear Evgeni explain, scrambling into the driver's seat. "Adamo was killed trying to drive them to safety. It was an ambush."

"Who?" Mischa demands, his voice nearly drowned by a sea of guards shouting out various positions and directions.

Evgeni looks at me as if noticing my presence for the first time. "Stay inside, Ms. Stepanova. Victor!" He nods to another man who comes up behind me, placing a hand on my shoulder. "Get her inside. Secure the property while we're gone."

The van starts to move, heading from the property with alarming speed. Even so, a cruel gust of wind throws Evgeni's parting words in my face, uttered in a tone I'm not intended to hear.

"My men are on the scene," he declares. "But you won't like what they've found…"

WILLOW

Night has already fallen when a commotion erupts from below, and I startle to awareness in a leather recliner positioned in between two small beds draped in pink sheets. A distant thud rattles the house to its very foundation—that of a door slamming. Even from here, I can sense the tension crackling in the air. Uneasy, I glance around the nursery, from the girls beside me, to Ivan asleep on the other side of the room. Marnie stirs, mumbling in her sleep, but as the seconds pass, neither child wakes up.

Gingerly, I untangle myself from the girls, gently interlocking their grasping hands together. As I slip from their room, my footsteps echo throughout the deserted hall, disconcertingly loud. Among them, I catch a series of muttering voices drifting from the direction of Mischa's study, but this time he isn't alone.

"It isn't proof," Evgeni warns, his tone neutral. I advance toward the doorway and find him standing before Mischa's desk, his back to me. My father sits slumped in his customary chair, his face in his hands. My heart aches as I take in what little of his haggard features are visible. In little under a day, he's aged an eternity.

"But my men were able to identify one of the attackers found near the market," Evgeni says. "He was already dead, but they are almost certain that he worked for—"

"The bastard taunted me," Mischa says over him with a cold laugh. Incredulously, he shakes his head, still laughing. The sound grows louder and louder, so booming that I'm sure it could wake the children. Suddenly, he stops, his gaze fixed ahead, beyond this room, I suspect, at something Evgeni and I cannot see. "That son of a bitch. Right to my face…he taunted me."

"I must insist upon caution, sir," Evgeni insists. "I don't have any right to advise calm after what happened today, but I—"

"Mouse," Mischa growls, his eyes cutting toward me. Before I can move, he crooks a finger, beckoning me closer. "Come."

The bodyguard clears his throat. "I will leave you two, sir—"

"Don't," Mischa says, letting his hand fall. "You talk. She deserves to hear this."

"I'd rather be sure, sir," Evgeni insists, displaying a rare hesitation. "My men will not stop until you have your answers."

"Answers," Mischa says with a scoff. He meets my gaze, his eyes so bloodshot that at a glance, they seem scarlet. Ablaze.

But I know him—if his wife or son were dead, he would be nowhere near this composed.

"They are alive," he says as if reading my mind.

An overwhelming wave of relief nearly brings me to my knees. Evgeni approaches me, grabbing my arm to steady me. As he guides me to a chair, Mischa continues. "I won't spare you the truth," he says hoarsely. "Not this time. Eli was badly hurt. He'll live, but they don't know yet what the long-term damage might be. His arm was shattered…" He groans, rubbing at his temples. After a second's pause, he says, "He's conscious at least. Anna is there with him. Your mother isn't so lucky. She is alive, but they had to take the baby early. Both survived the surgery, but for her own good, they had to keep Ellen sedated. She lost a lot of blood."

Despair clenches my lungs in a fist, but dread builds the longer I meet his gaze. He's telling me this for a reason, warning me to steel myself.

Because as painful as this is to hear, it's not the worst of it.

Not by far.

"They were attacked," he says. "And I could lie to you. Hide this from you. But I won't."

He slams his fist onto the table, knocking a pile of documents to the floor. As his eyes cut back up to mine, they burn fiercely, in a way I've never seen them. At least not in years.

Not since the day he acquired me as little more than a fearsome stranger.

"Tell her," he barks to Evgeni. "Tell her what you've found."

The bodyguard stiffens, his jaw clenched. "Sir—"

"Fine. I will tell her. They were attacked by Donatello Vanici's men," Mischa says. "And I love you, but this time… I won't show mercy."

He stands, pushing past his desk. My mind goes blank as my body reacts on sheer instinct. I scramble to my feet, reaching for his hand.

Turmoil rips through my thoughts, displacing any sense of logic.

All I can see is Eli and Ellen, covered in blood.

I see Donatello, the man who left me for dead.

And now I see Mischa, shrugging me off so violently I trip and land on my knees. Watching him go, I can't reconcile the fear constricting my chest, crushing the air from my lungs.

I can't breathe.

Can't move.

All I can do is try to scream.

21

DON

It's a good fucking day. Despite the rain pouring down and the fact that Vin is glaring at me from the top of the hallway steps, I'm determined to make it so.

"A good damn day," I say out loud, slamming my hand against the banister for emphasis. We've already packed our things, and between the two of us, the villa's foyer is a maze of suitcases. Admittedly most are mine rather than Vin's; his consist of just a few bags though the heaviest of the bunch. The boy likes his books.

"Good for who?" Vin grumbles. Shouldering a duffle, he descends the staircase to meet me. Without a fancy party to attend, he's exchanged the suit for a sweater and jeans. From behind his glasses, he looks every bit the doctor in training—one who is scowling at the fact that, while dressing half-asleep, I managed to put on the same pants from said fancy party, speckled with my own blood.

As well as judging me for the minor crime of oversleeping, causing us to run late and miss my morning whiskey.

But, I suspect he's pouting for another reason. Sure enough, he declares, "You're not the one being shipped off like some unwanted stepchild."

"Correction," I say, stepping forward to cup his jaw in both hands. I squeeze his cheeks and coo like a mother hen. As he wrenches out of my reach, I'm lucky he doesn't punch me. "You're being shipped off like my only child. My cherished baby boy. Be glad you don't have a mother here to pinch your cheeks. Though I may get teary-eyed when you finally leave, so take that as fair warning. Now give me a goodbye kiss."

"Knock it off, old man!" He winces, dodging my hand as I reach for him again. "You do enough fussing over me for ten mothers."

"Damn right. Now be a good lad and gather your stuff. By this time tomorrow, you'll be back in your dorm, crying with homesickness."

And I'll be somewhere outside of the city, crying over a shot of whiskey at the state of my finances.

"Whatever you say, Don." Rolling his eyes, Vin marches past me for the front door. A car is already waiting outside to take us to the airport, and with an exaggerated sigh, he heads toward it. From over his shoulder, he quips, "Since I'm your cherished boy, you should carry most of the bags, right?"

"Think again, smartass," I call after him.

The second he's out of view, the smile I've been sporting for his benefit falls. Fuck. Heavy with dread, I approach the room off the main hall that I've been using as a makeshift study. For the first time, I scan the pile of documents lying on the desk in a neat stack, left by Fabio, who worked all night to compile them. I look them over, hissing through my teeth. In a sense, they serve the same purpose as a white flag, ceding my control of the docks —and much of my income.

After Mischa's suggested "donation" to his daughter's conservatory, my disposal accounts will be all but drained. The rumors weren't exaggerating about the bastard's malicious streak.

God only knows how I'll scrape together enough to continue to cover Vin's tuition. He still has his trust fund, separate from any other accounts, but I'll find more. Even if I have to sell the rest of my assets piece by piece. I'll fucking find every last cent.

I form a fist at the thought of Mischa's ultimatum and smash it against the wooden surface of the desk.

"Everything okay, Don?" Vin calls out.

"I'm fine," I rasp back.

I'm not.

My knuckles smart like a bitch, but a grim truth dulls any pain I might feel—it could have been worse. Much worse. No matter the damage done to my pride, I'd be a fool to challenge these terms.

I would be an even bigger fool to waste any time. Turning tail and running now is the best course of action for everyone involved—regardless of whether or not I feel like a whipped dog in the process.

"Don?" Vin calls from the hallway, but the inflection in his tone catches my attention. He's alarmed. "Are you expecting a meeting or something?"

"A meeting?" I call back. Then I groan at the thought of Fabio dropping by to issue yet more stern mothering and fucking paperwork—I turned my phone off just to avoid his calls for a reason. The man is well known for his tendency toward overkill. Forcing another smile for Vin's sake, I head for the foyer. "Coming."

I've barely gone a step before I realize what he means—a sudden commotion erupts from the front lawn, but Fabio's arrival never draws this kind of fanfare. Or chaos. I break into a run, shouting for Javier as the piercing sound of squealing tires is followed by a sharper crack that chills me to the core.

As I near the doorway, I see the cause for myself—a black car crashing through the gate, speeding toward the house.

I know instantly the driver isn't Fabio, and my blood goes cold. On the list of potential suspects, one stands out, and I take a step toward the gun safe I've yet to clear out in the living room. Apparently, Salvatore decided to stop playing coy with his attempts on my life and try a more direct course of action. But no…

The second I see the car's model—a practical kind, not flashy and expensive—I know I'm off base. Only a professional would ride like this.

And not to discuss financial terms, either.

"Vin, get inside!" I demand.

He's standing on the front steps, watching the car approach. I barely manage to shove him behind me as the vehicle careens up the front path, swerving to a stop before the steps.

The door to the back seat flies open, and a man lunges onto the pavement without so much as a warning. Confusion roots me to the spot the second I see his face—this man doesn't work for Salvatore. Long blond hair streams down his shoulders, his expression cold, his identity chilling.

Mischa.

One look at his face, and I know he's not here to gloat over my capitulation. Recognition gives me a cruel taste of déjà vu. In his eyes, I see a blind rage I know all too well—the same look I saw in the mirror seven years ago.

It happens in slow motion. I see the gun he pulls from the pocket of his gray fatigues. See his hand aiming. Hear the shot…

The booming sound rips through my eardrums, and my mind goes blank.

Blood rushes to my head, deafening me to any sound.

I've been shot before—more than once. I know the fiery agony to expect. It hits like a crushing blow, taking even the strongest man off his feet.

I grit my teeth in anticipation of it, but as the seconds sluggishly tick by, I stay standing.

Snippets of action unfold before me, but I'm powerless to move.

Mischa jumps back into his car and drives off. Even in the brutal aftermath of uncertainty, I know I should be taking after him. Or preparing for another attack—no one takes one shot and walks away.

Unless I'm hit.

Gradually, sensation returns to my limbs. I run my hand across my chest, surprised when I feel no sputtering warmth of fresh blood. No fire.

Last time a bullet hit my collar, fracturing the bone, and I nearly blacked out from the agony.

This time…I don't feel anything other than an emotion I hate to acknowledge, resonating in my gut—fear.

Across the lawn, a man lies sprawled in the dirt. His dark suit warns that he's one of mine, and I dread knowing his identity. Javier? Another guard?

I can't be sure before I catch sight of someone else racing from the other end of the property, their lips moving, eyes wide. Javier. He sprints up the front steps, weapon drawn, but his eyes aren't on me—and whatever has his attention must be bad.

So bad the man pales, his throat cording around a shout.

Confused, I turn around…

And the next thing I know, I'm on my knees. Mischa shot me after all—I'm in a coma, hallucinating the unthinkable.

That's the only reason to explain this.

Because what I'm seeing isn't real. It can't be him. Not Vin, lying on his side, a puddle of scarlet seeping from his ear. He's too pale. Too red. Too red.

I call his name, hearing nothing but the surging pulse of my own heartbeat in response.

They say grief has stages to it, that there's a perfect name for every emotion. While it sounds nice in theory, it's all bullshit some doctor came up with while in his nice, neat office. Someone who never truly experienced the depths of that despair. Or known the brutal, violent kind of loss…

There are no fucking steps to follow, no pretty ways to quantify it. The shit hollows you.

There is only pain to judge the passage of time. One day, you can almost barely live with it. That's coming to terms with it, I guess. Or what you say to stay out of the fucking shrink's office at least.

The truth is that nothing will ever lessen it. Ever. Time merely soothes the sting, and alcohol may dull the ache, but the wound is always there, always smarting at the slightest touch. No amount of mourning ever eases it. You just linger there in the pit of that sadness, always waiting for it to consume you again—or you cling to the few people whose presence can distract from the pain.

I don't mourn Vin.

I don't weep and writhe in sadness. There is no point.

Throwing my head back, I just laugh. And laugh. Seeing my hands coated in his blood has me chuckling so hard I wind up clutching at my chest. Moisture spills from my eyes—an unavoidable, biological reaction. But they burn. Every fucking drop sears rivulets into my cheeks, branding me with the proof of my own goddamn weakness.

He's dead only because I failed him.

What a goddamn riot.

I laugh harder and harder until I'm on my fucking knees, braying at nothing.

But then it sinks in. I'm not in a coma. This isn't a hallucination. I never wake up. From the corner of my eye, I can see him, unmoving. So pale, his beautiful eyes closed, his nose—that signature Vanici nose—draining a trail of blood.

There's no way to quantify the loss—everything I've worked toward dies with him.

But some part of me must find that so fucking hilarious. I'm still laughing as I stagger to my feet. There's no aim in mind—just a need to keep moving. Breathing. I'll suffocate if I stay still. So, I pace the length of the room, watching the blood spread across the floor. I can smell it, salt, and copper. Taste it on my fucking tongue.

And Vin…

I can't look at him fully. Not yet.

I can't fucking look. All I can do is just register the silence. That looming, oppressive goddamn silence. The absence of his voice— I'll never hear it again. It's the same quiet that filled the air when I found Olivia and Nico.

And no matter how hard or how loudly I laugh…it never ends. So I shout. Scream. Yell until I can't hear a damn thing but the rushing of my own heartbeat surging through my ears like a fucking taunt. He's gone. He's gone. He's gone…

But then it's like my mind clears all at once, and I remember the culprit.

The animal who did this.

Mischa.

I lunge for the safe in the living room, rip it open, and practically teleport to the front door, a gun in my hand. I'm aiming it blindly, hunting for a target.

But he's already gone. All that's left are tire tracks ripping across the lawn and my own men scattered about. Some look wounded, but I don't even have the sense of mind to stop. Acknowledge them. Breathe.

I keep running, chasing a specter down to the end of the driveway. A noise finally pierces the fog encasing me—a gunshot. My finger throbs, cranking on the trigger, firing at nothing.

Again.

Again.

Again.

Doggedly, I'm racing toward the boundaries of the house. A car appears in the distance, and I aim for it, feeling my heart hammer against my chest. As it comes into view, I recognize the model—one of Fabio's.

It slows beside me, and the driver's side window lowers.

"God, Don…" His eyes take me in, widening in horror over my hands. My fucking hands…

I don't know what I say to him, but whatever it is makes him curse under his breath. "Let me see him," he says in a cautious tone. Then he drives, heading toward the house.

His reaction makes the reality even more real. Inescapable. Vin.

I'm frozen solid, gun still raised, chest pounding, heart on goddamn fire. I can't even look at the house. I can't…

But I can't leave Vin there, unguarded and alone. In a daze, I return to the villa, staggering into the living room to find Fabio there crouched beside the body.

I surge toward him, swatting his hands away. "Get away from him—"

"He has a pulse," the man says gently, rising to his feet. "We need to get him to a hospital."

"What…" He might as well have punched me. Struck dumb, I shake my head to clear it and croak, "What did you say?"

"He has a pulse," Fabio insists. He already has a cell phone in hand, rattling off a series of orders. "Bring a van around! We don't have time to wait for an ambulance. Now!" Turning to me, he gestures toward my chest. "Take off your shirt and apply pressure to the wound."

Apply pressure. While I'm not a doctor, I know that pressure won't help a gunshot to the head. It won't…

God knows I tried with Olivia. Even if it meant holding her skull together with my bare hands, I tried. Finally, I look over and groan aloud. Blood pools around him, clashing with the color of his skin. He's so damn pale.

"Fab…" My voice breaks several times before I finally get a coherent word out. "His head…"

"Don." Fabio grabs me by the collar, his eyes boring into mine. "Take a walk! Take a walk, brother. I've got this. I'll take care of Vin. You take care of yourself. Keep your head, Donatello!"

Keep my head. A task easier said than done. It's spinning as more men stream into the room, led by Javier, who clutches at his shoulder. Was he hit?

Meeting my gaze, he shakes his head before I can even ask him.

"A van is out front," he says.

"Good." Fabio strips his suit jacket and gently wads it around Vin's head.

I choke down the part of me wanting to demand he let him go. Leave him in peace.

As if reading my mind, Fabio meets my gaze directly. "We have to move him quickly. We can't take him to any hospital in the area. Not with the *mafiya*—" He breaks off and gestures Javier over. Together they lift Vin between them. "I know a man who owes me a favor," Fabio says as they head for the door. "He'll get the best care, Don. I will see to that."

He'll see…

I can't. The world goes dark, and I feel a bitter sense of dread. The same darkness that came over me when Olivia died.

When Safiya…

That thick, hopeless black.

The only way out is to breathe.

Suppress.

Feel nothing…

But rage.

In this moment, anger is the only cure.

Retribution—by any means necessary.

22

DON

"He's alive." It's the first thing Fabio says the second he steps foot into the villa, and it doesn't even register.

Alive.

That word lacks the connotation he thinks it has. After hours of silence, I've come to terms with what to expect. Hell, I've lived through this before. Seen the aftermath. Suffered this hell. You don't come out of a gunshot wound to the head alive. If anything, you exist—a shell fed by a series of tubes and machinery. Breathing, but not much more than that.

So no, I can tell from his face alone that even if he has a heartbeat, Vincenzo isn't alive.

Hope is a cruel fucking thing, gnawing away at my psyche regardless, daring me to believe—but I can't.

I won't.

"Donatello?"

Fabio steps closer. I haven't moved from the position he left me in, seated on the floor of the entryway. His jaw clenches as he realizes, horror flashing in his eyes. I look down and discover why. Fuck, my hands are sticky, covered in red. So much goddamn red.

The amount only proves my point. He's dead.

"He's alive," Fabio repeats, crouching to meet my gaze directly. I've known him for too damn long not to see the fear written across his face, contradicting the words leaving his mouth.

"Tell me the truth," I demand. God, I don't even recognize the sound of my voice. This cold, lifeless man. He's a phantom I thought I'd left in the past.

"I won't lie," Fabio warns. "He's in a coma. His condition is serious. There is no real prognosis."

"Where is he?" I start to stand, but Fabio sighs.

"Someplace safe with a doctor I know. One of the best in the world. But…" He grimaces before he says, "I think it's best if you don't visit him for now. Not with Mischa—"

"Why the fuck not?" I snarl, gritting my teeth.

He blinks. "Because Mischa Stepanov put a hit out on you." I have to give it to him. Somehow, he manages to sound gentle— like it's not the exact opposite of everything I've done my goddamn best to ensure.

"Why?" I demand, unable to keep the rage from my voice. The confusion. The hate. I'm too damn sober.

And at the same time, I'm numb.

"I gave him everything he asked for—"

"You tell me what happened, Don," Fabio demands with an exasperated sigh. "Did you call off the deal?"

"No," I croak, swiping my hand through my hair. Nothing makes sense. This could still be a dream if it weren't for the dull, throbbing ache in my chest, intensifying with every beat of my heart. No nightmare could ever feel this real. Meeting Fabio's stare, I say, "I did everything you told me. Every fucking thing."

Because like a fucking idiot, I expected the man to have some shred of honor.

Uphold his word.

One would think I would have learned by now—you can't expect mercy from an animal.

"What you need to do now is come with me. This is bad, Don," Fabio says bluntly. Moonlight from the windows ghosts over his pale face, enhancing the wrinkles exaggerating the corners of his mouth. "Very bad. I'm not an official part of the *mafiya*, but I've never been shut out like this before. Hell, I barely got any fucking warning. And… Did you do it?" He meets my gaze so reluctantly that even in this state, I'd feel some shred of guilt.

If I knew what to feel it for.

"Do what? Sell my soul to that motherfucker only to be betrayed?" The more I say it, the more real it sounds. I laugh again at the insanity of it. To work so hard to be a good man…

All to have it end like this.

"Mischa's family was attacked yesterday," Fabio says. His tone is comparable to a bucket of ice water being dumped over my head. Abruptly, he stands, putting his back to me. Both of his hands tear through his hair, his breathing heavy and labored. This isn't like him, the antithesis of the calm he tries to maintain. He's frantic. "His wife is in a coma—they don't know if she'll even live," he says. "His baby girl was born too soon. His son... The poor kid may be crippled for life. From what I heard, they were ambushed on the road and barely got away with their lives. Donatello... Tell me you didn't do it. Don?"

His voice echoes ceaselessly, but I stop hearing him.

In his place, I see another man, gloating over his own power. His smug, satisfied smirk should have alarmed me even then.

And guilt rips through me.

If I'd used my fucking head, I could have stopped him.

I could have stopped this.

"Donatello!" Fabio stands over me, his voice reverberating down to the house's very foundation. "I know you're not in the best mindset right now. But you need to trust me. You shouldn't even be here. I have a property out of the city where you can—"

"Salvatore." The name rips from me as I rise to my feet, heading for the door. Red paints my vision, and too many thoughts crowd my head. The dark, twisted shit I've spent years suppressing—the need to find the bastard. Make him pay. Make him bleed. "That son of a bitch."

"Don!" Fabio appears in front of me, placing his hand on my chest. "Where are you going? At least give me the gun."

I still have it, I realize, looking down. But I can't seem to relinquish my grip on the handle.

"Don," Fabio warns as I push past him. If I reply, I don't even know what I say. I just keep seeing that smug bastard. Hearing his voice.

"Wait! I have a car waiting," Fabio says, grabbing my arm as I approach the front steps. "I need you to get inside of it, Donatello. Get somewhere safe. I'll give you regular updates on Vincenzo's status, and we can figure out a plan later. Your safety is my first concern—"

"Vin…" As much as I love him, the pain is harder to process than the anger. My steps falter as I see him again, my poor boy. The blood. His fucking head…

Blown apart because of me.

No, because of Antonio Salvatore.

"I won't pretend like his condition isn't serious," Fabio warns, raising his voice until I look at him. "But he's alive. That's all that matters, and Donatello? He needs you to stay the same. Okay? Come with me and get in the car."

He tugs on my arm until I follow him. Nearby, a black car idles in the driveway, too expensive to be one of mine.

"Get in," Fabio says, opening the door to the back seat. "My driver Oliver here will take us someplace safe."

Oliver is a balding man who looks every bit the dutiful, professional type Fabio would hire. He barely even blinks when I raise the gun in my grasp and aim it squarely at his head.

From the corner of my eye, I see Fabio take a step back. "Donatello…"

"Out," I tell the driver.

With a glance at Fabio, the man complies.

"Don't do this, Donatello," Fabio begs, his hands raised. Even he knows better than to approach me. "Just let me handle this!"

I ignore him, claiming the driver's seat for myself. Before he can try to climb in, I put the engine in drive and step on the gas.

23

DON

I don't see the road. I have no idea which force is even in control of the fucking steering wheel. I'm not. My body may inhabit this vehicle, but my brain is somewhere else.

All I can visualize is Antonio Salvatore. Mocking me. Taunting me.

Over and over again.

My jaw aches from how tightly I'm gritting my teeth—but I bite down harder. The pain is the only thing I have to cling to. That and the rage.

Like an old friend, the icy, cold mindset of my past self takes over, and I let it.

I let the hatred narrow my focus, and breathing becomes easier. Thinking is suddenly more direct. My thoughts have meaning again, and the plan they spell out is so fucking simple.

If Salvatore wants to play politics by pitting me against Mischa, I will level the playing field. He won't get to declare checkmate with my foot up his ass.

The first step? Find him.

The potential options are too many to consider. Logic is a luxury I don't care to indulge in. Raking through my memories, I settle on one at random—he had a house, years ago, when I dared to call him "friend." I remember it clearly, some pussy fucking mansion in the hills where he could pretend to be a big man. I'm headed there now, watching the landmarks and street signs pass in a blur. It's like I'm possessing another man's body. A reckless asshole who speeds without a damn given for anyone else on the road.

A monster.

Eventually, that house appears up ahead, perched on an overlook that gives the bastard a clear view of anyone coming. I should slow. Park somewhere secluded and case the property for any weakness.

I only have one gun and hardly a full clip left. No extra ammo. No backup.

In a sense? No sane course of action.

I know from experience that Salvatore keeps at least a handful of *famiglia* goons around him at all times. He's always been a cowardly son of a bitch. Approaching him on my own is pure suicide. So, I keep driving, pressing on the gas as hard as I can.

Up ahead, a set of metal gates loom, barring the entrance.

But I don't slow.

Instead, I brace for the impact and catch myself laughing out loud as the front of the car careens into the barricade. At the back of my mind, I know that reinforced steel meeting the body of this car should be the equivalent of a tin can being crushed against concrete—but good old Fab. He invests only in the best.

My head rears back with the force of the collision, but the airbags don't even deploy. One side of the barrier gives way in a flurry of sparks and squealing metal, bent completely off its axis. The headlights illuminate the twisted chaos, but I wrench open the door and climb out, barely feeling anything.

Movement comes from my left. A guard? A Salvatore cunt? The gun is in my hand, and I aim and fire without a second thought. No restraint.

At the back of my mind, the new Donatello cringes, warning of the potential consequences.

So I aim and fire again until any other noise falls silent—in my head or otherwise.

Circling the car, I observe the gnarled wreckage of the gate. It's almost overly easy to wrench the twisted portion from its frame and shove it aside. Apart from a busted headlight, the car looks none too worse for wear. It's still running. My brain goes a mile a minute as I climb back inside behind the wheel. I continue forward up the winding driveway lined in fucking statues that cast shadows in the dark at full speed. They flicker like a chorus of devils urging me on.

Mama used to claim the road to hell is paved with good intentions. So I must be headed somewhere far worse.

There's nothing good in my soul now.

Just pain and bitter fucking amusement.

While I've scrounged for every penny, Salvatore's done well for himself. If male compensation for a tiny dick was personified by the number of acres, fancy hedges, and white marble a man owns, then Salvatore has a lot to make up for. It feels like it takes ten full minutes before I reach the house itself. A sprawling mansion, the place is ablaze with light that reflects off the parade of luxury cars parked on display in a circular driveway. A fountain bubbles in a small courtyard, and already two more guards come running.

I park in a bed of flowers and step out before they can fire. It's been years since I've shot at anything other than a stationary target at the range. For a second, I hesitate, recalling that promise I made all those years ago. On Olivia's grave, I swore it—I would change. Become a new man.

Repent for those old sins.

But that new Donatello? He didn't have his nephew's blood all over his fucking hands, or those images of Vin in his skull.

Ignoring him is as simple as giving in to the icy darkness creeping across my consciousness. I surrender to it gladly, letting it smother any regret. Any doubt. Inhaling deeply, I feel my grip tighten, trigger finger flex…

And it's too easy. Like slipping into an old piece of clothing, you thought you'd outgrown. Lo' and behold, it fits like a glove, ushering in a wave of memories. Paramount among them? How good it felt wearing it.

My brain doesn't even make the mental connection of aiming and shooting before both men go down. I keep moving, passing through the main courtyard.

It's a weak man's idea of luxury, as is the fucking row of marble steps leading to the entrance. I take them two at a time and kick open the front door before entering a spacious hall decorated in black marble and enough gaudy ornaments to stock some cheap-ass roadshow. The man likes animals. The place is a fucking safari of various creatures made of solid gold.

It's a world apart from Havienna's modest hallway, that's for damn sure. Especially on that day just over seven years ago. There were no golden figurines of tigers to gape at when someone entered my house then. My home.

There were only scattered toys and photographs. Safiya's dolls and Vin's books. Little Nico's burping cloths and his tiny blankets.

Not one damn item held them back. Made them rethink their course of action.

Like monsters, the bastards found my wife in the drawing room unprotected. As she shielded her newborn son, they shot her twice in the head at point-blank range and left her there.

And my fighter, my Olivia…she held on. For longer than any doctor was willing to give her credit for, she held on.

Stinging tears blur my vision as I blink, returning to the present. I'm the bastard now, advancing through a house that lacks any of the familial touches mine did—and my target is a lot harder to find. Antonio Salvatore isn't in the huge-ass living room that overlooks a swimming pool. Neither is he in a dining room with a glass table and a crystal chandelier.

I have to hunt for the motherfucker, letting instinct guide me.

Up a circular staircase where even more windows display the property. I can see headlights in the distance, and I laugh out loud. He must have a panic button, rigged to call for backup.

Good.

Panic is a drug more potent than alcohol. My nostrils flare as I breathe it in and round the corner of a wide hallway. I could aim to sneak up on the bastard, catching him off guard.

Or I can make him piss himself.

"Where the fuck are you hiding?" I call out.

A sudden noise draws my attention a few doors down. A glance through the doorway reveals what seems to be a master suite. Cautiously, I advance, spotting a large bed with silk sheets on one end, positioned near a row of mirrors. Vanity was always one of Antonio's many flaws. There's even a portrait of the man hanging above the polished mantel of a marble fireplace in the far corner.

I know even before I see him, that he's here—the stench of his cologne gives him away.

"You've lost your mind," Antonio Salvatore himself declares from the mouth of a doorway. Naked save for a towel slung around his waist, it seems that I caught him at a bad time.

Nonetheless, he has a gun in his hand, aimed squarely at me. But Salvatore was always a coward when it came to finishing a job. He preferred to have others do his dirty work.

So rather than shoot him, I meet his gaze squarely.

"You attacked Mischa's family," I say, surprised by how calm my voice sounds. Cordial, even.

His eyes narrow, and he sputters. "You've lost your damn—"

"Mind," I finish for him in a growl. "And you bet your ass I have."

My finger twitches. An explosion of sound rips through my eardrums as blood sprays across the glass door behind Salvatore. He falls back, his eyes wide, lips hollowed around a startled o-shape. Whether I've shot him in the chest or the arm, I don't care. I just know he's not dead.

Yet.

"Admit it." I move to stand over him, watching him cough and clutch at his side as I kick his gun out of reach. Wide, his eyes find mine, but while a coward, it appears he is still a smug son of a bitch. He spits at me.

Blood mixed with saliva lands against my pant leg, joining the stains already there. I'm wearing navy, and it's mottled with a million shades of a darker substance.

Fuck…

I sway. The room blurs around me as I paw at my side, spotting a splotch of scarlet there I'd missed. Hell, there's even more on my shirt.

Blood.

Vincenzo's blood.

"Ass…asshole," Salvatore croaks, drawing my attention back to him.

My nostrils flare, catching the scent of blood in the air—and the stench works on my brain better than any shot of whiskey. My vision clears again. All of a sudden, everything is so fucking clear.

Raising the gun, I fire again, aiming for his knee.

He squeals, and it's music to my ears. A melody so sweet it blocks everything else for the moment, and I'll do anything to make it last.

Crouching to my knees, I prod Salvatore's chest with a finger, narrowly missing his wound.

"Confess," I tell him. "To everything. Vin. Olivia. I should have killed you then."

"You don't have the balls to kill me," he rasps. "I'll have all of the *famiglia* on your ass. You'll be strung up just like that dumb bitch—"

I drag my finger over until it hits fleshy, warm wetness. Then I dig in with the tip of my nail so that beautiful song grows richer. I'm intoxicated by that tune. Laughing, I inspect my finger and swipe it across Salvatore's chin, painting him with the color.

"Red looks good on you, Antonio," I tell him. "And you don't want to confess your sins? The fuck if I care. Because I don't. Not really." Aiming the gun near his head, I watch his eyes widen, and the color drain from his cheeks.

It's a look I've waited seven fucking years to witness.

And…to be honest?

I don't feel a damn thing. Revenge is an itch reminiscent of hunger. Thirst. You can only satiate it for so long, but at the end of the day, it's in your fucking nature to. No reason to celebrate.

No reason to mourn.

Denying yourself is a game of control that only hurts you in the long run.

So I don't celebrate as I turn my pistol handle-first and whip the bastard across the face. He grunts, blood spraying from his jaw as a crack issues from the bone.

I still feel nothing.

Just a cramp in my hand as a grim curiosity sneaks into my skull.

"I wonder what your brains would look like, huh?" I ask him, gesturing to the pristine white, marble flooring. "Sprayed all over this wall. You've got some fancy digs here; I'll give you that."

I cock my head back to take it all in. A nice fucking place. Vaulted ceilings and black walls lined in gold crown molding and baseboards. Great acoustics, too.

I hit him again to experience the full effect, and he jerks onto his side, coughing up even more blood.

"Beautiful," I breathe, grinning in appreciation. "I think the place looks nice with a little red, don't you think?"

He doesn't answer.

Sighing, I smack his chin until he faces me.

"I said, what do you think—"

"Daddy?" That sound.

It's ice water to my senses. A gut punch.

I lurch to my feet, and for a second, the world shifts as reality descends. Where I am. What I'm doing.

"Kisa," Salvatore croaks, his voice thick, eyes fixated behind me.

Numb with dread, I turn as well and clench my jaw around a groan. A tiny girl stands near the doorway of the room. Curling dark hair, wide blue eyes. She looks young. Six or seven, dressed in a white nightgown, a fucking teddy bear clutched under her arm.

That look on her face is one I'll never forget. I saw a similar expression seven years ago.

But that girl came back to haunt me.

I see her again, my Safiya, laughing as movement flickers from the corner of my eye. I barely manage to avoid the kick Salvatore aims my way as he scrambles for his gun.

Before he can reach it, I pivot and hit him again. The blow lands so hard his eyes roll as blood splatters down his chin. Whining like an animal, he falls back, still alive.

A good man would leave now.

Let him live in the presence of his little girl.

That good man would pat himself on the back and call himself reformed.

Then that good man would lose every fucking thing despite that good deed. He'd never even see it coming.

Everything I've done has been for Vin.

And even if he's still alive…

I don't deserve him. I failed him once. If to protect him, I have to become someone else, so be it.

I advance so quickly my hand is around the girl's neck before I realize. She goes rigid, her eyes staring blankly. Still, she moves as I urge her forward and crouch down beside her.

"You have a beautiful little girl," I tell Salvatore in a voice so guttural I barely recognize it. "Kisa, is it?" I finger a lock of her dark hair and feel my stomach lurch. Damn… Looking in her eyes, the old Don rails, still there inside me.

But he's getting harder to hear.

"Don't..." Salvatore croaks, and I release the girl, turning back to him.

Propping my fist beneath my chin, I observe him skeptically. "Don't tell me you have a heart, Antonio? After what you did to my family? One would think you had no soul at all."

He grunts, and I lean closer only to realize that the gasping sounds he's making are laughter.

"Don't think I give a shit if you threaten her," he boasts, cackling maniacally. "Do it. Kill the little bitch. Her mother was a Saleri —the *famiglia* will just take it as an insult."

And I could. It's not like I hadn't done it before—used a child to prove a point. The Saleris are a powerful family, but so were the Vanicis once. Power didn't prevent an attack on us. As for punishing Salvatore in this way?

Gino Mangenello reacted similarly when it came to his daughter's life, smug and pompous, so convinced I wouldn't stoop to his level.

"Close your eyes, Kisa," I tell the girl.

She doesn't, her body trembling, tears glistening on her cheeks. With my hand on her shoulder, I manually spin her to face the wall before turning back to Salvatore.

"I could make you beg," I tell him, raising my voice to drown out his gurgling breathing. "Make you squeal and squirm. But you know what? Frankly, I'm too damn tired. All I want is proof. A name. An account. Whatever mercenary you used to carry out your plan. Tell me."

"Fuck off!" He spits again, this time, narrowly missing my cheek.

I don't even realize my hand is in my pocket until I feel it—the handle of a weapon I don't even remember putting there. All this time, I must have carried it with me in these fucking pants. Slowly, I withdraw it, watching the light play off the silvery surface of the tiny blade. *Tigre's* dagger. Safiya's dagger.

"I'm not going to kill you," I tell Salvatore as his eyes twitch toward the blade and back. "You 'kill' animals, like all those fucking toys you have around the place. There's mercy in that word. But what happened to Olivia? That was a slaughter. To Vincenzo?" My voice breaks. I can barely say his name. "That? That was murder."

Salvatore chuckles, and what I mistake for a grimace at first I suspect is another reaction entirely—he's raising an eyebrow. "Don't tell me that whelp is who got his brains blown out? I heard Mischa launched an attack... He just got the wrong man—"

An impulse seizes control of my limbs, and I'm too sober to even try to suppress it. I slam my hand down, driving the knife blade first into his chest. That glorious smell grows more pungent, that song rising to a crescendo. Howling, Salvatore jerks, his eyes rolling, but the wound won't kill him outright. Oh no...

"A name," I demand in a voice that resonates an octave deeper.

Salvatore falls silent as his eyes flicker in recognition. Despite everything, I have to laugh. That wasn't the voice of the good old Donatello I've spent the past few years pretending to be. It's a tone that feels more natural to me than breathing. The guttural cadence of *Il Mostro*.

"A name," I say, relishing in the resulting echo.

All this time, Salvatore's mouth has been wide open. He's trying to scream—he just can't find enough air. Poor bastard.

"Cat got your tongue?" I ask. Then, I rip the blade out to see if that helps.

And it does. He makes a sound this time, sharp and piercing enough to echo in a beautiful song. And that song…

I hum along to the melody—it's music to my fucking ears.

"Give me a name," I command a second time.

He gurgles. Croaks.

But not once does he look at his little girl, shaking with silent tears. Not once does he hold my gaze. Not for one damn second, does he show an ounce of regret.

"You won't tell," I deduce in disgust, rising to my feet. "You always were a secretive little cunt. You're just buying time until your backup arrives. But if you think I'll play your game? Think again. Blowing your brains out is a death far too good for you. But I'll spare your daughter the horror of watching you die. I won't give you the satisfaction."

Turning, I grab the girl by her arm and approach a set of doors on the other end of the room. Time is ticking, and I'd prefer not to waste a second. Still…

As her frightened whimpers reach my ears, some impulse makes me hunt for somewhere to put her. The new Donatello deserves that ounce of mercy. As suspected, the doors open onto a closet —but one so damn big I whistle in approval.

"Nice. Who knew there was so much money in being a lying cunt, huh?" I look back, but Salvatore seems too busy groaning to answer me.

The girl, I leave beside a hanging series of multi-colored suits, tailored finely enough to suit Fabio's most fashionable wet dream. She curls in on herself, her eyes so damn wide. I turn away, clenching my jaw so tight it throbs. As I do, I discover a promising weapon dangling from a custom rack—ties, all of them silk. Grinning, I grab one, a deep crimson which seems fitting for the occasion.

I return to Salvatore, winding the material between my fingers as I scan the room itself. It's an old habit—how I loved to ingrain every moment in my memory. I wasn't the kind of man to shy from his crimes.

I reminisce over them.

Salvatore's bedroom is admittedly one of the most boring places I've killed in. Apart from the king-sized bed, the bastard has a marble fireplace overlooking a view of the property. Not too far from where he lies is a doorway leading to a large bathroom with a sunken tub and gold fixtures.

And there, resting on a gleaming countertop, is an object that renders Salvatore himself nothing more than a liability—a cell phone. I approach the counter and grab it, stroking the smooth surface as I turn to face him.

"You always did like your devices," I say with my own chuckle. I swipe at the screen, unsurprised to find it locked by a passcode. "Laptops. Journals. With your shit for brains, you always had to write shit down to remember it later. Giovanni used to rip you a new one for that." I toss the phone into the air and catch it one-handed. "I suspect this will tell me everything I need to know, won't it?"

His expression alone is my answer—*hell, yes*. And if it's nothing more than a dead-end?

At the moment, I don't fucking care.

"I could say a speech, I suppose," I tell him, stooping back to his level as I slip the phone into the breast pocket of my shirt. "Draw it out. Make it dramatic. But I've realized one thing since we last worked under old Giovanni, old friend. You aren't worth the fucking effort."

Carefully, I raise the tie and watch understanding dawn across his face. The gun would be too quick. Quicker than Olivia suffered.

For him? I make it slow, taking my time to loop the length of silk around his neck. Taking both ends in my hands, I twist them together and tug, carefully controlling the pressure, watching every second.

How his eyes bulge.

How he flails.

How his face reddens before turning blue as he sputters for air.

I once told myself that revenge wasn't worth the damage it inflicted in the long run. A man can only sow so much evil in the world before it comes back to him tenfold. I wasn't much of a saint before Olivia died. Hell, to tell the truth?

I deserved to lose her.

I deserve to die.

But Vin didn't.

Even as Salvatore finally goes still, his eyes bug wide; it doesn't feel good enough. Grisly enough. Brutal enough. Hissing through my teeth, I kick the son of a bitch, hearing bone crack in response.

Apart from a slight throbbing of my big toe, I don't feel a damn thing.

No relief.

No satisfaction.

Just pain.

Swaying on my feet, I scan the room and find a wooden series of cabinets near the fireplace. My hands shake as I wrench open the doors of one. Sure enough, inside one is a fully stocked minibar. Antonio was almost as bad of a drunk as I am. I grab a bottle at random and down half of it before a sudden sound makes me drop the damn thing.

It shatters in a spray of scarlet liquid as I look over to the closet. The doors are open, and a tiny figure stands there watching me, her eyes so wide, just like Safiya's.

Safiya…

I traumatized her in much the same way, though I let that girl live even if in hell. But now? This dark, twisted impulse warns me not to make the same mistake twice.

"Kisa?" I ask her gruffly. "Is that your name?"

She doesn't answer.

"I could let you go," I tell her, advancing on her position. "But in seven years, you might come back…"

I crouch beside her and look into those eyes…

And even the icy mindset I crave can't break this last bastion of the new Donatello.

Hissing, I grab her, throwing her over my shoulder.

Unlike Safy, she screams. Pummels me with tiny little fists. Each blow lands harmlessly as I cross to the bar and shove a bottle of clear liquor into my pocket.

Grunting with the effort, I carry her down the stairs and out of the mansion where what I assume are *famiglia* reinforcements fan out across the lawn, guns drawn.

My, how the mighty have fallen.

In my day? Three times as many men would have been already stationed on the property in fucking uniform. These men wear jeans and shirts as if scrambled here from a night at the bar.

"Get down, you son of a bitch!" A man calls from a group of at least four.

One look at the girl, and they fall back.

Aware of that, I shift her tiny body, holding her in front of me, my arm around her waist while I keep the gun trained in my free hand.

I'm not fool enough to think it will stop them—hell, would it even stop me? Regardless, I keep moving, carrying her right to the car. One of the men steps toward me, and I fire without thinking. He goes down with a howl, clutching at his leg.

"Salvatore's dead," I say coldly, preempting any other threat.

Against me, the girl stiffens, and my steps falter...

I didn't even have the balls to tell Safiya as much back then. I couldn't even give her a reason to her face. Why I sold her. Why I needed to hate her in that moment.

Because her father betrayed me.

But the truth is more twisted than that. Crueler.

By hurting Safiya, I wasn't hurting Gino.

I hurt myself—and God, I *needed* to hurt.

"Don… Donatello?" one of the men calls. I brace for a shot, but none comes. In the dark, I vaguely recognize his face as a *famiglia* lieutenant. Luciano.

"Come after me if you want," I declare, approaching the car as they watch. I head to the driver's seat and find a lever to pop the trunk. Still keeping the girl within view of the men, I move toward the rear of the vehicle and drop her inside. She's fallen silent, curling onto the floor of the compartment.

For a second, guilt almost levels me, slicing through the haze of rage.

Before it can take hold, I slam the lid and turn around. All this time, my back has been to the men, but they haven't moved, even as their comrade groans on the ground.

And deep down, I think I know why.

That name I've struggled to outrun. That reputation I've tried to redeem.

An identity I know now I can never fully shake.

Under *Il Mostro*, the *famiglia* was untouchable, an outfit unrivaled. Even now, it seems some men still remember those days.

"If you want to see the *famiglia* respected again, then wait for me to call," I say, letting my voice ring out.

As I return to the driver's seat, no one fires a single round.

Even as I drive away.

24

WILLOW

The Donatello I knew was a man who, at his core, embodied everything I grew up admiring. Strength. Wisdom. Most important? Kindness.

I still remember the first day I met him, hiding behind my biological father's pant leg as he paraded me before his boss.

The memory hurts to relive, and I've resisted it so bitterly until now.

Gino Mangenello was the type of man who saw those in his orbit merely as tools. Even me. At my young age, I knew my worth—to him, I was more of a doll than a daughter. A toy he could use to curry favor.

Or a pawn he could leave on a shelf in the meantime.

That day, his friend "Don" had stared down on me from behind a massive desk at the old complex he and my father "worked" at, a sprawling mansion outside of the city. What they did exactly? I didn't know, only that Donatello was a man that even Gino—a brutal drunk who raged at everyone weaker—deferred to.

Fully aware of that reputation, I'd been so shy in his presence. So curious of this man, my father so respected.

I remember inspecting every inch of his loose-fitting gray dress shirt with the sleeves rolled up to his elbows. It was ugly. The first two buttons had been left undone, revealing a sliver of his chest and a tiny gold cross he wore back then. Cautiously, I'd observed the bold features that shaped his face, and the pink lips pressed studiously in concentration as he inspected a set of documents. The second he looked up, I didn't feel that strange disconnect I did when most people observed me, knowing that I was different.

"Dumb as a fucking rock," Gino used to gripe. *"Retarded."*

He growled at me, using his fist when he couldn't understand me as easily as he wanted. Honestly, the reactions of others were far worse to endure. They would exaggerate their features and speak too loudly as though the dramatics made up for the fact that I couldn't talk back.

Maybe it made them feel better. They could project onto me their own intentions as though I were a pretty, smiling little puppet.

Donatello Vanici didn't. He eyed me as though he knew exactly what I was thinking. With a dark eyebrow raised and his head quirked, he could see every thought and feeling written clearly across my face.

"Your father told me about you, Safiya," he'd said to me sternly that very first day. "He said you were a quiet, mindful little girl. I can take one look at you and see that he was wrong."

Gino had stiffened, laughing nervously while I'd gone still in horror, my tiny cheeks flushing. It was a directness that no one had ever presented me with, and I was sure he would use it against me.

Already, I could sense the beating brewing if this meeting went poorly.

But with a booming laugh, Donatello surprised me again. His face transformed in an instant, and he withdrew a handful of sweets from nowhere, presenting them to me on his massive palm. "You look like you enjoy fun, eh? And even silent, you aren't shy about what you're thinking. Is my shirt really that ugly?"

Instantly I knew that he was different, a man apart from my father or the others he associated with.

Perhaps, I remember hoping, a man I could trust…

And even though he left me. Forgot me. Couldn't even recognize my face as I stood before him; I know one truth in the pit of my soul, despite how hard it stings to acknowledge—the man I knew would never send his thugs to attack a woman and her child.

Much like he dragged me into Nicolai Baryshnikov's lair himself, he would mount such an assault. If he wanted to harm Mischa, he would do it himself. No one else.

In a way, Mischa is the same, and his absence chills me to my core, distracting me all morning though I do my best to put on a smile for the children.

They're worried.

Marnie and Aljona cling to each other, barely touching their toys while Ivan lurks in the corner of the nursery, a book under his arm. By bedtime, Mischa still hasn't returned.

Tension poisons the air, and I suspect even the children can pick up on it, though they don't mention their father, or Ellen, or Eli once.

At least until I tuck Aljona beneath her blankets and she demands, "Where is Mama?"

"She's sick," Ivan says matter-of-factly, already having crawled beneath his own blankets.

Marnie whimpers. "Sick?"

I shake my head, smoothing back her curls as she ignores her own bed and crawls in beside her sister. Holding each of their hands, I remain beside them until they finally drift off.

"I don't need to be tucked in," Ivan says as I stand and inch my way toward his corner of the room. Nonetheless, he submits to a kiss on the forehead.

Beyond the nursery, moonlight illuminates the darkened hallways, casting shadows that sway like phantoms. One looms over me as I enter the wing of the house overlooking the front entrance. My imagination runs wild, transforming the swaying shape into a solid figure, one so tall I have to crane my neck back to take him in. Fathomless, his eyes meet mine accusingly.

He's not real. I know that.

Still, I hear him in my head. *You wanted your revenge, Safiya?* he taunts. *Well, you've gotten it. How will Mischa enact it for you? A shot to the head? A knife to the throat? Either way, he won't fail like you did.*

His rich laughter haunts me as I advance toward a row of windows with a view of the main driveway. I have a clear look at the road from them, and at a glance, I can tell that Mischa hasn't returned yet.

He's probably washing the blood from his hands, the specter of Donatello murmurs near my ear. *Don't pout. It's what you wanted, isn't it? Me dead—though you can't even be honest with yourself as to the real reason why?*

I shake my head, fighting to ignore the thoughts.

But they persist, feeding on the unease building in my stomach with every second that Mischa remains gone.

You were jealous, that voice hisses, impossible to escape. *It wasn't that I threw you away that hurt you so much, Safiya. It's that I kept Vincenzo. I always loved him more than you. Always. You knew from the day I took you in that you were nothing more than a burden, always on borrowed time.*

I can see that very day unfolding before me. My father had made me pack a bag, telling me that I was going on a "vacation" for a little while.

But we never went on vacation.

And, given his lack of a suitcase, he wasn't coming.

On our way from our small, cramped house, we'd passed by mother lying on the couch, too drunk to acknowledge my leaving.

Even now, my heart flutters as I recall that very first day that I saw Havienna, that big beautiful house in the countryside. A pair of oak trees had shielded the front path, perfectly framing the stone cottage with its big red door.

Donatello himself met us on the front steps. As he descended them to greet me, he tripped over a cracked piece of stone and cursed. "This damn place. It's falling apart."

But to me?

Then and there, I knew one certainty—it was paradise.

Laughing, his wife Olivia had scolded him from the doorway, "Language in front of your little guest, Donatello." Her laugh was infectious, sending him into his own raucous bout of mirth.

And I just remember standing still, watching him. Dappled by morning sunlight, he was a figure unlike any I'd ever known, and as our gazes met, he smiled in that reassuring way. Even the memory makes me shiver. One quirk of his upper lip, and I would feel so safe…

As my father drove off, he crouched to my level, taking my small suitcase in his hand.

"I won't lie to you," he warned. "I can take one look at your face and realize that you understand what's really going on. You aren't here on 'vacation.' You are my guest. For as long as you need to stay here, you are welcome."

And looking back, I realize something the little girl I used to be had been too naïve to understand. Even then, he always left a route for him to rescind his offer whenever the urge struck him.

But you can admit that day didn't come out of the blue, the phantom of him hisses. *Did it?*

No.

The day Olivia died was the day the Don I knew changed forever. He'd been colder after, more prone to isolating himself in his study rather than spending the evening playing games with

Vincenzo and me like he used to. Most telling? He never once looked me in the eye as if avoiding the truth he knew he'd find there.

I had been so worried about him.

Because as well as he could read me, I could interpret him just as adeptly. I knew him. Deciphering every nuance to color his expression came as naturally to me as reading the words in a book. I understood how to read his many smiles. How to scour his face for a hint of softening.

And I knew the way his eyes narrowed when he sensed my presence after Olivia's death—a reaction he never displayed before. How he'd stiffen when I tried to meet his gaze. There was more to his response than grief.

And, even at that age, I knew that few men knew the way to Havienna. Knew that Olivia would be there.

Knew how to truly hurt Donatello Vanici.

And somehow, in my heart, I knew why my Don's love for me turned to something else overnight. Hatred.

Because my father's betrayal led to Olivia's murder.

A flash of bright light snaps me back to the present. Beyond the window, a vehicle approaches, driving slowly up the long winding road leading to the house. My heart pounds against my ribcage as I recognize the shape of the sturdy van—one of Mischa's.

Turning on my heel, I race down to the main entrance just as the massive doors open in tandem. I stop short before I even realize why.

The smell reaches me first—a sharp scent I've never sensed from Mischa before. Alcohol. A lot of it. Shadows drape his form, obscuring his expression, but he stands rigid, moving slowly in a way I barely recognize. I step forward as a million fears race through my mind. Is he injured?

Slowly, he turns in my direction, his head cocked. I wait for him to speak. Acknowledge me. Anything.

But all he does is keep walking, trudging down the hall toward his study without a word.

On his heels is another man who races through the main doors, closing them behind him. Evgeni. He takes one look at me and sighs, shaking his head.

"You should go to bed, Ms. Willow."

He heads after Mischa, leaving me alone in the entryway. Silence falls again, seeming so unnatural in this large house.

The same quiet fell over Havienna the first night Donatello mourned his wife. How he could even manage to stay in that house, I'll never know. I remember how he hugged Vincenzo to him as though God himself couldn't tear the boy away.

As for me...

He didn't make me pack a bag like my father had. He didn't feed me some lie about a "vacation" that would span the better part of two years. Donatello said nothing to me at all until we finally reached our destination, a foreboding, unfamiliar fortress far from what had become my home. I recall clinging to his hand so tightly it hurt, desperate to find the warmth in his touch I usually could.

But he was stone that day, ice-cold as he wrenched his fingers from mine.

Then he left me there.

Tears sting as I blink them back. Swallowing hard, I find myself creeping down the hall in the direction of Mischa's study. Paces down from the room, his voice reaches me, so gruff and hollow, his accent thicker than ever.

"You can hold your mothering," he growls, presumably to Evgeni. "It's already done. Have your men patrol the perimeter tonight. I wouldn't put it past him to retaliate soon."

"Yes, sir," Evgeni replies in a crisp tone that makes my breath catch in my throat. I know him well enough to predict his expression even before I near the doorway and peer inside. He stands beside Mischa's desk, his hands clasped behind his back— but as expected, his expression is constricted, visible in the moonlight streaming in from the window. I don't think I've ever seen the faithful bodyguard so troubled in the presence of his employer.

The two men stand in the dark apart from the silvery glow emanating from outside. Mischa leans over his desk, his hands braced against the surface. Head lowered, his hair falls wildly down his shoulders, obscuring his face.

"You want to say something," he snaps. "So say it."

"Vanici may have been behind the attack, but going after the man directly could start a war that I doubt you truly want."

Mischa scoffs. "It's too late for your scolding—but I'm sure you know that."

My blood runs cold. I turn, bracing my back against the wall for stability as the air sticks to the inside of my lungs.

Donatello...dead? It's a reality I've told myself over and over that I wanted. The only way to move on from him. Forget him.

I try to picture him lying lifeless, those dark eyes closed forever, his laugh silenced—and I don't feel an ounce of joy or satisfaction.

I just feel cold.

"The man will want his revenge," Mischa says, and something in his tone draws my attention back to him. With difficulty, I focus on his voice, trying to decipher the words he says. "And he can come after it if he wants. He will lose more than his son."

Confusion rips through me as my brain tries to identify the unnamed figures. *He* as in Donatello. And as for his son...

Vincenzo.

Maybe I've always known, the same way I know Mischa and how he responds to his enemies—violently and callously, rarely striking them head-on at first. He prefers to make them suffer. The same way he kidnapped Ellen to prove a point to her first husband. He wouldn't attack Donatello directly.

He'd do the next best thing and attack the one person whose loss would hurt him the most.

I barely register wandering down the hall on trembling legs. My fingers flex against the icy wall as I brace myself in some distant corridor.

Left in turmoil, my thoughts are a tangled mess of fear and doubt. Donatello gave me away without a second thought. Then he martyred that girl and turned her into some kind of saint. But now?

All I can do is think of him.

His pain.

And his rage.

I know Mischa well. I once knew Donatello even better. If Vin is really gone, nothing will hold him back.

And no one.

*N*icolai Baryshnikov was a tall man with piercing green eyes that seemed to cut through me like a knife. He ruled his domain like a tyrant, one with a vicious streak who preferred for those under his control to *resist* his commands.

Then he could break their will to the point they never questioned him again.

To such a man, even a little girl was nothing more than a tool to be utilized as he saw fit. And yet…

Looking back, I can admit that much of his brutality might have been for show. Those first few weeks in his custody, I was beaten and put to work around what little of his complex I was allowed in—just a few rooms and the kitchens. But as an adult with the knowledge of the true horrors this world has to offer, I know it could have been worse.

And Donatello expected as much. He didn't give a damn about what might happen to me.

He wanted me broken.

Brutalized.

He wanted me dead.

I shouldn't shed a single tear for him—and I'm startled to realize that I'm not. I don't sob or weep even while my steps carry me into another wing of the house. All the same, my body rebels against my mind.

I'm in my room, crossing to my bed without understanding why. At least not until I sink down and feel underneath the frame for a crumbled item I vaguely remember dropping here the day I was brought home from Havienna. My fingers curl around it and, trembling, I lift it, straining my eyes to view it in the dark —a business card with a number printed on it.

A number that's entirely useless considering that I don't have a cell phone—according to Mischa, I don't require one. While at school, I'm rarely alone. Any communication between us was always done with the aid of a bodyguard's device.

Still, I stand, moving toward the servant's entrance, my mind racing.

Mischa owns several vehicles for various purposes. Most are kept in a large garage several yards from the main house. The second I creep down the narrow hall before the back exit, murmuring voices catch my ears.

"I'll take the first shift on the perimeter," a man says, "then I'll switch to the gate. New rules say that everyone takes double shifts. No inch of the property goes unpatrolled, so cut your break short, so I can charge my battery, lazy ass."

"I'm guarding this entrance," a man replies with a yawn. "I've been outside all damn day."

"Alexi is watching this side of the house," the other man snaps. "So, you'll be on the south lawn."

A heavy sigh echoes in the wake of the warning. "Let me at least take a shit first," the second man replies. "Don't touch my phone, either. You can wait to charge your own. Your little girlfriend can wait five damn minutes for you to reply to her sexy little photos, eh?"

"Asshole."

Both men storm off, their steps echoing in the opposite direction. Cautiously, I creep forward and spy the narrow room off the entrance where the servants sometimes take their breaks. Attached to a cord in the wall is a plain, black cell phone. Without thinking through the consequences, I dart forward and grab it.

Silently, I backtrack and retrace my steps to the main hall. Apart from the servant's entrance, there's a side door on the other end of the house for deliveries. Sometimes, Eli and I would play here, dashing down the halls.

A sturdy lock on the door complete with a passcode always left it less patrolled than the other entrances. Eli, as smart as he is, figured it out by the time he was eight and spied on a servant accessing it.

Even years later, that same code works, and the door opens with a musical ping. Cautiously, I creep out into the west side of the property. Flashing headlights betray a passing van. Another in the distance reinforces the previous guard's observation. Mischa's set the entire security on high alert.

To evade them, I have to rely on the skills I haven't used since childhood. The three of us used to play hide and seek on every stretch of this vast property—me, Mischa, and Eli. My favorite hiding spot was an oak tree near the very edge of the property. If I climbed it high enough, I had a clear view above the stone wall lining the perimeter.

I find my way there in the dark, treading over the damp earth of the west lawn. I'm barefoot, wearing nothing but a pale sundress Ellen bought me two summers ago. Why I chose it now, I don't know.

I don't even know why I'm trying to find a way out at all.

Or what I plan to do afterward. Finding Donatello now would be insanity. Reckless. Suicidal. Besides, he could be anywhere.

And yet…

I'm running through the shadows, trying to evade detection.

Maybe it's a grim need to see his face. To gloat?

Or to grieve.

After everything he's done to me. Everything I've been through since his return.

I deserve to see him now, no matter the reasons.

Or so I tell myself.

And there is one place he would go—the one structure haunting us both.

25

DON

*H*avienna laughs as I approach, the place where everything began. Once my haven, these old stone walls were the last place I experienced my family intact—and the hell where I watched it fall apart. And now? This house is the very purgatory where my Safiya returned with a vengeance.

It's an irony even someone as twisted as Antonio Salvatore couldn't devise. The little cub grew into a tiger, and she got the revenge her parents could only dream of.

Damn her.

Damn...

As the moon rises high in the sky, I park near the abandoned garage behind the house and climb out, staggering toward the old structure. All it contains now are canisters of lighter fluid and dust-covered wood for the fireplace.

With the liquor bottle from Salvatore's in hand, I head for the house, leaving the car behind without even looking at the trunk.

This damn house. It mocks me as I enter through the kitchen in utter darkness. Even after seven years, I know the floor plan by heart. This modest room with its old appliances was where Olivia spent more time burning our meals than preparing them. Still, it was in her nature to try something over and over until she succeeded.

Safiya was the same way. She excelled at proving wrong anyone foolish enough to doubt her. And yet, at her core, she was sweet. Kind. A girl who strived for peace above all else. Vin, as good as he was, could be stubborn, prone to grudges from time to time.

But never her. Not Safiya.

At least, until now.

I don't think I've fully let myself process it. I haven't pored over the mental image of her all grown up, trying to compare it to the little girl I knew.

With the speed of an old man, I move to the staircase and climb it, wincing at the memories. Her room was the last on the left, beside Vin's.

My heavy breathing echoes in the air as I curl my hand around the doorknob. Turn it. Push it open.

A cloud of dust swirls to lift, illuminated by a stream of moonlight. I don't bother to switch on a lamp. Even in the darkness, I can tell it's the same. Her pink walls. The wooden bed frame pushed against the wall. Her nightstand—even her old bell is there, something Vin devised for if she needed help, and no one was in view.

But that's all that remains of her. Everything else I had packed up. I had been too much of a coward to do it myself, assigning Fabio to the task.

All of her books, her toys, her little dresses. Gone.

And, like the pathetic son of a bitch that I am, I wish I had them now. Something to tie me to that lost little girl, my Safiya.

Something tangible to torture myself over.

As it stands, I only have my own fucking memories. With a sigh, I raise the bottle I took from Salvatore's. Crouching on the edge of the tiny bed frame, I drink.

And drink.

Intoxication isn't the aim this time—just relief. Numbing myself numbs those memories of her, if only for a second.

But this place persists, driving the past into my skull despite my blurring vision and fractured thoughts.

My girl. My sweet, innocent Safy.

I will never forget the look on her face the day I left her behind.

But another expression creeps into my skull, supplanting it. A beautiful woman with haunting dark eyes who, in every sense of the word, is a stranger. A woman with a face so enchanting that I hate myself for the thoughts that crept into my skull as I saw her. That body. That supple mouth.

In some ways, Safiya's supposed future self is a fitting punishment. I threw her away, but she survived, finding a man who could protect her better than I ever could. A man who could give her a world she would never have access to as a Vanici.

A man who protected her. Cherished her.

Killed for her.

It should be Mischa's blood speckling my chin right now, not Antonio Salvatore's. Mischa, whose demise dominates my fantasies. Mischa, with his perfect, cherished family hidden safely behind their high walls.

I could show him how easily such a fortress can be breached. How it would only take a few bullets to shatter his carefully cultivated paradise.

And how that pain could drive any man insane.

The loss of sanity is something you don't realize at first. Not until the day you're guzzling whiskey just to keep your thoughts clear.

But what's the point?

I could hurt Mischa. Hate him.

But my head is spinning, throbbing badly enough to outweigh the rage. To rectify it, I grab the clear bottle resting at my feet and drain it. Then I stand and leave this room, trudging back down the hall without any clear destination in mind.

I'm outside again, observing the house in the moonlight. I used to dream of torching it. Setting the entire damn thing ablaze and watching it burn.

But Vincenzo loved it. I kept it, hoping to give it to him one day when he could do as he wished with it. Maybe raise a family here. Salvage the darkness that tainted our once beloved home.

But now?

Those dreams die with him, and there's nothing left to hope for. This goddamn house should go the same way.

I march to the garage and grab the red bottle of old lighter fluid along with an old book of matches. At the back of my mind, I doubt I even have the balls to go through with it. Still, I carry it back into the house, moving blindly from room to room. Eventually, numbness sets in, turning my limbs to lead. I find myself slumping into a chair, my gaze unfocused.

I'm in the study of all places, sitting in the same chair I left the little imposter Safiya in. If I breathe in deeply enough, I can still smell her. Fresh. Like a field of fucking roses.

It's so real.

And then I see her, pale and slim, she hovers near the doorway. A plain dress makes her the most innocent apparition. A hauntingly beautiful one as well. I snarl at her. Then I sigh.

"I knew you'd come," I tell her, pointing the tip of the bottle at her face. It's a cruel twist of irony that she's beautiful.

She blinks, shock painting her delicate cheeks pink.

I stand, approaching her unsteadily. My hand finds that cheek, cradling it against my palm. Her lips part beneath the pressure of my thumb, and I can't silence a groan. So pink. So pretty.

She could be real…

"Come to laugh at me from hell, Safiya?" I ask her, brushing my lips along her jaw. My brain is a cruel fuck. I can smell her more clearly, how I think she'd smell anyway. Fresh. Sweet. Her warmth is an echo biting through my numb fingers.

It's the goddamn alcohol that does this to me. Makes me imagine her so damn clearly. Makes me notice things a man like me never should about a woman so young. My Safy…

I cup her chin with one hand and rake the other through her hair—though it's not like she could run away. She's paralyzed, this apparition. Her eyes meet mine, so wide. So goddamn bright.

Another groan rips from me as I press my forehead to hers, sensing the small body trembling against mine. She's afraid of me, this phantom Safiya.

And she should be.

I fist my fingers brutally through the thick strands, drawing her closer. I can hear the air entering her nostrils and leaving her chest in little pants, but even in my head, she doesn't scream.

Good.

I press her against the wall, inhaling at the way she feels. Small breasts, narrow hips. I cup one against my hand and hiss in amusement. It's disgusting how slight she is. How delicate.

"You are a sick son of a bitch, Donatello," I tell myself.

But I can pay for my sins in hell—I'm already on my way there.

"You came to watch me die, Safy?" I open my eyes to find her staring back, but again my own imagination surprises me. Wetness glistens on her cheek, and I swipe my finger against it, marveling at the glistening residue.

Something in my chest clenches, but I force whatever emotion it might be away.

"No!" I growl against the hollow of her throat. "You don't get to haunt me like this, Safy. I want you to laugh. Smile." I close my eyes and open them again, expecting it to happen like magic.

Her tortured frown would be replaced by a ghoulish grin. She'd laugh somehow. It's all in my fucking head; what does logic matter?

But she can't even give me that. She watches me in horror, her eyes so damn wide, her chest heaving, lips trembling.

And I'm too weak. Too drunk. Too tired.

"You know what is worse than knowing you're alive?" I ask her, following that sweet scent to the crook of her shoulder. Shamelessly I inhale, keeping her pinned in place—though she doesn't fight. "Do you?" I laugh, but the sound echoes back like a mongrel's howl, pathetic and wild. "It's that you're so damn beautiful. I wanted to fuck you, Safy. How sick is that?"

It's a reaction fit for a degenerate. A pathetic fool who failed anyone foolish enough to love him. Over and over again.

"Do you want to know why I did it?" I tell her, a confession admissible only now. Here in Havienna. "Do you?" I murmur against her ear. But she won't answer even in this form. "Because you would hurt. Losing you would hurt so bad, and that pain would be enough, Safy. Enough to keep me going. Make me fight and kill those bastards where they stood. I would have crumbled without that pain."

I stroke her delicate jaw and search those eyes for any hint of understanding. More tears fall silently, each one more disarming than the last.

"I loved you so much," I confess, my throat tight. "So much. You were my little *principessa*. I would have done anything in the world for you. Anything… But I needed to hate you, Safy. Because if I could lose you, I could survive anything."

But I was wrong. I didn't survive what I did to her. All this time, I haven't been living, just crawling through time, barely coherent enough to witness it passing.

And now with Vin gone…

"I'll join you soon, the real you." The little girl who doesn't belong to Mischa Stepanov. "I'm sorry, Safy. I'm so sorry."

But, as always, she doesn't do a damn thing other than watch me, tears streaming from those beautiful eyes. I swipe at them, again startled by how real they feel. How wet.

"It's the alcohol," I murmur to myself, laughing.

But curiosity is a twisted fucking thing. I press against her and hiss through my teeth. She feels real, so small that even touching her like this feels dangerous. Like I might break her. Crush her.

And she would deserve it.

"You did it, Safy," I say. My fingers twitch for that slender neck, but I stop myself, only to laugh. Even against a shadow of her, I hold back, cringing in guilt.

No more. Gritting my teeth, I encircle that column in both hands, forcing her to meet my gaze. Slowly, I squeeze, watching those eyes go bug wide. Her hands fly to mine, clawing weakly, but she doesn't fight like the real girl would.

She just watches me, sobbing silently, and I realize just what emotion she's conveying. No hatred.

Just pity.

"You took it all away, didn't you, Safy?"

I let her go and return to the desk. Grabbing the bottle of lighter fluid, I wrench off the cap and nearly choke at the goddamn smell. I fumble for the matches in my other hand. When I turn around, she's still watching, her eyes even wider, and God damn me for the observation that crosses my mind—horror on her is so lovely. I hate myself for appreciating that. How perfectly my brain can represent this grown figment of her when I've spent years banishing her memory.

"Here's to you, Safy—" I lift the bottle in a mock salute. Then I upturn it over my head. The liquid clings to me, dribbling over my nostrils and down my lips. I smell nothing anymore. Feel nothing. Laughing, I inspect the book of matches and hunt for the best one, and I find it; a defective strip smaller than the rest.

It will be a bitch to light, and I deserve the struggle. I rip it from the packet and prepare to strike it.

The force that slams into me is so slight I barely notice it. Regardless, the matchbook slips from my grasp, tugged free by slender fingers that shouldn't have the strength to do so. I take them back, but that insistent touch persists.

I'm insane. Laughter rips from me so violently I clutch my stomach. After all these years, I've finally lost it. But of all things for my brain to conjure, this one is beyond belief even for a desperate man—Safy, stopping me from ending my miserable life.

She claws at the matches, wrenching them away. But it's even easier to snatch them back. Her warmth comes as a greater shock this time, as does the solidness of her limbs. Her touch. Those eyes.

"If you want to watch, just watch," I growl, readjusting my grip on the match. "Enjoy the show—"

She lunges at me; this time, her weight knocks me back against the desk. Tiny nails gouge at my forearm as she tries to steal the matches again. I lash out with the back of my hand, and she goes flying.

But she doesn't vanish. Curled on her side, she stares up at me, blood dribbling down her chin. Real, red blood…

I clutch my skull and blink just to clear my vision. This is too damn much. Too surreal. But when I return to that spot on the floor, she's still there.

"Fine." I crouch and snatch the bottle of fluid, crossing to her. I overturn it, dousing her in what little liquid is left. She gapes in shock, her damp hair clinging to her slender shoulders.

"We both can die if that's how you want it." I rip a new match free and aim the tip against the back of the matchbook, but I never move to strike it.

She grabs at my knee, straining the fabric of my pants. I can feel her nails. Her trembling. *Fuck,* I can feel the pulse surging beneath her skin.

"Damn you…" I sink to my knees, cradling my head in my hands. "What the fuck do you want from me? Tell me!"

She's silent, of course.

So goddamn silent.

"You want me to suffer, is that it? I can't even die. You want me to stay here and suffer for what I did to you."

Softness flutters against my cheek. It's not real, but I react to it anyway, opening my eyes to find an endless pair staring back. I reach out, brushing my fingers along that beautiful cheek, down to her throat. I encircle my fingers around it, gripping tight, so hard her eyes bulge.

"Is this what you want?" I ask her.

She bats at me, but I shove her down, pinning the specter to the floor. With both hands, I squeeze so hard… I could break her neck if she were real.

"If I kill you, Safy, will you finally go away?"

Her limbs jerk beneath me, her pink cheeks losing their color, her lips parting wordlessly. But even now, railing against the shadows, I can't hurt her. My hands slip from her skin, and I sink against her, even more alarmed by how real she feels. Air wheezes in and out of her throat, her body limp, eyes still staring.

I seek out refuge against her shoulder, pulling her against me so that she can't turn away. My sick brain makes her react to me how she never would in reality. Her fingers fist through my hair, her breathing heavy.

And even though she's a phantom, her nearness has an effect on me it shouldn't—a calmness deeper than what a joke from Vin could instill.

A grotesque amalgam of peace.

Horrible, mind-numbing peace.

26

WILLOW

I'm in a dream. A nightmare. In it, I leave the safe protection of my family home and venture into a world of darkness.

Draped beneath the shadows, I walk right into the lair of a monster—a tormented beast who seems determined to destroy me.

But somehow, I wind up lying in his arms, tasting blood on my tongue, suffering his scent in my lungs, unable to move. I'd consoled myself with the lie that I was here to gloat over him. To relish in my triumph and watch him suffer as I once suffered.

But as his breath fans my throat, the tears falling from my eyes won't cease. The silent sobs wracking my chest only grow in intensity, each one threatening to launch my heart from my ribcage.

But the physical pain is a welcome distraction from the agony clawing through my mind, scrambling any coherent thought. Horrified, I can only lie here and bear the onslaught.

Watching Donatello Vanici in the throes of madness should draw laughter from me. Not sobs. Not guilt.

His pain shouldn't hurt this much.

Closing my eyes against him, I try to examine my emotions. This man betrayed me. Abandoned me. Hurt me in ways I never thought possible to hurt.

Until now.

I could always comfort myself with the idea that what I'm feeling is jealousy. In the end, Mischa wrought this revenge, not me.

My pounding heartbeat resonates through my eardrums as if to counter that lie. For the same reason, I didn't kill him at the hotel, and the reason why I came here in the middle of the night…

I'm here because he always had a hold over me.

And now… I'm at his mercy.

Shivers wrack my body as he stirs, groaning. My cheeks flame as the masculine sound ripples through me, raising goosebumps over my skin. The only other man I've ever been this close to is, well him.

His knee is between my legs, his hands clasped behind my back, locking me to him, chest to chest with his mouth against my throat.

He mumbles something unintelligible, and I jump as sturdy warmth brushes my shoulder.

"You," he croaks in a tone I barely recognize.

Shock startles me into opening my eyes, and I tremble at the sight that meets them. A nightmare would be preferable to this

—Donatello so close. He's awake, his eyes unfocused and wild, his breath tinged with a sickening amount of alcohol.

And lighter fluid. We both reek of the cloying substance.

"You can't be here," he tells me, his voice hoarse. "You aren't real…"

He sounds so convinced. So…angry—at himself for daring to envision me, this corrupted version of his precious Safy. Frowning, he runs his thumb beneath my nose and frowns. Red paints the tip, and he shakes his head with a hollow laugh. "This blood isn't real." But confusion shatters the confidence in his voice.

I'm hurt, marred with the physical injuries inflicted by him. My throat aches, bruised by his touch. My nose smarts, and I can taste the hint of blood on my tongue. Fear should embolden me to resist him now. Fight.

Not stare.

Like a man utterly lost, he shakes his head, his nostrils flaring as he looks down, eyeing our close, entwined bodies. Something dark crosses his gaze, tightening the line of his mouth, exaggerating the wrinkles crinkling the skin. My breath catches, watching the nuances of his expression shift and change.

Gone is the wild pain that made my heart ache in the face of it.

Bit by bit, the focus returns to those piercing eyes, honing them into narrowed slits. Abruptly, he withdraws from me and stands. Without his heat, I'm freezing, my teeth chattering.

"You're not real," he says, breathing heavily.

But with every breath of air to enter his lungs, I know that he can sense the same pungent odors that I can—things far too real to exist in a dream.

Or a nightmare.

Blood.

Tears.

Lighter fluid.

Something in my belly unfurls, urging me to move. *Run!*

I barely twitch a muscle before his hand flies out, latching onto a fistful of my hair. Grunting, he drags me to him, heedless of the pain blazing across my skull. Tears sting my eyes, but I'm alarmed to realize that they never stopped falling.

Blurred, his shape looms above me, his lips a pinkish smear moving, his voice a growl.

"You aren't real," he insists. "But if you are…" He tugs me to my feet so swiftly stars dance across my vision. I stagger, desperate to find any traction over the cold wood beneath my feet.

He's unmoving, but as my vision clears, I'm more confused than ever.

Why am I here, facing this man?

Because, whoever he is…

He is not Donatello Vanici.

Bloodshot dark eyes glare into my own, slicing through me with the ease of a knife. That mouth, composed of lips I used to easily goad into a smile, flatten against me, and I suppose he lets me go more out of shock than mercy.

"Safiya."

Hearing that name stings—again, there's so much reverence in it.

Lowering his gaze to the floor, he sighs. "Willow Stepanova. But no," he says, shaking his head. Turning his back to me, he laughs, and the sound is chilling.

It's a madman's wail.

"Willow Stepanova wouldn't come to me, no. Unless it's to gloat. Your father got your revenge, didn't he? Didn't he?"

I flinch in the face of his shout—that brutal baritone I've only heard once before as he bellowed at a man who made a mistake that cost him money.

"Is Mischa waiting for me, outside, huh?" He grabs my arm and storms into the foyer so quickly I have to stumble to keep up. Still laughing, he throws open the front door, glowering into the pale dawn light.

"Come out, come out, Mischa!" He shouts, hauling me after him down the front steps.

It's a twisted reversal of our first meeting. That day he helped me up these very steps, his touch comforting.

Not restraining. Now, his nails dig in uncaringly, no doubt drawing blood as he hunts for enemies among the trees swaying in the morning breeze.

"Come out!"

Despite how loudly he demands as much, no one comes to meet him.

He wrenches me around to face him. "Where is he? Waiting to take his shot?" Shoving me back, he steps forward, his arms outstretched. "Take your fucking shot, you son of a bitch! I'm ready."

My pulse surges—I'm terrified. But not for the reasons I should be. I can hear the honesty in his voice. The desperation.

He's not cockily boasting.

He's begging.

One touch—I don't even realize I'm doing it, swiping my fingers along his forearm.

He jumps violently, whirling to face me. His constricted expression reveals that he would prefer to take a bullet from a gun. Anything but have me touch him like that.

Like I don't hate him.

He snatches my arm, pulling me against him. Our chests slam together as he forces eye contact, staring me down. Whatever he finds in my gaze makes him scoff. Then utter a cry in between a groan and something more primal. Guttural.

His free hand ghosts my cheek, his thumb tracing the curve of my mouth. Each stroke of his thumb applies more pressure as understanding shapes his exhausted features. It's like watching a corpse come back to life.

Fire ignites in those fathomless irises. Color returns to his cheeks, giving his golden skin more definition, and finally…

His finger quivers against my skin, and he releases me.

Before I can think to move, he grabs me again, capturing my waist in both hands. In a quick motion, he hauls me over his shoulder, marching across the property.

I'm too stunned to react the way I should. My hand curls into a fist that lands harmlessly against his back, but by then, he's already approaching a car parked alongside the old garage.

The front is horribly dented, the windshield cracked, but he opens the driver's side door without hesitation and finds the release for the trunk. He carries me toward it, and I struggle, but when I see what lies in the bed of the compartment, I go limp, my lips parted around a gasp I can't voice.

Huge blue eyes meet mine, glazed with fear. They stare from a small face, shrouded by tousled black curls.

It's like looking into a mirror. One that reflects the worst-case scenario and taunts me with it.

A girl. Donatello has a child in the trunk of his car. A girl wearing only a nightgown, her trauma apparent.

Grunting with the effort, he shoves me in beside her, and I barely have time to curl in on myself before he slams the lid down, drenching us both in darkness.

Through inches of metal, I hear his voice, gruff with burgeoning rage.

"Safiya. Willow—whoever you are. You should have stayed safe in your cage," he says, sounding more monster than man. "Your father took my son from me. My heir. But you? You will give me another."

The way he says those words, along with their implication, roils my belly. He can't mean it. He can't...

A thud slams against the lid of the trunk as though he slapped it. "I'm going to break your wings, little bird," he promises, distorted by the barrier between us. Nonetheless, the malice in his tone is crystal clear. "I'm going to take pleasure in ripping them off."

His footsteps echo in ominous tandem before I feel the car jolt as a door opens and slams shut. Around me, the engine roars to life, punctuating the silence along with a muffled whimper near my ear.

And then the car itself moves, taking me to only God knows where.

As the captive of a man I no longer recognize.

~ **To be Continued in Queen of Thorns** ~

AFTERWORD

You have finished book one of Donatello and Willow's story. Do you want to see where it all began? Check out the War of Roses Trilogy!

XV: Fifteen: War of Roses Trilogy Book One

Kidnapped, Ellen must do whatever it takes to survive her cruel mafia captor, Mischa. Will he break her— or will she outsmart him?

WHEN HATE BECOMES OBSESSION...
Mistaken for her beautiful half-sister, Ellen Winthorp is taken captive by a madman who declares that she will be his "fifteen": the fifteenth victim of a vicious mafia blood feud. Armed with only her instincts, Ellen must resist her captor for as long as she can—which is easier said than done the more she's exposed to the complex man beneath the beast.

Because Mischa Stepanov isn't a mindless monster—he's a wolf, and she's the unwitting doe caught in his midst.

Unraveling the torment of his past may be her only hope of salvation...

Or the secrets uncovered may destroy them both.

CHAPTER 1 OF XV: WAR OF ROSES TRILOGY BOOK 1

Noise…
Chaos…
Briar…

The first thing I'm aware of is that I'm blindfolded—a fact that could be a blessing in disguise as my thoughts blur and jumble together. Only one coherent question escapes the fray: *Where am I?*

No answer comes to me immediately. My straining ears can make out only a few words muttered nearby in unfamiliar voices. Deep, *masculine* voices.

Various smells irritate my nostrils as well: sweat, body odor, male. *All* male. God, *where am I?*

I try flexing my shoulders only to wince. My hands are impossible to move, tied behind my back with something rough. Rope?

Oh, God.

Familiar terror gnaws at my belly as moisture gathers in my armpits and sweeps across my palms. At least, now, I have an inkling of my fate. I'm trapped in another one of his games. My nostrils flare with renewed purpose: seeking out *his* scent.

He must have hired lackeys this time; foreign body odor drowns out the stench of his cologne. I can't smell him.

But you can survive this. I fall back on the mantra that has gotten me through every day for sixteen years. *You can survive, Ellen. Focus, Ellen. Breathe, Ellen.*

Ten hours—that's how long I endured last time. My resolve had nearly splintered by the end. I'd almost given in. Almost.

But even psychological wounds eventually heal and leave tougher scar tissue behind. I can last another ten hours with Robert. My brain makes that distinction as the barrage of scents dissipates, revealing one that overpowers the rest: a man's. I taste the nuances in his stench rather than smell them—he's *that* potent, composed of a multitude of different things.

Cigar smoke.

Vodka.

One scent in particular makes my heart stop. Salty and sweet, it's almost as familiar as the flowery perfume wafting from my skin now. *Blood?*

Robert never smokes. He doesn't drink. Whenever he hurts me, he always washes his hands before and after. It is our routine, and he is nothing if not predictable.

No. This is someone new. Someone taller, whose shadow completely blots out what little detail plays across my blindfold. His footsteps are steady. Heavy.

"This her?"

I sense the outline of his fingers before the callused edge of one grazes my forehead.

"You made sure?"

His voice is deep. Almost *too* deep to be intelligible: a series of grated, rumbling notes. There's an accent tucked among them— something thick. Eastern European? Briar had a maid from there once. Sonja.

Sonja liked to read Jane Eyre. She liked scribbling love notes to Robert Sr.'s men before fucking them in the broom closet late at night when she thought no one was looking. Sonja liked a lot of things before Robert took a liking to her.

But another figure from my memory possessed this accent as well. Even though his words were hissed in a whisper, I still remember. *Breathe!*

"Bring her."

Those two words snap me back to the present. Unfamiliar hands grab my shoulders, cinching the soft silk of my blouse. *Briar's* blouse. She dressed me in it lovingly, remarking on how the color complemented my eyes. Our eyes, the same shade of light blue.

"Move!"

A tug on my shoulders hauls me upright and unseen hands shove me forward. Every sound echoes. Four footsteps, including mine. The biggest man takes the lead, I suspect, his gait rhythmic against creaking floorboards.

In contrast, the men holding me dig their nails into my skin and scurry toward an unknown destination. A rusty squeal seconds later conjures the image of an old door opening, and the footsteps trail off.

"Move!"

Something rams into my side and I stagger for balance until my cheek strikes a hard surface. It's warm. *Human.*

"Get her on the bed."

Those harsh hands return to my shoulders to fulfill the command.

"Sit her on the edge…like that. Cut her hands free."

A metallic hiss sends a shiver down my spine—then *pain!* Fire courses through my fingertips as circulation returns to them. I long to flex each one, but I know better. Instead, I keep them close, settling them onto my lap.

These men kept my skirt on, at least. Her skirt. The hem comes down past my knees, and I've never been so grateful for four inches of satin. It will buy me more time.

Ten hours. I've already lasted ten minutes. *You can do this,* the courageous part of my soul whispers. But then that voice dies in the wake of two more words uttered in that guttural cadence.

"Leave us."

The two smaller men scatter in the direction we entered—but it's all wrong. No. No. I don't smell Robert, and he'd never leave me alone with another man. Not his lackey. Not even his own father.

Most alarming of all, this man certainly is no Winthorp. His voice isn't familiar and this house doesn't smell like any property on the familial grounds.

They took me from the motorcade…

Fire sears through my skull as memories return in snatches. The clearest one is of her face. *Briar.* So beautiful, dominated by that pure, sweet smile. "I want you there," she insisted. "We're sisters, after all."

Sisters. I cherished how that word sounded in her soft cadence, tucking that moment inside myself like one of the trinkets hidden in my secret cache. Love was more precious than a button or rock I'd stolen away. Those four words meant everything. *I want you there.*

But the memory of that moment serves as a weak antidote to the terror paralyzing me now. More bits and pieces come back.

I was in the car—the beautiful limousine for once, instead of one of the servant vans that took up the rear. For part of the way, I was even sitting beside her while she braided my hair. "We look alike now," she wistfully remarked, beaming at our reflections in the polished windows.

We look alike. The phrase haunts me. As if I could ever look like Briar, with her lighter ringlets and her creamy skin. The only feature we truly share is our eyes. Our mother's eyes. Large, round, and blue. In every other respect, she takes after her father, with a beautiful aristocratic nose and a graceful neck. Every Winthorp possesses the same subtle characteristics—markings of the blood, they like to claim. Good blood. Blue blood.

I take after my father, whoever he is.

Briar loves to tout our tentative resemblance anyway—especially to her benefit. *I* am the one the maid saw sneaking out back two summers ago. *I* am the one who scurried out of the room of that visiting businessman one winter.

And now…

We look alike.

"Take off the blindfold." That voice…

I swallow hard, uneasy. Robert has found a new monster to play with. Someone who shares his flair for the dramatic. *But where is he?* My tormentor always relishes this part of the game. How he enjoys savoring my fear as I try to piece together where I am. Admittedly, it wasn't this hard before; he never strays too far from the property.

His favorite lairs are the boathouse, or the deserted crypt, or the east wing. I could always hear the bluebirds chirping throughout the grounds, no matter which corner of the estate he deemed my chosen cell.

My ears strain, searching for that faint, familiar song. This time of year, they're nearly deafening, able to be heard in even the farthest reaches of Winthorp Manor.

Two seconds. Three.

I hear nothing.

"Take off the blindfold."

The harsh rasp of syllables steals my breath away. I know anger on Robert. On Robert Sr. Even on Briar. They stutter. They shout. They scream.

None of them ever exude their impatience to the point where I can sense it in the air. Or taste it: copper on my tongue. This man isn't a Winthorp.

The realization coaxes my body into action. My sore fingers finally contort, trembling after what must have been hours of captivity. Whoever tied my blindfold snagged bits of my hair in the process and every tug on the knot at the base of my neck rips tiny strands loose from my scalp—comparable to my pathetic hopes being ripped from underneath me one by one.

I don't hear the bluebirds.

I can't smell Robert's favorite cologne.

When I finally get the knot loosened enough to uncover my eyes…

I see hell.

Mother used to say it was beautiful, forsaking the teachings of the local priest. "Hell is a rose," she used to murmur, her gaze turned inward, wistful and distant. "A flawless one, with all the life sucked out of it. The thorns have become knives. Its leaves have swallowed up the stalk. It's grotesque. It's deadly. But never forget that, underneath the violence, it's still beautiful."

He is beautiful. Or he was once. Blond hair draws my attention first—a sun-kissed gold in places, darkened with age in others. It's been clawed back from his face into a ponytail longer than mine was before Briar trimmed it. His eyes are that dangerous color between blood and brown. Like a flame, they catch the light filtering in through a sloppily boarded-up window beside him. His face is angular. Chiseled. Stone. Every feature is sculpted to convey just one emotion: determination. The way an owl might watch the mice scurrying underfoot in the stables. Or the way Robert used to look at me.

The way the devil looks, I presume, as if he has all the time in the world. More than ten hours.

An eternity to torture me.

~ Continue Reading XV ~

A WORD FROM THE AUTHOR

Hey there!

Thank you so much for reading! If you enjoyed the story, please leave a review and recommend the book to any friend you think would love this twisted world. You'd have my eternal gratitude. Even a short sentence goes a long way!

Then, come join the rest of us dark romance lovers in my Facebook Group where you can get snippets, sneak peeks of upcoming books and even help vote on aspects of future novels.

Come to the dark side:
https://www.facebook.com/groups/lanasbeautifulmonsters/

WANT MORE STUFF TO READ?
Join my newsletter and get a **free book**! Plus, you get to stay updated with any new releases, random giveaways and exclusive sneak peeks!
https://www.lanaskybooks.com/newsletter

Other Novels: https://lanaskybooks.com/

FREE BOOK - JOIN MY NEWSLETTER

DARK, TWISTED ROMANCE

Join my newsletter and get a **free book**! Plus, you get to stay updated with any new releases, random giveaways and exclusive sneak peeks!

https://www.lanaskybooks.com/newsletter

ABOUT THE AUTHOR

Lana Sky is a reclusive writer in the United States who spends most of her time daydreaming about complex male characters and parenting her Cockapoo Joey. She writes dark, twisted romance across several genres. Her titles include everything from mafia romance to vampires.

facebook.com/AuthorLanaSky

twitter.com/lanasky101

amazon.com/author/lanasky

pinterest.com/lanasky101

goodreads.com/lanasky

instagram.com/lanasky101

bookbub.com/authors/lana-sky

tiktok.com/@author_lana_sky

www.ingramcontent.com/pod-product-compliance
Lightning Source LLC
Chambersburg PA
CBHW070638310726

48982CB00001B/321